ENTANGLEMENT

to Mo

Ann Douglas

Also by Douglas Thompson

Ultrameta: A Fractal Novel
Sylvow
Apoidea
Mechagnosis

ENTANGLEMENT

DOUGLAS THOMPSON

Entanglement
First published in Great Britain by Elsewhen Press, 2012
An imprint of Alnpete Limited

Elsewhen Press, PO Box 757, Dartford, Kent DA2 7TQ

www.elsewhen.co.uk

British Library Cataloguing in Publication Data.
A catalogue record for this book is available from the British Library.

ISBN 978-1-908168-05-4 Print edition
ISBN 978-1-908168-15-3 eBook edition

Printed and bound by CPI Group (UK) Ltd, Croydon, CR0 4YY

CONTENTS

CONTENTS

Candide, amazed, terrified, confounded, astonished, all bloody, and trembling from head to foot, said to himself, 'If this is the best of all possible worlds, what are the others?'

– Voltaire, *Candide*
(translated by Tobias Smollett)

FOREWORD

In July 2018, a talented young scientist named Gene Vesberg is working at the Large Hadron Collider near Geneva, Switzerland. Wandering the inside of the 27km concrete tunnel during down-time for maintenance, he opens a hatch and puts his head inside the quaintly named 'beam pipe' and finds himself wondering what would happen to the brain of a human being caught in this position by accident, were he to receive a stream of near light-speed protons straight through the hippocampus.

He remembers reading how Albert Einstein's preserved brain has been dissected and analysed at various times since his death and found to be missing the *parietal operculum* and *lateral sulcus*, suggesting a facility for unusual degrees of connectivity between regions, quite literally a lateral thinker. Whether such connectivity could have been forged through practice and mental exercise or merely a genetic accident or gift, remains a moot point.

Following the perverse principle of retro-causality, déjà vu, Gene Vesberg now realises in a flash of terror that he has wandered overly-far from the tunnel entry point and has just heard the door close and lock, the power systems firing up. Panicking, he drops his clipboard and pen and runs frantically back towards the entrance, shouting out in desperate protest.

A moment later he is enveloped in blinding white light and heat.

~

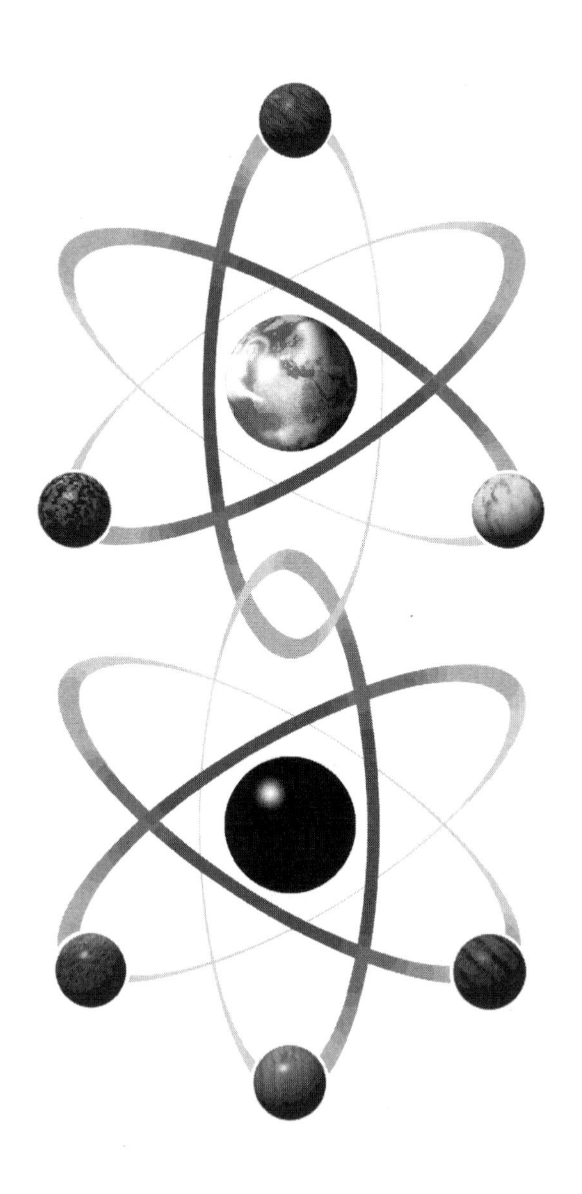

PREFACE

Of the missions undertaken, only fifty per cent found planets with life on them. Of those only ten per cent proved to have life sufficiently evolved to have language and culture.

This book deals with only that net five per cent of targeted worlds within the 'Goldilocks zone' of suitable star systems identified by NASA.

ENTANGLEMENT

...And then he came to know the dead so well
It was as if he, through her, became their kin.
He let the others talk

Did not believe, and called that land
The well-appointed, ever-sweet
And made it fit for her own feet.

– Rainer Maria Rilke, *The Death Of The Beloved*
(translated by Nina Allan)

A hundred years ago, the great tides of probe-spores were unleashed from Mother Earth, and for several weeks she looked like some exploding puffball of seeds, a dandelion head unfurling in the solar wind. Within all the apparent chaos of fuel and hardware however, there was precise purpose, which has become apparent over time. Each probe was aimed on a separate trajectory, each to travel out towards a different candidate among our nearest neighbouring star systems, each known to hold planets likely to harbour life.

No human being travelled in these devices, nor did any need to, for each carried a chamber of quantum-entangled sub-atomic matter, whose twin remained here on Earth within the space future travel bank, the Telepedrome, as it has become known, the purpose-built NASA base in the Nevada desert. By a simple method of displacement upon entry and exit, whatever is added to one chamber is instantly created in the other, whatever the distance. The principle was well-known centuries ago, even by Einstein, who called it "spooky action at a distance". Only immense patience and hard work has been necessary to make theory reality.

This year the first of these probes reached their destination, the planets orbiting the Gliese 581 star system, a red dwarf sun, and I finally received my orders to report to the Nevada Telepedrome and prepare for insertion into one of the Gliese-twinned chambers, and thereby to instantly 'travel' to the surface of an alien world twenty light-years distant, from where robotic messages and images have already been revealing a rocky surface with liquid seas and signs of microbiotic soil life.

But 'teleport' is, strictly speaking, a misnomer and 'dupliport' would be a better neologism. My self on Gliese 581g will be physically identical to me, but unable to move or think, essentially a zombie, a golem, a mandrake man, until my self back home on Earth is made to enter deep and carefully-maintained sleep; to enter a coma, in other words. Then and only then, will I open my eyes on Gliese 581g, sniff the air (so to speak, through my elaborate breathing apparatus) and be able to walk around and look for new life forms.

So, contrary to centuries of science-fictional speculation, there is no space travel as such, no need for suspended animation and travelling bio-domes, whole communities in space. Only one science fiction writer got it right: Ursula Le Guin, with her concept of the 'Ansible', whose name the real device now carries in her honour. The quantum-entangled matter chamber is pretty much exactly what she envisaged, delivered by the strange miracles of sub-atomic particle interactions, except that it can *dupliport* not just information, but objects and even life, but with one mysterious qualification: life arrives, but minus its soul.

*

We have given this planet a new name already, myself and my colleague Lieutenant Pleznick. We hope NASA will adopt the term as official some day. To us this world is 'Somnos', a sleeping planet, where (paradoxically, since it is tidally locked) in all probability no life-form sleeps at all. An orb of brown swirling gases, nitrogen oxide rain and yellow sulphur rocks. The sky is pink of course, ruled over by a blood-red sun and a host of irregular-shaped moons, evidence perhaps of an asteroid collision a few million years ago, the jagged edges still not smoothed by time and gravity.

The probes reported a city-like construction about seventy-five miles from here, and 'tomorrow' (I use the term loosely; my spacesuit's chronometer still splits time into terrestrial twenty-four hour segments) we will investigate. Perhaps it is some kind of mushroom field or mineral crystalline accretion, and we will be disappointed. Or perhaps it is something even more unthinkable or unimaginable than the wonders we have already seen: the settlement of living beings, as intelligent as ourselves.

We comfort each other, only half-jokingly, that the dangers are only half here: if these bodies are injured and die instantly in some accident or attack, then our minds will 'magically' find themselves back on Earth and wake up startled in our original bodies. But we both also know that this is not strictly true. The rules of Entanglement dictate that if I lose an arm here, that arm back in Earth would be destroyed at the exact same instant, and that if my body were burned to a crisp here – before the

Telepedrome operators could be alerted to douse my body with suitable coolant (making me 'magically' non-flammable on Somnos) – then I would simply die, with no body left in either world to contain me.

The bigger question of where such a soul, deprived of any body, ultimately migrates to, remains a mystery, even to our so advanced and enlightened civilisation, which is now conquering the stars at last.

*

My colleague Pleznick is beginning to concern me. Last 'night' I went home, by the simple trick of sleep. I was awoken on Earth, where I could greet my family through the glass walls of the Entanglement chamber. My wife and I spent several hours joking and playing with our children, and although I wish I could have held them in my arms rather than merely gesturing through glass, the experience was restorative. Pleznick, on the other hand, refused to 'travel' home and take 'shore leave'. How can NASA approve of that? It can't be right for any man's mental health. He says he slept but that he told NASA not to wake up his Entangled other self. I quizzed him and he said that he has no family that he wishes to see. This sounds very sad I know, but I somehow found it hard to believe: not a brother, sister, or parent, friend, nobody that he would enjoy talking to in person back home? I'm sure NASA knows what it's doing, but I feel like I need to know this guy more, and dig beneath the surface. I don't want anyone losing their marbles on my watch. He only joined this assignment at the last minute after Mark Selwyn's illness, and I haven't had the customary lead-in time to bond with him as a 'partner'.

*

Today we reached the 'city' and that is just what it is.

Incredible to think of millions of people back on Earth watching this through our helmet cameras in real-time, the first contact with another apparently intelligent race. I say apparently, because their language and gestures are so unintelligible, it's like listening to dolphins or whales, but computers on Earth are now already working around the clock on de-encryption and translation software for us.

The *Somnons* (Pleznick and I are happy that people back home seem to have latched onto our colloquialism) are brown-skinned and on average about four feet high, with long fish-like vertical mouths and large blackish eyes on the side of their heads; more prey than hunter, to follow terrestrial anthropological assumptions. They seem to eat root vegetables, and a lot of red mushrooms, and indeed their architecture to our eyes at least, seems almost a homage to the mushroom form. Scientists on Earth are getting very excited about this. First thoughts are that the architectural mushrooms that form their houses and palaces are a hybrid of natural and Somnon design, like coral reefs back on Earth, some fusion of mineral and biological, whereby they have learned to divert and expand a living form into a building material, while still keeping it alive.

Early days and first impressions, but compared to the rape we inflicted on our own planet, this seems like an impressively gentle and renewable technology, and consistent with the hypothesis, touch wood (to coin an old Earth phrase) that these natives of Somnos are very peaceful and consequently accepting of our presence among them. It seems a little patronising of me to say so perhaps, but my impression is that this society is a primitive agrarian economy, akin to Amerindian or Polynesian races on Earth before collision with the white man. But we have strict rules. We will do no harm to these people or their culture. Only study them and try to understand, then leave them alone again.

Did I forget to mention their bodies? Despite walking upright the Somnons have four crablike lower limbs and three arms, central one of which seems to function like a trunk or antennae, with which they incessantly touch as they chatter to each other and tentatively explore us.

Pleznick seems to have been particularly taken with these locals, and they to him, and it's been good to see his spirits lift today, and see him forget whatever has been the source of the melancholy darkness I've seen within him.

*

Unbelievable progress and new wonders. I feel like Howard Carter stumbling upon Tutankhamun's tomb with his torch and famous pronouncement: "Wonderful things".

The Somnons led us today to a great central palace where we met what appeared to be their rulers, an inner circle of particularly thin and old beings, wrinkled with age and connected to various bubbling tubes, whether carrying life-giving elixirs or information, we were unable to tell.

The 'mushroom' architecture of this hall was hugely elaborate and decorative, on a par with any of the great cathedrals of England or France, and the walls were full of what we think are books or records, semi-transparent crystals that the Somnons place into a kind of slot on their abdomens and then attach their third arm to until it glows. The effect is bizarre, as if they are living record players, turntables of the old twentieth century variety.

We have the disorientating impression that these beings are much more intelligent than we at first thought, and that our value-system is too Earth-based to be able to understand them properly.

*

Speechless. A paradox. The translation software came

through from Earth along with devices to help us create Somnon sounds from smart-boxes on our chests. Suddenly a veil is lifted on a whole ancient culture and two worlds look at each other and gape. We are now able to show them live images of people and cities back on Earth and to begin to explain ourselves and learn from them. We constantly emphasise that we will leave their world in a few weeks and that no colonisation is ever intended. I'm not sure yet that they understand our Entanglement technology or the implications of that, both good and bad: we need not arrive in huge spaceships holding many people; provided they never destroy our Entanglement chambers here on Somnos, we can theoretically return at any instant, with no warning.

* * * * * * * * * * * * *

Listen. This is Pleznick now. I have taken over command. My sincere apologies firstly, to his wife and children and to planet Earth in general, for my having killed Walters. It was however, necessary, since he would not agree to allow what I plan to do next. Likewise, the destruction of the full-size Entanglement chamber was necessary to prevent you from sending other astronauts to interfere and stop me. Now, I can no longer return to Earth and you can't send anyone after me, for another hundred years. Only the 'Ansible' still connects us, that miniature miracle, predicted by the great seer Le Guin. I know you won't disconnect it or attempt to blow it up or set the probes against me. I know that much about human nature: the defining characteristic of our pernicious little species is that we are insatiably curious and nosey. And here you all are, peering into Somnon culture like fevered peeping-toms, lapping it all up, terrified that I will cut the transmission. Well, don't worry, I have something to show you. Something important for you to try to understand.

In the meantime, and for the rest of my life, you have my twinned body in a permanent coma back on Earth. And as an extra precaution, I don't intend to fall asleep, just in case you have some extra trick with which to wake me up and trap me back there. Don't worry, I packed a lot of coffee!

I know I'm in no position to make demands (threaten to kill myself and thereby cut off this flow of information?), but please take my twinned body out of the Telepedrome and place it in a bed next to my beloved wife Julia in her intensive care ward in Westland Hospital in Maryland. She is in a permanent vegetative state, since the car accident, and so it seems somehow appropriate that our two 'zombie' bodies should lie there together, keeping each other company, however uncommunicatively.

*

My understanding of their language and culture is increasing by the hour, exponentially. Maybe some of those liquids they keep offering me, the ones you told me and Walters were nearly safe to drink after that last analysis, maybe they're doing things to my brain, good things, expanding my cognitive capacity. They certainly seem to stop me requiring sleep. Genius! How did they know that was exactly what I needed? Did I actually tell them that? I don't think they're telepathic (how could they be when we think in mutually incomprehensible languages?), but they do seem extraordinarily empathetic.

*

Their planet being tidally locked, as our astronomers predicted two centuries ago, means we have only seen the light side of their world so far, the Red Realm as the Somnons call it, which always faces the sun, no nights or days, no seasons. But a hundred miles beyond here, across what they call the Mouth-Eye Mountains, the other hemisphere begins. The moonlit, hidden world of perpetual night, of brown nitrogen-dioxide cyclones and constant rains and sulphur sand-storms. The Somnons tell me that this land contains their souls, that it is where they each go when they die, and sometimes unhappy souls come back. You might think this laughable superstition, but they devoutly maintain that sometimes wraiths are seen wandering through their mushroom-cities at night, strange white ghost-like beings who have become disorientated and drifted back across the forbidden border from the netherworld, the Grey Realm. They are said to be disturbed and disturbing, unable to rest, tortured spirits, those who have died prematurely or violently and come back to seek answers, or closure.

You think this is primitive and religious, but there is an astounding similarity with our own folk-myths surely, in a culture so distant from our own. And, more to the point, they have shown me these creatures. Twelve hours ago I touched one with my own hands before it fled away. I am told that sometimes wraiths will seek out the house of a particular citizen, and stand over his body because.... here's the crunch: Somnons have coma victims too. And when that happens they send a priest traveller out under special license, over the border to search in the Grey Realm for the lost spirit of the living person, and then lead this wraith version back over, bring it home, and when it touches the body of its sleeping twin, it fuses with it, passes into it, and the patient wakes up and recovers.

So you see? For Julia, for hope, for the love of God, I have found a new mission here. This is why I had to mutiny. Walters just wouldn't understand.

*

My native guide for the journey seems to be a female, but

what am I saying? The term is meaningless here of course, so why am I using it? She is merely one of the two apparent sexes of Somnons, both vastly different from men and women, but I already like her immensely. Her name I will translate as *Lanyleirtis*, although half the actual sounds are more like clucks and sucking noises to human ears, so it's all a bit arbitrary. She must be some kind of high priestess. To the Somnons, travel to the Grey Realm is a religious rite, as much a passage of the soul and mind as a physical journey. She is puzzled by the weight and cumbersome packaging of the Ansible that I'm carrying with me, curious about its function, but tolerant of its intrusive presence.

The landscape is beginning to change, the yellow deserts and red mushroom forests of the Somnon heartland giving way to lusher wetter vegetation, brown and purple trees and a kind of leaf-creeper ground cover like seaweed. Terrifying lightning strikes rage on the mountain tops ahead in the dark shadow of the nitrite storms. Clouds change from brown to yellow as nitrogen dioxide cools to dinitrogen tetroxide then back again. We have to climb up and through that maelstrom to reach our destination.

*

I don't know the rules of this culture, and that is very dangerous, albeit that the Somnons seem so peaceful and friendly. Too friendly. Has Lanyleirtis been assigned to me as a wife or something? As we rested fourteen hours ago (no sleeping of course!), she started caressing me with her third arm and kissing my spacesuit with her voluptuous fish-mouth, while emitting a weird song through some kind of tendril-lined gills on the side of her chest, followed by puffs of an odd pink gas. I found the effect bizarrely enchanting and nearly relaxed so much that she was about to take my breathing apparatus off. I would have died within minutes of course. I had to explain to her very carefully after that how different my physiology is and how different our two planets are. How the cold temperatures and nitrogen-rich air are beyond the range of human adaptability.

I am confused to have to admit that I found her two large blinking eyes, filled with sadness as I told her how alien I am, enormously attractive. But of course, nothing can assuage my sense of loss, my love of my Julia, frozen, sleeping icy princess lost on a distant world, beside my other body, as I hope you have arranged things.

*

This is Pleznick, Earth. We have a wraith here, Lanyleirtis is appalled, screaming hysterically and keeping her distance, but I've trapped the thing and I'm holding the Ansible instrumentation up against it, scanning. Can you analyse this thing? You need to work out what its chemical and atomic composition is. Don't you see? This is a soul, a ghost, a spirit. Solve this enigma and you may very well have the key to life on Earth also. If souls migrate here to a darkened hidden hemisphere, then where might they go on Earth? Maybe they live all around you there, but simply cannot be seen in our atmosphere. On this so-different world, somehow they are both visible and corporeal. You have to try to understand and learn from this.

*

Earth, why have you remained so silent? Still working on it, or don't you like what you've found out?

Reluctantly, and although still shaken, Lanyleirtis has led me deeper into the Grey Realm, a forbidden world. An entire year on Somnos takes only thirty-seven days. We must have orbited the red sun twice already and yet remained plunged in perpetual night. Only the orange light on the moon fragments give us a clue as to what we're missing, as they drift through the clouds, throwing dappled changing light patterns, like nightclub strobes.

About forty hours ago as we rested, Lanyleirtis told me about one of her people's myths about the origins of those nine irregular moons. Somnons tell their children that they are jigsaw pieces (I translate loosely) that one of their Gods (the 'monkey god' although I have yet to see their equivalent of a monkey, a less intelligent version of themselves living in the hottest regions of the Red Realm) created by smashing up the Orb of Knowing, a sort of crystal ball, in a rage of frustration because he could not understand the meaning of the universe. It was the supreme God-being, 'Zea' who had given the monkey this privileged opportunity for enlightenment, and when the monkey threw away this chance, Zea condemned the monkey to confinement on Somnos. This is why there are so many storms and thunder and lightning, the children are told. This is the rage and despair of the monkey god as he travels the world repenting and regretting, tearing his hair out, alternately begging with Zea and railing against him, pleading for another chance to see the crystal ball put together again so that he might have another opportunity to understand the universe. But Zea always refuses.

Somnons seem to set great store by the concept of knowledge, by which they mean spiritual understanding, not just the scientific accumulation of facts, which they see as a kind of vanity. Their monkey god festival is celebrated every year by an exchange of small puzzle games and telling to each other of enigmas and riddles. Lanyleirtis tells me that it's not the solving of these puzzles which Somnons cherish but the opposite: the sense of mystery and unknowing which creates in them a sense of humility, a character trait they admire above all others.

*

We have reached the first wraith city. Astonishing. Instead of mushrooms it appears to be made of semi-transparent crystals that flicker with electric pulses, in some way related to the lightning perhaps. The inhabitants are silvery translucent versions of the Somnons themselves, and Lanyleirtis insists that they are each equivalents of the living beings we left behind in the sunlit world. She has begun talking to them, overcoming her fear, asking them directions. She says she intends to take me to meet her 'dead' mother, to prove her point and make me believe.

Everywhere we walk, spidery white cobwebs blow and accumulate over us, from the branches of some kind of black leathery trees. I am sending you a sample to analyse.

*

It may be true. She has found her mother, and although these creatures have no tear glands, I think I now recognise their equivalents: a shivering in their upper limbs, accompanied by a sweat of green moisture on their hind legs. The 'gills' also palpitate, just as they did during what I took to be amorous or sexual arousal.

*

Am I going mad? Today I thought I glimpsed humans among the crowds in the wraith city. I pursued them, on three different occasions, but never caught up with them. How could such an insane thing be possible? I killed Walters. Does that mean that Walters' soul is here? Insanity enough. But I thought I saw more than one. I have asked Lanyleirtis to ask a question of her mother or of one of the leaders of the wraiths. There's a lot here I don't yet understand, but I feel a kind of panic at times, as if logic itself is slipping away from me. Is everyone here all the Somnons who have ever lived? – Or do they each in turn return to new bodies, when babies are born on the daylight hemisphere, like reincarnation?

*

Yesterday we travelled all day, to use the term loosely, to meet the wraith's leader in the eastern hills. I say 'east', but what is west or north or south in a world such as this? North is here, away from the red sun, and south is where I came from, to me at least.

Exhausted, I unwittingly dropped my guard and fell asleep for a moment, but was not returned to Earth. I take this as a good sign and am very much relieved. Have you given up the idea of tricking me, back there on Earth? – Followed my instructions regarding my other body? – Not burned it and destroyed me out of spite at least, I see.

The wraith leader told me to my astonishment that there are indeed humans in this realm. He says that a few began appearing around the time of the arrival of our first probes, and being a polite race (like their daylight counterparts) they ignored the probes and accommodated the new people. How can this be? The probes only contained Ansibles. Can human souls (invisible on Earth) somehow migrate through these devices, and were they somehow attracted to them like moths to a flame?

Who are they all and can I meet them? I asked excitedly of course, but my question puzzled the leader. Wraith-Somnons have neither names nor fixed abodes apparently, they merely wander endlessly, talking to themselves. They find each other only through feelings, strong emotions like love or hate, and thus Lanyleirtis had found her mother. Can the method and effect work for me I wonder, or for my fellow humans in this alien place? Of course, nobody knew the answer.

*

An answer. Wraith-Somnons like Somnons themselves,

only live for their equivalent of fifty of our Earth years, and then their souls instantly re-emerge as new-borns on the sunlit hemisphere. Thus is this peculiar world held in equilibrium.

Why are you still so silent, Earth? What did you find out about the wraith data I gave you? Are they made from Muons and Higgs-Bosons, anti-matter or electromagnetic plasma, dark matter? What might their equivalent be on Earth, and how would you detect them?

Well, it's you that needs to find out now, not me. I resigned myself to death here the moment I destroyed the Entanglement chamber, I understand that. I only hope that you will have the sense to use the data I sent you and… and what? Find the soul of my beloved Julia and re-unite her with her sleeping body? Unless…. What if…?

*

Yesterday I tripped and fell from a sulphur rock outcrop and a sharp fragment tore through my survival suit and pierced my chest. I was unconscious for four hours, and yet I am alive. I threw myself off another cliff this morning, to check an astonishing hypothesis. I am immortal. I have dispensed with my survival suit and breathing apparatus, I no longer seem to feel cold. Am I breathing nitrogen? It feels no different. The white cobweb-filaments that drift everywhere here have been slowly accumulating on me, I can no longer brush them off.

*

I have made a calculation. The surface area of this hemisphere is 11,822,510 square miles. If I walk 50 miles a day for the next 236,450 years I can traverse it all in search of Julia or the other human spirits. If I am immortal, such a task is easily feasible. I no longer seem to have to eat, just as well since my protein pills have been running out.

*

I walk endlessly every day now, across dark wastelands under electrically-flickering storm clouds, lashed by brown rain, travelling between white crystalline cities. Above me always, the jigsaw pieces of the fragmented moons slowly twist and interlock and pull apart like luminous sad birds, indolent fish in the depths of a bored eternity. I am no longer afraid to sleep and dream, and when I do I sometimes imagine myself putting all those pieces back together again, reconstructing the puzzle and at last finding out the sublime meaning of all this, these strange torments that I live through in these darkening days, so far from all sunlight and understanding.

Somewhere at last I may find my beloved Julia, or at least another human soul as lost as I am, if God wills it. But which God, and over what realm? – Or are all realms the same one? – Now and always?

And why are you so silent, Earth? You who put me here, sowed me like a seed, casual casting of a handful of life, spattered across the universe like milk or honey? I killed my brother and I have a long time to reflect upon it. Is this my punishment, how you ostracise me, cast me off into the black abyss of space? Am I now disowned and disavowed? I cannot bring my brother back to life, though his spilled blood cries out from this alien soil. Will I meet him here again and will he and you forgive me? – Or I forgive myself?

*

Lanyleirtis is getting old and frail. I think she may die soon. But she is not sad or afraid as a human would be, but jubilant, overjoyed at the prospect of returning to the sunlit world. Does that mean she died when she came here? – And have I then also?

She has been a good companion, my dear friend these last long months and I will miss her terribly. But my own journey has no such end in sight. I walk and hunt and search through every land and all the many faces that I meet, each day, looking for an answer, for recognition, for hope and hope returned.

And meanwhile I know I live, not just here but somewhere else, on another world, where I sleep peacefully, I must trust, side by side with my Julia, my Queen. *Et in Arcadia Ego.*

And have you still nothing to say to me, Earth – my mother, my father? Are you ashamed of me? Or are you proud? Or are you no longer there? – an emptiness, an absence, empty void?

Have you solved my puzzle yet?

Signing off,

– Walter S Pleznick

*

(NASA Explanatory Postscript):

Walter Pleznick was actually Entangled out to Gliese 581g alone. The companion astronaut he refers to was therefore imaginary. This impairment of his perception and sanity seemed to begin from the very moment he set foot on alien soil. Perhaps even more rigorous psychological testing of Telepedrome candidates should be considered in future. Perhaps the teleportation principle has unknown side-effects or limitations when used over such enormous distances, for this, the first time. Or perhaps the dualism of the tidally-locked planet itself produces some immediate schizophrenic disintegration of the unprotected human mind. Whatever the case, much of Pleznick's testimony remains unreliable. His destruction of the full-size Entanglement chamber did not however, as he suggests, put back manned exploration of this solar system for a century, but for a mere three years, since other chambers were sent to the neighbouring planets of 581d and e. Our probes and Ansibles remain intact on 581g, and continued aerial mapping and analysis do correlate with much of the topographical and meteorological phenomena he describes, including the presence of large 'mushroom' and 'crystalline' structures which may theoretically be settlements of intelligent beings.

Pleznick's body died on Earth six years after his semblance's first 'touch down' on Gliese 581g, thus indicating his demise by unknown causes on the alien world. As recently reported in the national news media, his wife Julia miraculously awoke from a ten-year coma last April, and has since lodged an application with NASA to undergo training for the Telepedrome space programme.

~

DISSEMBLANCE

(The following is narrated during a car journey across the Nevada desert, by the driver, a federal agent named Jack Downey, to his passenger a reporter called Becky Lee Falconer).

The early dupliportation experiments went badly wrong. Things had seemed fine with fruit flies and white lab rats. A quantum-entangled mouse lifted up by a human hand in California would magically levitate inside its glass cage in Oxfordshire. One fighting with a rival over a block of cheese, would creepily interact with nothing, on the other side of the Atlantic. So NASA raced ahead into trying the first human, an eager science student looking for extra money, made sure he had few family, made him sign the forms. They thought they botched the first Entanglement, then the second, so kept going, but all had worked, just not predictably.

By the time they stopped, the experiment in disarray, they had created eleven versions of Guy Lecaux, all of varying quality and stability, distributed across the planet's surface.

At first, Guy could only inhabit one body at once, and pass instantly between them, his mind teleporting only upon falling asleep or fainting. But the situation deteriorated over time. Simultaneity, disparity, dissolution and disintegration took hold.

In New York, his face was mostly gone. A field of grey static, flickering, pixels rearranging, in flux, like digital interference. He kept out of sight, in raincoats and broad-rimmed hats, found himself disassembling in rain showers, interacting with the lights on Broadway and Times Square during long evening walks. Nearly lost his left arm to a cathode-ray tube, sucked into the electron storm in an old TV repair shop in Queens, had to go stand on Three Mile Island to rebuild his hands.

In Tokyo he was raped by modem – split open three-way with his semblances in Brussels and Lima. Dangerous singularity meshing him with traffic noise. He remembered his girlfriend and went to find her, all three bodies boarding different planes to London. Stopped at customs, only one got through, by dissolving through several walls and an aircraft hull. Emergency landing at Paris Charles de Gaulle, screaming tourist pointing to white electro-ghost slipping along the aisle floor like luminous piss. Bled into the Autopilot and phoned himself to Surrey. Inhabited the network for six years before downloading in a disused railway siding in Swindon, from an accretion of stolen mobile phones connected up in parallel, electromagnetic meltdown of social networks, texting of DNA.

He lived again and hid himself in a Teflon suit, kept cover of darkness. Found Amy at last in East Croydon, but his legs were gone from the knees down. Imperfect translation, Berlin semblance was resonating with him, his movements being taken over remotely like a deranged Pinocchio operated by distant hands. Taken into hospital as suspected epilepsy patient, he escaped through an oscilloscope, ECG heart beat trace like Morse code, digitised street to street through webcams. Found her again in Greenwich Park but dissolved among the pigeons and ducks as she looked on, screaming. Energy haloes breaking up, feathers and flutter of wings, each bird taking a different part of him up into the skies and stars, over to the trees and down into the autumn leaves.

He became the essence of London, remembered days, trampled underfoot. Amy smelled him everywhere, in rain-damp mornings and late afternoons of exhausted, exalted light. He was neon, lipstick, magazine stands, all ephemera, gesture, glances, lost moments, fragments of touch, overheard snippets of music at Saturday morning markets. She could find him only when alone and despairing, on long walks two-hours-in, in the light on clouds, burning cigarette butts discarded at bus stops by people moved on, in cooling coffee cups left behind at lonely café tables in unprofitable thoroughfares.

She turned to prostitution then drug addiction, every form of annihilation and loss. In the needle's winking eye at last, she downloaded or uploaded herself or him, what's the difference. At the moment of orgasm with a stranger, she found she could disassociate herself, disengage briefly from the physical as Guy had done permanently, and in that fleeting window of non-being touch the horizon, kiss the sky, circumnavigate the globe and find him again as she cried her little death, crucified on the winds of time. The strangers always seemed to leave with something of Guy invisibly smeared over them, cross-meshed into their fabric, implanted by osmosis. She thought for a while she might be bringing him back to life a little with every fuck. Guy and Amy.

Their faces and souls became billboard images moving in Leicester Square, cryptic giants etched over city maps, shapes in fog, refugees in peripheral vision, posters of the missing, dead police files, smiling girls, models in magazine adverts twenty years out of date, stained by rain and semen.

Meanwhile in Berlin, the action moved on. His missing legs after walking alone at night for a year, downloaded two fragmented semblances from Warsaw and Rome. Completed himself, but never quite stable, he lived in subways and detuned radios, white noise, EVP. The CIA were on his trail now, agents in all the target cities. One of them, a woman Gina F, found him in Rome and followed him to Turin. They met and embraced on the banks of the Po in early February, swirling in chill fog. She followed him through the dreaming arcades of Nietzsche and De Chirico, one eye on the Alps and the Basilica of Superga, white snow-like dream of innocence and peace, unattainable, found he broke up at city boundaries, her arm reaching right through him, a prisoner of the grid, of human static. Every power-cut he died a little, his essence bleeding out towards elemental nothing, the ultimate terror of human silence. The collective unconscious was keeping him going, like WiFi, Infrared, afraid of being undreamt. He needed her, his open file, on-going, a story, any story.

In a hotel room in Milan they attempted sex, but he meshed with her and became her, screaming. The startled maids understood nothing. He began a new life as her, but her old colleagues tracked her down, suspicious.

Years went by. Her body died in public, heart failure on the marble floor of the Galleria, within sight of the Duomo, passers-by coming to her rescue. His ghost emerged, disengaging to startled gasps. Late afternoon light thrown through muted glass, filigree pattern across him, he became Milanese shadows for three decades, plaguing tourist photographs and shortwave radio.

The space programme had moved on, the technology mastered. His semblances in Detroit and Buenos Aires had been quietly consolidating, one a tramp, the other a serial killer. Both fused through a police file in Mexico City, the face unstable, liable to contraflow with another dying fragment in Moscow that blew through streets as torn newspapers.

Finally they caught up with Lecaux in Los Angeles. He had wandered Sunset Boulevard for decades, cross-contaminating with celluloid re-masterings, Hitchcock, Humphrey Bogart, decayed films from military installations, Roswell, the 1950's, wind blowing through empty film sets. At the desert's edge, he would tremble like flimsy Drywall, on the threshold of dissolution as dusk approached, gazing up at the stars.

They found him in a derelict apartment, limboed between developments, one boom and the next, construction and demolition. Four agents with back-up on the way, encapsulated and sterilised then condensed him into a foot-square steel box of electromesh, after a brief maelstrom involving swirling curtains and frayed electrical wires, blue flashes, two agents electrocuted, minor burns and an epileptic fit followed by four years of psychotic episodes for both of them.

They had found Lecaux watching television in the empty room, amid the pools of rain and turned-up carpets, rotting detritus of abandoned construction work. No power, the television was wired to his wrist, feeding on his own ebbing life force, a century in the dying.

The screen was showing the arrival of the first probe-spores on Gliese 581g, the eager astronauts reporting to the Nevada Telepedrome for upload and dupliport, pacing the shining polygonal corridors in their safety suits and pig-masks, glass chamber doors springing open in futuristic ease, antiseptic anticipation. He hoped they would make it, intact. He had paid the price for their ambiguous journeys, to walk on distant worlds, twenty light years distant.

He would be a footnote in history he knew, scrubbed out, as he awaited the stealthy steps in the corridor outside his ruinous apartment, a state secret obliterated, a man who never was, the cost of progress. Not fully alive, how could he ever die now? Detuned radios, malfunctioning televisions, schizophrenic's day-mares, would forevermore be suspect. But like Marilyn or Kennedy, he would be data-safe, culture-encoded, bound, stitched, integration-encrypted, irresolvable left-over fraction, non-divisible, residual, background radiation. He smiled, as he pressed the remote control and the picture faded, as the door was burst open, dissolving himself in silver static.

~

IN TIME LIKE GLASS

An astronaut is a scientist first and an explorer second. So went the current doctrine. Bill Whitmore had always favoured the unproven suggestion that 'déjà vu' was just some kind of electrical short-circuit in the brain rather than evidence of second-sight. But in doing so, he was ignoring something else he knew: that electrons can travel backwards in time in quantum mechanics, and electrons are the medium with which thoughts are transmitted between human neural-synapses.

When the first video from the robotic probes on 55 Cancri k were shown in terrestrial television via Ansible, Bill stopped in his tracks, his heart leaping in confusion, reaching for his wife's hands to steady himself, the foundation of his world shaken. They turned the TV up.

In an instant of revelation that he would try to suppress and deny later, he realised that he had been having recurring dreams for the last six months, of talking to alien beings closely resembling the bipedal horse-like creatures he now saw distant glimpses of, moving around in green velvet robes, in ruined stone cities, on a planet with twin suns.

Two minutes later the phone rang. It was NASA.

*

The future had arrived. Every generation probably thinks so, but Gene Vesberg was sure of it. And more than any other man on the planet right now, he was in a position to know. That position was Executive Director of NASA's Telepedrome programme, but today was his day off. He sat in his back garden in a deck chair and looked up at the blue sky and clouds, content to sit and dream until night fell and the stars appeared. The stars… hidden up there, but no longer abstractions, unreachable points of light, mythological patterns and portents of fate. Now they were destinations, reachable, but even better than that. *Instantly* reachable, doorways to other life forms and civilisations, all the knowledge mankind had ever wondered after, the answers at last. And surely by knowing and learning about humanity's counterparts, some kind of picture of God, *his* or *her* self, would emerge. The reasons for life existing at all, would be within our grasp.

For the moment, Vesberg relaxed and sipped his whisky and lemonade and listened, smiling, to the sound of his neighbours' young children at play. Hazel and he had never had children themselves, and despite his memory of his father complaining about the noise made by him and his sister as children, he found now that he rather loved the screaming and crying coming from over his suburban fence and hedge. He had never even seen his neighbours' children, such was the hedge height and seclusion of the neighbourhood, and now it occurred to him, a strange thought, that they were invisible, personal ghosts of a future he would never have. As they played and laughed and cried, he imagined them in front of him.

*

Children. Even on Earth, many life forms don't share humanity's rigid scheme of sexuality and child-rearing. Wolves, forefathers of man's so-called best friend, regulate their pack hormonally so that only one dominant pair mate and reproduce and the others defend them. Bees of course are all female and sterile, save for a few drones at the hive, where the queen churns out larvae around the clock, like rice grains.

Such was Vesberg's stream of thought as he drove the next day and approached the checkpoint gate at the Nevada NASA compound. The bee analogy pleased him. There in the distance sat the Telepedrome building: polygonal and hive-like, gold as glistening honeycombs in the early morning sun.

Vesberg's excitement and satisfaction today were palpable: the time had come for the second dupliportation, this one to 55 Cancri k. Lessons had been learnt from last year's fiasco on Gliese 581g. The astronauts would be plural this time, two being safer than one, one female one male, and psychologically better tested and prepared.

There would be no breakdowns or blowouts, no letting-down of the extraordinary Entanglement technology by the sad frailty of the human element. Reports would be sober and reliable, the information sent back professional, dispassionate, scientific. A new benchmark would be set, and humanity would learn something useful about the meaning of the universe in which it finds itself.

As Vesberg paced the hexagonal corridors, he watched the 'cells' of the beehive being made ready, sterilised and washed-down for Bill Whitmore and Angela Sanchez, due to arrive at midday. The media scrum were already assembled outside, and the Gliese 'cell' would be kept cordoned off, well out of sight, where Walter Pleznick's original body still lay in coma, unrevivable, twitching occasionally, arms moving, legs stumbling, striding on a distant planet whose secrets in all probability only he would ever know now until the day he died.

At midday exactly, the hermetic steel doors were swung

open and Bill and Angela walked in out of the blaze of Nevadan sunshine and flashing cameras. They both turned around one last time to wave, then the doors swung slowly shut, restoring an eerie calm and cool to the waiting scientists, over two hundred NASA personnel on hand to greet them, and these only the tip of a global iceberg of expertise ready to assist the mission.

The truly hard work had been done a hundred years beforehand, by those scientists who had isolated all the many thousands of kilograms of quantum-entangled matter necessary and blasted it off in probes towards the target star systems. Those assembled today were still full of admiration for those earlier men and women, who had embodied the vision and dedication to undertake such a grand project, even as their planet had remained enmeshed in so many petty wars. None of them had lived to see this day, but perhaps they, and every other human being who had died since, had done so knowing that the seeds of mankind's lifelines had been sown, and been that much more exalted by the hope that offered.

Soon Bill and Angela, or Whitmore and Sanchez as protocol demanded they be referred to, were strapped into their glass chambers within one steel hexagonal cell with the in-room cameras running, and fed a live video-feed of the surface of 55 Cancri k. There, the robotic probes with Ansible cameras monitored the weather outside and the temperature and pressure of two identical glass chambers, ready to receive the astronauts' semblances.

After a short countdown in which the watching world held its breath, the chambers in which the astronauts lay slid forward on rails and entered the two apertures in the steel wall in front of them. In the symmetrically opposite cell, on the other side of the wall, their bodies began to emerge into the identical glass chambers containing the quantum-entangled matter. Transparent as air, it was if nothing particularly special were happening.

But simultaneously, from the head down, their bodies had begun to appear on 55 Cancri k, to the gasps of astonishment of ten billion viewers. Nobody ever got used to this bit: the effortless absurdity. In less than a minute, perfect body doubles of Whitmore and Sanchez were stretched out on their cushioned silver mattresses within their glass chambers on 55 Cancri k. These were not holograms, but corporeal, living, physical, real.

Vesberg cleared his throat and spoke into the microphone from his control room just outside the source cell. *Dupliportation completed successfully. Life signs normal. Whitmore and Sanchez, how do you feel? Can you open your eyes now please?* Again, the feeling, almost palpable, of a whole world jumping in ecstatic fright, unseen, outside, beyond the silent walls of the Telepedrome. Each body simultaneously operated its puppet on the alien world. *Now lift your left arm please. That's fine. The right leg now also.*

Top of the world, Ma! Whitmore joked, still only able to see the terrestrial room around him.

Look, Mom, I'm on 55 Cancri k! laughed Sanchez, on two worlds, in bizarre interstellar stereo.

AISC procedure commencing in sixty seconds... Vesberg intoned, the phrase always holding a chilling finality: Artificially Induced & Sustained Coma.

Whitmore mumbled: *Night, night, Mom...* But NASA made no such levity in response. Sleep as a metaphor for death was too near the bone in light of the complications with Pleznick. This was the most delicate and ultimately semi-mystical part of the process after all.

The discovery that a human nexus of consciousness could only inhabit one body at once, and was able to bypass the normal laws of space-time in order to maintain this restriction, had proved too useful to resist making use of. But did anyone truly understand it? To do that, scientists would have to have understood what consciousness itself physically was, but ultimately consciousness was the only tool they had with which to do that. A slippery conundrum. Explanations had been cobbled together, good enough to bluff the man in the street, but to the scientific community the issue remained a private embarrassment and source of contention. The electrons conveying thought in one brain had been created perfectly in another, so why not the whole character and experience? But something was missing in their equations, something that sleep somehow resolved. That which has not yet been fully understood is dangerous to play with. But how many lives in medieval history had been saved by applying blue bread-mould to wounds, long before anyone knew the active element was penicillin?

After five minutes safety margin, the process was deemed over. A sort of gentle alarm clock sounded on 55 Cancri k, and Whitmore slowly stirred then sat up, not even blearily. His various life signs: heart-rate, breathing, blood oxygen levels, were being anxiously monitored on earth in response to each of his movements but, to Whitmore, all was normal and calm, just like waking up at home. His straps were loosened and he was walking about the silver room, looking over apprehensively at Sanchez, who appeared to be having something of a Sunday morning long lie-in.

Meanwhile on Earth, the sleeping originals of the two astronauts lay serene, twitching occasionally as if in deepest dream sleep, and doubtless many people at home were wishing that they too could have dreams as exotic and outlandish as those about to unfold.

Whitmore was gently nudging Sanchez, as he had now been instructed, speaking quietly into her ear. She moaned and mumbled softly, rubbed her eyes, then sat up. All of planet Earth, forty-one light years distant, sighed in relief, a wave of cheers of joy and celebration going up into the deadening silence of space, to see this one woman wake up at this moment. They had both made it.

*

The robotic probes on the alien world had done their preparatory work well. Otherwise Vesberg wouldn't have sent two of NASA's best scientists of course. There were not just life forms nearby, but intelligent ones by the looks of it, a whole city of them, just twenty-five miles away from the 'landing' site.

But as the steel doors slid slowly apart and Whitmore and Sanchez stepped tentatively out under the blazing green sky lit by the binary suns of the 55 Cancri star system, Vesberg realised he still had a doubt in his mind. Given that the probes had effectively made contact already and informed the Cancrians of the imminent human arrival, why were there no aliens there to meet them?

Sanchez: The green skies and vermilion clouds are the first and most striking things to hit you. Television images and high-res' stills via Ansible just don't capture the full visual shock experienced in person. And the smells? How can I explain that? OK, it's all a bit distorted by my augmented oxygen tank pissing up a tube in my left nostril, but I think maybe it's the chlorine-rich air and other trace elements, hence the green skies. Underfoot it's kind of like the Atacama desert or something. All grey, grey stones for miles on end, very hard, quite compacted and easy to walk on. Actually the grey stones look quite green to me, but I'm guessing that's down to the colour-distortion in the atmosphere, which I'm already getting used to, and when I next wake up on Earth I'm going to find everything really blue or yellow in comparison. There's some kind of pale blue vegetation in the distance and we're heading towards it.

Whitmore: The probes have prepared us for the appearance of the aliens, loosely speaking, that of pale grey upright horses with long heads and huge brown eyes, attired usually in long garments like velvet cloaks. The second pair of arms at their waists appear largely vestigial, although they occasionally use them to hold onto each other during what may be cultural rituals, but there's a lot here to try and understand. The computers back on Earth have already unravelled what they believe are some basic greetings in their language, but it is our approach and interaction itself which will hopefully generate enough words for NASA to unravel and decipher and then in a couple of days maybe we'll be communicating.

Tomorrow we will meet them, having walked all day today across their grey stony deserts, approaching the leafy jungles of blue and turquoise 'ivy-weed' of their tropical zone, within which sits the principal city already identified.

We are already finding many impressive ancient stone ruins amid these jungles, of a very recognisable and consistent architecture. The stone seems to be akin to something metamorphic on Earth, like marble but with high quantities of germanium and yttrium in it, giving it a colour and weird texture quite unlike anything back home. The carvings on these stones are very ancient and beautiful, strange curvaceous designs and symbols. Blue 'birds' fly through this jungle, landing on the stones. At least we think they're birds. When we approached one it screamed and plunged straight to the ground (a fall of at least 15 feet), lodging its beak into the soil, then exploded, turning itself inside-out and blowing weird black pollen spores everywhere. It seemed dead after that, but the pollen seemed almost sentient, more like flies or wasps perhaps, than merely inanimate seeds on the wind.

Sanchez: So these are the Horse-men, as the terrestrial media have dubbed them. The first meeting was stressful and dangerous. They are about two feet taller than the average human but our appearance must seem deeply bizarre to them, because there was a lot of panic followed by displays with makeshift spears, and crowds approaching us in mock charges. We kept our cool. And though Whitmore seemed to be inspiring me with his stolid bravery, he told me afterwards that he'd thought it the other way around. I think he really meant it. Nice to know sexism might be dead, here on an alien world at least.

Whitmore: Equinans, that's what we'll call them, and their planet: Equis, of course, a world of walking horses. Sounds humorous, except that they are actually quite frightening looking, and seemingly pretty sombre in temperament. Our de-encryption programs are catching up by the hour, both at listening and at projecting back translated phrases from the soundbox on my chest. Their leader's name sounds like Vislnqua Dvewmo, a tall handsome creature in a particularly fine deep green robe. They led us to his palace after convincing themselves that we were harmless: a beautiful very old stone building with the same curvaceous architecture, many arches and hoops. The gardens surrounding the palace looked as if they had been what we would call 'formal' once, but had long since fallen into neglect.

We asked Vislnqua about this, and he told us that his palace and all other major buildings of their civilisation were built many centuries ago by a preceding culture, whose knowledge of carving has been lost.

Sanchez: Maybe it's because I rode horses a lot as a teenager, but I feel a great empathy for these creatures, more so than Whitmore does, I suspect. There was an enormous melancholy in Vislnqua's eyes and voice last night at sunset, as he stood by the open windows of the summer palace. It's always warm here. The dual suns, one yellow, one crimson, setting into the purple seas beyond the turquoise sucker-jungles, were a breath-taking sight. I hope video captures something of it for people back home, but the reality of it is something else, with the cooling breeze of evening on your neck and the strange calls of the exploding birds and ratchet lizards (who move by winding themselves up like gyroscopes then spinning forward in circles). Don't even ask me about the slug-skunks. If I find any in my clothes tonight, you'll know all about it.

Vislnqua took me down into the basement to view a kind of art gallery of leaf and sand paintings by his ancestors, while Whitmore stayed behind to play with what we think were some of the leader's grandchildren. I was stunned by what I saw. The technology around us, such as they have, is scarcely more than medieval (in our terms), but in the paintings I saw what looked like metal machines, things like cars and aeroplanes, even spacecraft perhaps, but to my surprise then shock: neither Vislnqua nor any of his advisors were able to tell me much about them. How can they be so ignorant of, even uninterested in, their own past? They offered to go search for other records to retrieve the information I wanted, but I could see it was getting late and didn't want to bother them.

One last shock: when I returned upstairs, Whitmore was holding what looked like a huge wrinkled orange melon with yellow spots on its skin. When he let it go, it hovered above the floor somehow, like it had some kind of bio-electromagnetic field of its own. He told me it was the key to Equinan reproduction, where all the children and grandchildren come from. I thought he meant an egg, but no. In effect he meant it was the other sex of the Equinans. They 'grow' in sacred groves in the jungle, where they are carefully tended and protected. But in order to reproduce, Equinans must couple with some kind of orifice that opens up in the fruits every six hours. Then the fruit rapidly matures and splits apart, blowing tiny fertilised seeds on the wind, which catch on the skin and hair of passing Equinans, eventually lodging themselves in their blood stream and coalescing into some kind of embryo in their upper stomach, to then emerge from a slit in their chests after many months gestation. Without these fruit, the Equinans cannot reproduce. We'll need more DNA tests to confirm it, but 'Sexual Dimorphism' Earth-style doesn't come close to this! The 'horses' and 'melons' are the same species? My mind is boggling at how this could have evolved and at what the full implications of it are. For a start, nobody can know who anybody's children are.

Whitmore: Things took a further turn for the bizarre this morning. We slept in beds of 'Sactrya' leaves on the palace floor last night, but when we woke up in the morning all the Equinans had lost their memories completely. Vislnqua no longer knew he was King, nor even what the palace was for. All his advisors looked at us in alarm, squawking and defecating (red pellets shot sideways from apertures on their lower knees), apparently no longer remembering what we were or how we got there. We had to flee for our own safety. Outside we found the Equinans who had operated a primitive timber rickshaw for us, puzzling over its meaning, unable to operate its mechanisms, consulting wall murals nearby for instructions.

Our planet of walking talking horses, is also one of forgetful horses, so it seems. I believe the expression for what I feel is 'a loss of centre'. Sanchez and I are in a state of increasing panic regarding the strangeness of this world, and heading back to our base-camp for safety and time to think…

*

Back at the 'landing' site, safely returned to their Entanglement chambers, Sanchez and Whitmore took a night's sleep and thereby woke up back on Earth in the Telepedrome. Vesberg was there to greet them in person, along with their respective spouses and children, with whom they were able to interact through the glass. For a week their families and ten billion other Earthlings had been able to see these sleeping bodies move arms and legs, sleepwalkers mumbling incoherently, trying to run; shadows of their real activities as enacted on Equis, as 55 Cancri k would now be known.

*

Vesberg had to take leave of the Telepedrome at short notice during the second week of the mission. His wife's mother had died, relatively unexpectedly (despite her age) and Hazel was distraught.

After the utter absorption and immersion of working with the other scientists in Nevada, Vesberg found it immeasurably strange to return to the humdrum middle-

American town of his wife's upbringing and the mundane concerns of mundane human beings.

But, despite the sadness and upheaval of the situation, the contrast ultimately proved insightful. There was much talk at the funeral, and during the wake thereafter, of everyone's memories of Hazel's mother. And it struck Vesberg with renewed astonishment how much unhappiness was given to human beings on account of their memories. Mrs Scottsdale had been an old woman, her busy daughter had only seen her once every two or three months. How big a part of Hazel's current life had she actually been? But clearly this was not the point. The crying at the funeral was not just for the loss of an old woman, but for the memory of a younger one also. Indeed, perhaps what the grief was really about was everyone's lament for time itself, the idea that anyone had to age and die at all; that happy childhood memories could never be brought back to life again. Subconsciously, subliminally, to take things to their most extreme: could everyone present be said really to be weeping for themselves; despairing in terror at the prospect of their own impending demise?

Memory was a strange thing, as was anticipation of the future. The only thing that linked these two sources of woe seemed to be the present, an elusive and fleeting concept which, fortunately, was mostly their complete opposite: a source of joy and consolation. Maybe the mysterious inhabitants of 55 Cancri k had something going for them.

Back home, Hazel showed Vesberg one of her late mother's most treasured possessions: an ancient-looking book of the poetry of Robert Burns, in which, coincidentally perhaps, he found these words written by the Ayrshire Bard on the occasion of turning over the nest of a field mouse with his plough:

Still, thou art blest, compar'd wi' me!
The present only toucheth thee:
But Och! I backward cast my e'e,
On prospects drear!
An' forward, tho' I canna see,
I guess an' fear!

*

Having been allowed another few hours of genuine sleep after their families departed, Whitmore and Sanchez were returned to the controlled coma state and woke up again on Equis.

Whitmore: Remember that old 20th century movie, 'Groundhog Day'? Today we ventured in again towards the city of Glydnosprost (as we now know it is called) and found the events of last week eerily repeated. Again, nobody knew who or what we were, or recognised us in any way. Again everyone was frightened. Again we had to subdue them with diplomacy (using a much-improved command of their language at least) and were eventually led to meet their leader. Our hearts leapt when we saw Vislnqua, hoping to be recognised but, dismayingly, his amnesia too was total. His character remained unchanged at least; good-natured and open-minded, curious about us, gentle and tolerant of our differences. I found myself wondering if human leaders would have been so calm in a similar situation. We showed him film of our previous visit (which astounded him) and made the best of the hours we had left, before the next double sunset, to explain again about ourselves and try to understand how this seemingly amnesiac world can exist and go on functioning.

Sanchez: I think I found the explanation this time: in the basement painting. I believe that the advanced civilisation that built the stone palaces decided that memory made people unhappy. There are pictures of something like mass inoculations, sort of laser lobotomies performed on the whole populace. For at least a thousand years now, the Equinans have lived in complete peace and harmony with each other and with the natural world around them, freed from the burden of memories, past regrets and grudges, or the torments of future longings. Each Equinan lives only for the day in which he finds himself, and by yielding occasionally to the instinctual whim to copulate with a piece of levitating fruit, ensures the survival and perpetuation of his race. This is a society where no mother or father or other filial bonds can be known for certain, and thus all Equinans live as brothers, sisters and cousins, freed from familial jealousies and clan rivalries.

Standing again with Vislnqua by the tall arched palace windows, as the twin suns went down, their gold and blood melting into purple fire, I felt something give way inside me suddenly, as if I were living in some weird dream, the dream of a strange child, myself perhaps. For a moment I saw Vislnqua as the spirit of my favourite horse as a child: 'Brising', somehow come back to life as a horse-man on this distant world and imparting wisdom to me. After all, how much do horses back on Earth remember or regret of the day before, or trouble themselves with thoughts of the day after?

Tears filled my eyes as I tried to explain to Vislnqua what he was missing, how humans thought of themselves within the huge span of chronology, the astonishing joys and terrors we experience because we see ourselves in time. But I felt like a square talking to a straight line about space, or a cube even, and I saw that in this world **we** were the exotic and strange ones, the fabulous freaks.

No, Vislnqua said, *I simply cannot conceive of it. You talk to me as if I have lived many lives and will live many again, like your word for 'reincarnation', and this strikes me like superstition, or a religious belief, not a tangible or helpful reality. You talk of relationships to other beings, that I have secret brothers and sisters and mothers scattered among the people I see around me, and this too seems an unprovable abstraction of dubious moral assistance. To me all Equinans are equal...*

*

Vesberg sat in his back garden, gazing up at the daylight moon, waiting for his old friends the stars to appear again and make themselves known. He was writing up his final report on the 55 Cancri k mission.

Whitmore and Sanchez had got out just in time. Thank goodness for all the digital data recordings, because had anything been left to witness statements then God help them. Whitmore had no memory of the entire mission or of any of his life beforehand, but back on Earth was at least able to remember each day and the next again, and was now slowly re-accumulating knowledge such as spelling, maths, and who his children were.

For Sanchez, the problems were worse, having somehow completely 'gone native' and acquired the inability to remember any more than each individual day she lived through. Strangely however, both astronauts, but particularly Sanchez, seemed extraordinarily happy with their situation. Even their families thought so, through their tears and confusion.

Vesberg listened to the neighbour's children playing and crying again, his invisible non-existent ghost offspring running before him in his imagination, and pondered the philosophical conundrums that the Telepedrome programme seemed to be progressively throwing up, almost as many as its scientific challenges.

Vesberg fingered the censored pages he had decided to withhold from the public report:

Whitmore: I switched our headset cameras off and kissed and embraced Sanchez. She responded passionately. For a moment I was tempted to take our suits off and have sex, and let the Equinans enjoy the spectacle. I know, I know, don't frighten the horses. But they would only have forgotten it all anyway. NASA however, might have been less forgiving. It's hard for people on Earth to share this: but Sanchez and I were both suddenly overcome with the emotional revelation of what we humans are, the unique flaws and advantages of our condition. My memories, our memories: we have so many of them, so sad, so happy. How could we ever let them go? What would that be like? Is it imaginable?

Sanchez and I looked at each other longingly and wondered... if we made love then forgot about it completely afterwards, would knowing that was going to happen, the forgetting, make the moment more or less poignant?

And would reading this note afterwards, and not knowing if we ever did make love, would that be more or less haunting than if we knew, if we remembered?

*

Vesberg sighed. Did memory make men and women happy by and large? Or mostly sad and wistful? A wood dove cooed in his favourite Cedar tree, as if in answer. Animals got by pretty well it seemed. They merely existed, happily and vibrantly, in the ever-present revelation of the here and now.

The voices of Vesberg's neighbours' children pleased him, even the screams and bawling over the falls and grazed knees, because this reminded him of childhood, happy memories, nostalgia. He looked at the clouds: dreamy ice cream, white candy floss in an eternal blue sky, blue as the deep remembered sea, lazy hot summers as a child. The wistful longing of life, always looking forward. Of course, young children have very few memories, of very little of the not very much that has yet happened to them. How ironic. Vesberg's nostalgia, his memory, he suddenly saw, was for a state without memory. Thus was it a love that sought to extinguish itself in some sense, obliterate its own viewpoint and centre. And so might not all life, despite the pleasures and terrors of its dramas and trials, be ultimately just such an equivalent longing, for the absence of life, for infinite sleep; the sweet slumber of an exhausted child after a long day in summer? Life and death, two binary stars, orbiting, pulling and feeding on each other, keeping each other in eternal motion, wakefulness and sleep.

Thus, in the laughter of children, in the epitome of life and love, did Vesberg unexpectedly find the revelation of the meaning and beauty of death. He hoped it might prove a comfort as he grew older. But something else that the Equinan leader had said echoed in his mind: about reincarnation. Was it James Joyce who had said that history was a nightmare from which he was trying to wake up? On some future mission, to some other world, might humanity yet meet some race whose memory and sense of time far exceeded ours? What was the sad litany of war and revolution on Earth after all, if not the evidence of amnesia, of a failure to wake up?

~

4

THE FRUITLESS ONES

It happened again. Alone in his office after lunch, Vesberg saw an apparition of Guy Lecaux materialise in the far corner. In a former generation, the incident would have been seen as madness or the supernatural, but the history of hideous quantum experiment failures meant that Vesberg knew only too well that he was looking at something real.

As Lecaux screamed and mimed silently in the corner, his image breaking up and repeating like a faulty film, Vesberg picked up the phone and called the Pentagon. *I thought you said you'd canned this thing, that Lecaux was contained, doused, history? What do you mean 'residuals'? 'Afterimage'? How long might this go on for? Decades? I have the rest of my life to live, you know, and the small matter of the most important exploration project in human history to oversee. You want me to go mad? Driven loopy by electro-ghosts? Sick leave? What do you mean? Resign because you boys fucked up? Dream on. Try harder, get this sorted why don't you?*

Vesberg hung up, sighed and tentatively walked over to the corner. Lecaux was gone, but had left ash traces, Hiroshima-like, his shadow image, an indelible charcoal trace on the wallpaper. Vesberg touched it with his index finger and shivered.

*

Vesberg paced the familiar silver corridors again, in his white coat, like a grand physician, the world's cameras running. Roll up, roll up, what have we here? Curt Farango and Carol Dwight, boy and girl, man and woman, entering through the big doors in their NASA survival suits. Two by two like Noah's ark. Mister Vesberg sir, you don't think the Cancri k incident should sound a note of caution about mixed sex missions? Those reporters! Their ignorant jibes still rang in his ears. Just because the last lot went loopy and ended up fucking like rabbits doesn't mean that this one will. Does it? Resort to the old strategy? Send a man alone, Robinson Crusoe, and watch him lose his marbles in slow mo'. If this one fails, we'll send girls only, promise.

The big doors slammed shut, banishing the bright light and sound. Dwight and Farango were strapped in and the count-down began, ready to push the big plungers. Bingo! 61 Virginis f. The realtime Ansible-cams showed the semblances appearing on a rocky orb 28 lights years distant. Deep coma drugs kicking in. Goodnight Nevada.

*

On live television back on Earth, the world watched agog as Carol Dwight stepped out into the pale lilac dawn of 61 Virginis f. Tall, tree-like vegetation swayed above her in a yellow hazy wind which seemed to make the sun blink. The trees had large black leathery leaves at their tops, which flapped like wings. The lower reaches of their trunks were bare except for occasional polyps which looked like branch stumps but upon close inspection actually turned out to be wet red eyes or mouths, some kind of organs, perhaps sensitive to light.

The pollen blew everywhere, driven by the winds. Dwight tried to take samples, but the spores were accumulating all over her suit, turning her yellow and fluffy, as if rolled in corn flour, ready to deep fry. Caught off-guard by this increase in pollen activity, Nevada strongly recommended caution and withdrawal, in case the particles choked her air filters.

*

Dwight stood with her arms around the thick smooth trunk of a Virginis tree, like a visiting tourist, while Farango took a souvenir photo of her.

It feels somehow sentient I think... Dwight moaned dreamily, *these trees seem to have characters, don't you think, can't you feel that?*

I think we have to get out of here soon. Head west until we find that citadel structure the probes told us about, look for intelligent life.

Dwight began crying. *Oh Curt, it's weeping now, this time I can feel it, can't you? It's singing a sad song about remembered summers...*

What the fuck? Farango gasped, some weird grassy tendrils at his feet had just clutched at his ankles and begun wrapping themselves around his legs. He kicked and writhed and cut himself free. The constant warm winds had blown a huge lake of pollen all around his feet now, and something was happening to him.

A flash of red behind his eyes. Anger, rage, as he kicked out at the tendrils, he heard them screaming out in pain, heard but did not hear, in a way he couldn't quite explain to himself. He looked at Dwight and was suddenly filled with distaste and fury. He found her ugly, irritating, alien, he wanted to reconfigure her somehow, mould her clay. Smash and tear at her, until she resembled something.... something else that he couldn't quite remember. But what?

He moved towards her raising his hands, scowling, and she cried out in wild terror. Something in his expression suddenly utterly foreign to her, as if she had never seen him before.

*

It's happening again... Vesberg sighed, despairing, over dinner at home with Hazel.

What is it, Gene? What's eating you?

Another planet, another meltdown in astronaut reliability. What am I missing in all this? What crazy rule of consciousness is this we're coming up against? Something like Schrödinger's cat, is that it? Consciousness can't encounter consciousness without contamination, alteration, transformation...?

But I thought there was no intelligent life on Virginis, Gene?

Yes, so did we all. So we still do, officially, but there's something freaky afoot again in this mission, I can feel it in my bones. The astronauts are experiencing mood swings and visions when they stand near to plants at certain times of day. I'm beginning to feel that there's some kind of native intelligence they're encountering, just one so vastly different, physically from ourselves, as to be non-understandable.

Oh, but how exciting, Gene! But that could be wonderful. Hazel exalted, throwing the Sunday roast down on the table with a triumphant smile and a flourish.

Yeah, bloody great.

Why the sarcasm, Gene?

Safety, human lives, human minds and sanity, Hazel. If we lose one more astronaut, I'll lose my job. This program is turning out to be a little ***too*** *exciting.*

But only Pleznick is presumed dead, Gene. Whitmore and Sanchez are alright, aren't they?

Try telling their families that.

*

I don't think it's the plants, Carol. It's the pollen... Farango said, as they stepped out onto the vast Plain of Circles, as it had been dubbed by NASA from previous aerial reconnaissance. Like Nazca back on Earth, the huge desert arenas seemed to make little sense at eye level. Decorative art by intelligent life, or some weird kind of wind trails, or something akin to crop circles back on Earth; the jury was still out.

In person, this close-up, some stone monuments could also be seen, circles and slabs with round portals through them, aligned with each other, miles apart, some in enormous arrays like silent, transfigured armies.

This place spooks me, Farango said.

Your turn to get hysterical and childishly unscientific then, eh?

Farango touched his face, nursing the swollen cheek and black eye he had received from Dwight. *Yeah,* he frowned, *it keeps doing that, doesn't it? It's hard to keep it together.*

The wind blew again after a bored lull. The grass was almost absent here, almost true desert, arid. The sky was purple at this time of day, noon, the landscape orange and green. Pollen blew in across their feet then gradually intensified. Some of it poured through the holes in the 'portal' stones. The ground seemed to shake for a moment and Dwight and Farango looked at each other.

The pollen intensified, then the wind rose to a howl, several howls at different pitches, through all the many different portals.

Music! Dwight shouted over the din, wading through the yellow seeds, *Could that be what this is? Some kind of enormous musical instrument?*

*

Jake Whitmore opened the door to Gene Vesberg and led him through the hallway back to the living room where he could sit him down to greet his father.

Bill? Remember me? Gene Vesberg? How are you doing these days? How's your recollection and re-education going, coming along nicely?

Bill Whitmore looked at Gene with the eyes of a four-year-old child. In front of him were building blocks, colourful toys, large wooden letters of the alphabet. The rudiments of phonemes and syllables seemed to be being taught today.

Hallo... Vespy. You come genn? Bring the ka?

Car, he means your car... Jake prompted, smiling. *He was very taken with your red sports car last time you dropped by. I promised to buy him a model one just like it. Not done it yet though, keep forgetting, thought he had too. Shit, that reminds me, I need to buy more nappies soon too.*

Tut, tut. Vesberg chuckled, good-naturedly. *No swearing in front of baby. You remember Uncle Gene, don't you, Billy boy?*

Oh yeah yeah... Bill giggled, putting his thumb in his mouth, and reaching for his juice bottle, fumbling with the rubber teat, salivating down his chest.

You decided what you want to be when you grow up again, second time around, Billy boy?

There was silence and both Jake and Gene looked at their charge expectantly. Gene wondered where the wife was, then remembered the sociology report that detailed how she had fled to her mother's house, unable to cope with the new situation. Hopefully just a temporary blip. Only 17 years old, young Jake was coping remarkably well, an example to everyone. Surely Mrs Whitmore would return once her husband's speech became coherent at least, out of curiosity as much as love.

Assonut! Bill proclaimed wildly at last, scratching the grey hairs on his forty-seven year old head, and Jake and Gene laughed and applauded whole-heartedly, eyebrows raised in delight, wondering if this was spontaneous or if one of his nursemaids had taught him it as a trick.

*

The winds had stilled, the pollen clouds dropped to the desert floor. Dwight and Farango were no longer alone. The new silence was expectant, stultifying, terrifying, shocked.

Back on Earth, people were waking each other up, running through to their televisions to turn on in disbelief, quivering in fright. The trembling of the operators of the Telepedrome was greater however: had the decision to allow live video broadcast of the missions really been entirely wise?

Within each stone now spun spheres of pollen, which one by one like miniature tornadoes, morphed outwards in sinewy trails and reconstituted themselves into humanoid forms, starting at the feet, working upwards to the head. The process eerily echoed the dupliportation process itself: how Dwight and Farango's semblances had begun appearing within their Entanglement chambers a few days earlier. This was clearly intelligence, technology even. Had something observed their arrival, so that it was copying that process now?

The figures, six of them, now completed, began to move and the astronauts jumped in terror, running towards each other's arms like frightened children.

The figures slowed, seeming to understand this reaction, modulating their progress to obey the subtle rules of human territorial ballet, opening their hands in gestures of peace and welcome, encircling only by 180 degrees so at allow the comfort of perceived escape.

They were pure pollen, no eyes or mouths, living silhouettes, shadow men. Unable to override their primal instincts, the astronauts took up their defensive positions and raised weapons, while Nevada yelled in their ears not to threaten the approaching figures.

*

The man from the FBI pulled up a seat and sat down opposite Vesberg in his office. *You seem agitated, sir, have you experienced any further Lecaux manifestations?*

No, no, not since we last spoke. Vesberg slammed his notebook shut nervously, biting his lip. *Look, I'm sorry, officer...*

Agent. Agent Downey.

Mr Downey. I know I called you out in effect and you're here at my instigation as it were, but something major has come up today as you are doubtless aware.

Downey raised his eyebrows.

Don't you watch television? The latest mission? 61 Virginis f?

Downey shook his head. *No, sir, too busy for entertainment. My wife watches the soaps all evening.*

Entertainment? Vesberg could scarcely contain his astonishment and indignation. *We're talking about finding life on other planets. There's some kind of first contact in progress now, although we don't understand it.*

I'll get the highlights at the end of the week, and my daughter follows it at school with her classmates. She mentioned something about it at breakfast. Can you show me where the Lecaux trace occurred?

Downey followed Vesberg to the corner and whistled, producing a small camera from his jacket inside pocket then taking notes.

Will he come back? Vesberg whispered, almost to himself. *Are there other afterimages of him, ghos...* he stumbled for the right words, *–manifestations of him, showing up in other locations around the globe?*

Not anymore, that are getting reported at any rate, as far as I know, sir. It's just here left now.

When will it stop?

Downey sighed. *Well, doc, you invented this black magic. Will your dudes on Virginis be coming back?* Downey watched Vesberg's dismayed frown, then continued without waiting for an answer. *The last few international Lecaux sightings were over five years ago now, 'sightings', but some of them could have been whackos, the Elvis effect and all that, jumping on the bandwagon. But you're what we call a reliable witness.*

Well, I'm glad to hear it, Vesberg laughed at last, stealing a glance at a wall monitor and checking the time.

*

Farango had lost his nerve and fired off a round of energy pulses into one of the figures, but they had passed straight through. When the hands of pollen had made contact with their brows, both he and Dwight froze then went limp, then began to shake and undergo convulsions. They were being shown pictures, data-streams of vast amounts of knowledge, history, technology, emotions, battles, cataclysms. Their brains were struggling to cope with the input speed, let alone comprehend or memorise any of it. Only a few words escaped their mouths, offering NASA clues as to what was happening to them: *Incredible... information... contact... exchange... struggling...*

Fifteen alarming minutes later, it was over and the six figures, holding up the crumpled figures of Dwight and Farango gently let them go, laying them down onto the surface of recumbent stone slabs to rest. They walked apart and began to move back towards their stone portals, but then the yellow wind picked up and blew them each apart, unravelled them into the air itself and they dispersed to the four corners of their peculiar world, returned to pollen, a million seeds, alive with potential, numb, unfeeling, sleeping, blind.

What the devil were they? Organic or technological? Vesberg asked excitedly into the microphones at NASA, pacing the floor, hands in his hair like a deranged Einstein, exasperated by the blank faces of all his advisors. *Please God, not another amnesia job,* he muttered to himself, *not another mind-wipe on the next world up. What would be the chances of that?*

As if waking up, he looked around the control room and saw that everyone else was busy analysing the life signs of the astronauts, as they had been trained, unconcerned for the moment with the bigger picture that was assailing Vesberg.

A cheer suddenly went up as one of the astronauts regained consciousness and addressed Nevada: *We need to come home,* Farango was suddenly saying, the voice tone reassuringly sane and controlled. *I need a pen and paper or something, I feel like I've just absorbed about ten centuries of facts, I'm going to need twenty years of peace and quiet to regurgitate all this for you, and I maybe only understand one tenth of it.*

Dwight was awake now too. She cleared her throat and began speaking, but what came out was like nothing any human being had uttered or heard before. It was audible but unintelligible. Extremely fast and high-pitched, almost like an old dial-up modem.

But in the control room, Vesberg screamed aloud and leapt backwards from his chair, pointing at a corner of the room where he suddenly saw Lecaux emerging through the chest of a junior scientist, gesturing and miming something obscure. Vesberg was hospitalised for a month, and the control room footage inconclusive as to what he had seen.

After four subsequent years of attempted de-encryption by teams of linguists around the world, the first paragraph of Carol Dwight's databurst was (controversially) translated as follows:

Autumn came in the high temple, our hearts became stone. Blood sun rose beneath the rib cage, too full. We tired of clothes of flesh, the old ways. The wind takes us, crossing horizons to where the dark seas weep. Memories of ancestral landscapes, murmurs in the grains of sand. How to contain it? The centuries of longing, bravery forgotten, tales told, blood spilled in ancient troughs. The stars come down at last and we, weeping like dawn birds, kiss them in the wet dew of moonrise. We feel them, new seeds, press them to us, but they will not grow. They too are many, like us but cannot join, their oneness broken, long buried or forgotten. Their star weeps in agony but not in longing for those, lost, whom it has scarcely touched. Let their rain fall but in this desert they are sweat wiped from a brow, forgotten warriors in a tale without heroism, untold. Cold, the fruitless ones, whose seed will never grow.

Since then, Curt Farango, able only to pass on his information in correct chronological order, has so far not progressed beyond chapter one concerning the geology of the planet's early history.

~

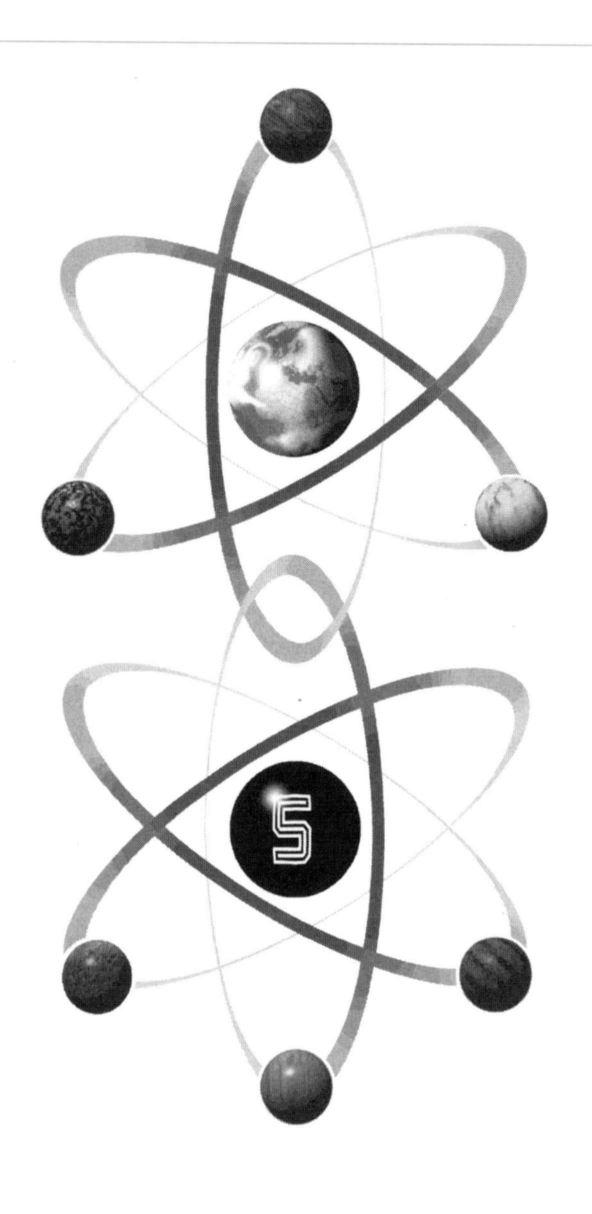

MERALIS

It was five years before the next mission that found life, and fortunately so perhaps, given the particular practical difficulties it would present. Meralis was an entirely oceanic planet, one of several moons orbiting a beautiful red gas giant reminiscent of Saturn, which in turn orbited Upsilon Andromedae. This and the other moons, each startlingly coloured, were visible, rising and setting at all sorts of times of day, from near the surface of the waters. We say waters, but the robot probes (self-adapted from flotation devices) confirmed an ocean constitution of Hydrogen, Nitrogen, Oxygen and Carbon which is to say, a sort of amino acid soup, within which the possibility of Earth-like life was deemed highly likely.

The press jokingly asked the astronauts whether they could swim or not and Hal Bruford, famously retorted that if he "fell out the boat" he'd rather drown before he could get eaten. His lieutenant Sara Janacki, as it happened, had won a bronze medal in her youth at the Canadian Olympics.

Vesberg, still troubled by visions of Guy Lecaux, not all of which could be corroborated by eyewitnesses or forensics, now increasingly relied on his rapidly promoted deputy Hillary Fording who helped in every way she could to keep the lid on the mental health rumours concerning Vesberg.

The Entanglement chambers were floating on the surface of the mostly calm seas of Meralis, when the dupliportation sequence began. On arrival, Bruford and Janacki prepared for a high-pressure dive, with oxygen tanks and floodlights. They would also anticipate having a small submarine, after a further few weeks of manual work on some specially adapted probes, capable of taking them down to the ocean floor in some of its shallower areas.

Horrifically, within fifteen minutes of diving, both astronauts were attacked by something resembling giant catfish. Back on Earth, Bruford's left leg and forearm disappeared, leaving teeth marks on the wounds, then his remaining body slowly turned black and decomposed, indicating his probable fate as being digested inside a large fish-like stomach. Janacki's body however, remained intact and pristine, although totally out of contact from the moment of the attack. Attempts were made to 'bring her back' by waking her on Earth, but these were all unsuccessful, indicating perhaps that she was fully conscious on Meralis and entirely engaged in some activity below the water's surface. The five-hour limit on her oxygen tanks was however, a cause of growing anxiety.

*

Janacki: They saved me from the Brivalgherd's jaws. Poor Bruford, God I hope he didn't suffer or ever know what hit him. I am surrounded now by The People as they seem to call themselves. My suit computer is doing a reasonable job of gradually improving its translation of their noises. Time is of the essence. They seem to have knowledge of atoms and molecules, which might enable me to explain to them what oxygen is. Could I describe its atomic number to them, would that work? I need to get them to understand my need to either return to the surface or get breathable oxygen from somewhere.

I wouldn't put that beyond them though. There is a whole underwater city down here, some kind of fantastical coral reef, but our size, with doors and windows, carvings, elaborate architectural styles beyond imagination. I have shot half an hour of video but I want to conserve battery strength for God-only-knows what… whatever I have to do to get out of here and back up to the surface.

But come to think of it, the air up there isn't particularly breathable either. Gas or liquid, what's the difference when it's not your mix? It's the movement you notice here, the way that I and these creatures are forced to move, a kind of swimming prancing motion. They have long trailing limbs, large eyes and mouths, and flat thin vertical bodies like scaly fish. They twitch and flicker as they move, blowing bubbles out of what I think are gills on either side of their throats. They are all turquoise and see-through. I can see their vital organs beating within. I feel so isolated and frightened. I need to get back to the surface again.

*

Bruford being dead, meant his body would be removed from the Entanglement chamber, and a replacement astronaut prepared for a manual rescue mission. There was widespread concern and distress on Earth for the Janacki family, who Vesberg personally invited to the Telepedrome for counselling and up-to-the-minute briefings. Sara's husband Claude and their two children Philippe and Albert, along with their maternal grandparents, were all accommodated within the residential wing and visited daily by Vesberg like a kindly uncle.

They were allowed to visit the Entanglement chamber and view their daughter at close proximity through the glass, while Vesberg prayed that a giant piranha wasn't poised to take her head off from 27 light years distant.

Afterwards, Sara Janacki's tearful mother put her hands on Vesberg's arm: *She's like sleeping beauty there, Mister Vesberg, I was almost scared to wake her...*

Gene, please call me Gene, Mrs Janacki.

But you're sure you've tried everything? You can't suddenly jolt her awake with an electric shock?

I'm afraid not, Mrs Janacki. That's not how Entanglement works. If we electrocute her here, we electrocute her on Meralis, with God knows what consequences, after which her sleeping body out there might only be in even greater peril. And fatal damage to one body would be fatal to both. Only if she returns to the original chamber on the surface of the planet could we safely bring her mind back to Earth. But I'll be honest with you, we have reasons for hope. Reasons to believe she is in the hands of some kind of intelligent beings. Her oxygen supply should have run out three hours ago, but she is still very much alive and breathing, so something or someone must be helping her or...

Or?

Well, I don't think I have any other explanation actually, it's a miracle, almost, to use a very unscientific term.

*

That night, before going to bed in his on-site quarters, Vesberg watched some television, but a Lecaux manifestation emerged from the screen and electrocuted him, throttling him with holographic hands and arms, setting fire to the carpet. The fire brigade and ambulance were called, the room sealed off, and Hillary Fording made temporary acting director of the Telepedrome the next morning.

*

Janacki: They did it. They expel oxygen, something close to an air-like mix, through their gills. They bottled it up in brown leather-like bags and refined it, then refilled my tanks with it. It stank at first, but I've gotten used to it. I'm alive, that being the main thing.

My computers have evolved to fluent communication levels now, emitting sonar-like noise from my chest box, deep infra-sound roars, mostly beneath my audible range, but I see them as water ripples.

They're not hostile as such, but they seem to be interrogating me, examining me, disbelieving of my stories. I say I am from the sky and beyond the sky, from a distant orb, but they seem to have no conception of this. In their folktales, only demons and angels can live in the sky up where the marbles play (the colourful moons that they can see when the waters are clear and calm at noon in midsummer). The idea that I can live up there, and come from a world where intelligent creatures do… all this is far-fetched in the extreme to them.

*

Hillary Fording, with a nose for a good story, brought forward Bill Whitmore's official rehabilitation date and sent him out to Meralis as Bruford's replacement. The press and the public loved it. After twelve hours of intensive repair and alteration work, he was able to take the converted probe underwater in submarine mode, using the homing beacon in its nose to try to locate Janacki.

He triangulated a grid reference, but was unable to dive

any deeper. He could make out vague ragged reef-like citadel forms in the smoky depths beneath him.

Fording and her team came up with another brainwave, and re-programmed the orbiting satellite to rotate its photovoltaic wings on its next pass and bounce a focused photon beam down into the area of ocean in question, over a 50 minute window.

As sun and probe rotated towards alignment, the world held its breath.

*

Janacki: I am understanding them at last. My eyes have been adjusting to the greater gloom down here. They are so beautiful. Gossamer thin, transparent, gently pulsating. I swim among them, gallery after gallery, tier upon tier of curvaceous stalagmites, carbonate mineral accretions, centuries old, carved, adapted, coloured, studded with jewels from the deepest ocean.

I witnessed their mating ritual. The female is half the size of the male and swims right through him, in by the mouth, out by the anus. Once to become fertilised, second time to then lay her eggs inside him. He then carries the young until birth. But does that make him the male or the female? Surely that beats human sex, to be able to completely swallow your partner, or be completely contained within their warmth?

Thus eating, for them, is at times a deeply erotic experience, more than we could ever imagine. Their charming king, Vaichandu, half-jokingly offered to swallow me the other day, and I nearly accepted.

As we speak, all our words become circular ripples emanating from our bodies, like blowing smoke rings. Vaichandu introduced me to their greatest poet, Fifklertrir. Their poetry seems to often consist of the subtle art of manipulating these rippling circles by minute amounts. Thus their language fuses perfectly the aural and the visual. We swim endlessly through these poems and through the serrated palaces, tall crevasses giving glimpses up to the light on the surface, hundreds of feet above. Shoals of little fish of every colour of the rainbow dart here and there, over our shoulder, between our feet. Some of them give us electric shocks as they swish against us. Others change colour while they look at us, as if displaying their moods, signalling their thought sequences.

Vaichandu and his consort Selpertertal are beginning to believe my stories, or at least to summon larger and larger crowds to gather around us whilst I tell them. My stories emanate from my chest and I can see their content spread out and make contact with row after row of Meralans, their eyes widening, their visible organs leaping with delight in their silvery blue see-through bodies. I struggle of course to describe our lives on Earth in terms they will all understand. Yesterday I described the United States' White House as a big white cave and the United Kingdom's Houses of Parliament as a particularly dead coral reef filled with conversational piranhas.

Vaichandu and Selpertertal were so overjoyed with my performance, that one ate the other, by which I mean of course that they had sex publicly. I tried not to blush and after the second pass asked them how many children they would produce from this coupling and when. Fourteen thousand, in ten days they said, then it dawned on me I had been swimming through everyone's nurseries for the last week.

Before I went to sleep, with my brown Gurpeefra Fish oxygen bags beside my sponge pillow, Selpertertal kissed me on the forehead and asked me if I still wanted to return to the surface. To my amazement I realised that for a moment I had quite forgotten about the idea.

*

This morning I awoke to find the citadel in turmoil. A huge swinging blade of light, about twenty feet in diameter, was slicing through the reef, burning off terraces and cornices, incinerating Meralans, cutting others in two. Vaichandu and Selpertertal and I stood on the balcony of the royal terrace, wept and watched in disbelief the destruction unfolding below. Crumbling palaces, clouds of smoke and steam, great seething crowds of maimed and dying, panicking, darting back and forth in desperation. The scythe of light seemed to be coming closer, as if looking for us, for me perhaps. Oh God, had I brought this upon my innocent hosts, who saved my life in the first place? I urged them to leave with the others, before everything was destroyed and the blade scythed through us. But they had not the heart to leave. Like our ancient custom of a captain going down with his ship, they said their whole lives had been spent there, so many fond memories crumbling to dust before their eyes. They could not bring themselves to abandon their own past and happiness. They had no appetite or curiosity for any other future. All was lost.

*

The light beam, like a great roving eye, finally found me. Trying to protect my hosts I ran out to meet it, my arms and eyes wide open, screaming up into the tyrannical sky, until my oxygen mask slipped off. All went white and hot then black. I am blinded now.

*

Now Hillary Fording had three patients to look in on. The

Nevada Telepedrome was starting to feel more like a residential care home than an instantaneous interstellar travel hub. Gene Vesberg was recovering though still heavily sedated, buoyed up by the news of Janacki's (almost) safe return.

Bill Whitmore's family were at his side in on-site intensive care, where he was being treated for the after-effects of severe decompression sickness, having heroically taken the sub-probe to beyond its depth and time limits in order to retrieve Janacki. Despite his performance, he still had a mental age of only seven. If he ever woke, he could probably run for President.

In the front room, Fording opened the door soundlessly, looked in on the scene and after a few minutes departed unnoticed. Sara Janacki sat up in bed, her hair gone prematurely grey, her eyes open but burned-out white, pupil-less, a priestess, a sorceress, a seer, arms spread out, holding forth in dramatic gesture and word, to her awestruck husband and children. The wonders she had seen in a distant world she could only struggle to describe in words now, just as she had tried and failed to do the reverse, before the weird aquatic audience in that realm of waves and fishes. Though the task was hopeless, she would burn like a mystic for many days to come, trying to share her inner light with those still trapped as she had once been, unable to see anything but the familiar world around them.

~

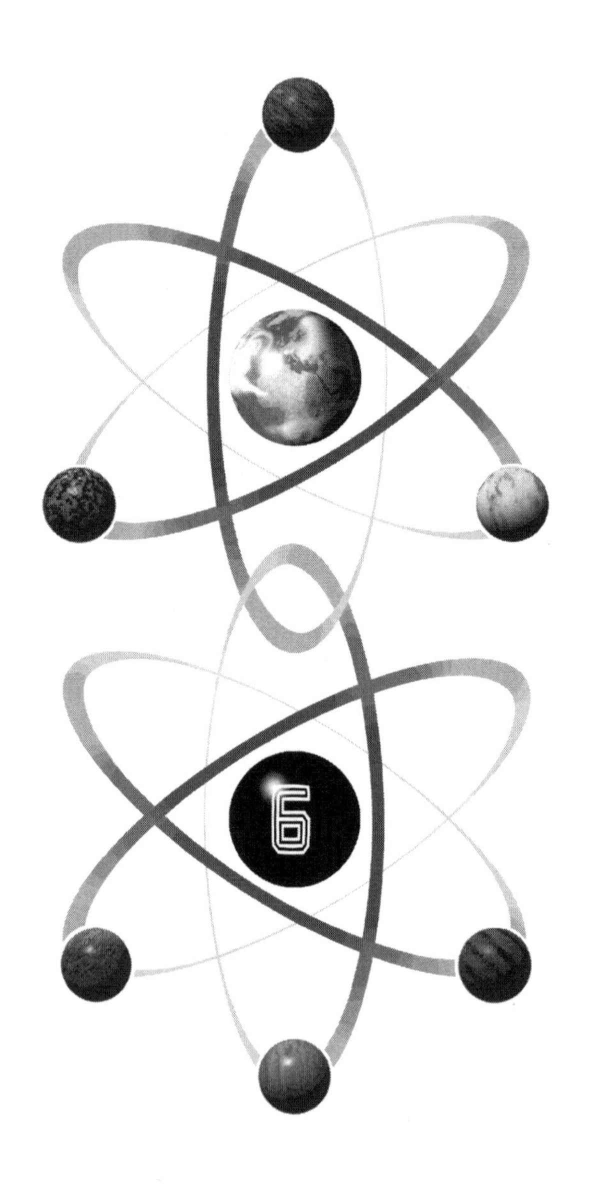
6

PROFILE

(Becky Lee Falconer's profile of Gene Vesberg and Hillary Fording: ***a special Telepedrome feature for International Geographic:)***

We've all seen it on TV. The shining silver corridors, the bee hive cells gradually filling up with sleepers, twitching, straitjacketed bodies of highly-trained men and women, dreaming of distant worlds. Dreaming and being, simultaneously of course, the bizarre miracle of Einstein's '*spooky action at a distance*', put to use at last on the grandest of humanity's grand projects.

But what of the individuals behind this gargantuan undertaking; a project described by the New York Times only last week as "a step forward from the construction of the great pyramids, a veritable Valley of the Kings where regal sleepers are worshipped by adulating millions"? The quote has some unfortunate connotations to it, relating to death and entombment of course, and it was these misgivings, highly relevant due to the rate of NASA fatalities in recent years, that I put to Hillary Fording, acting head of the dupliportation programme, when I caught up with her in her spectacular glass office with its polarised views onto the surrounding desert; an eagle's nest of a place.

Fording, a household name and face over the last six months, is much more charming in real life than the public persona we see at press conferences. She is highly cautious on the subject of fatalities and at pains to describe safety procedures and the many hours she and the original project leader Gene Vesberg spend with relatives of astronauts.

The last twenty years have irrevocably changed our understanding of what human beings are, she smiles, her trademark grey trouser suit and silver hair catching the light like some metallic angel. *Not just because of the other intelligent species that we've met, but because of the bereavement counselling, the family conferences, the vast teams of support scientists working at high speed to respond to the information being fed back live. Coming up with answers and ideas, translation software and planet-specific tools.*

We've learned I think that human beings are closer to ants than to albatrosses. By which I mean that we are pack animals, like wolves at their best, we need to be together and work together. It's a paradox, but none of us are truly ourselves when utterly alone, and then again neither can many of us be ourselves when immersed at the centre of crowds with whom we have no empathy.

What I mean to suggest is that grief, the loss of one human life, is unbearable to an individual, as an individual, but that to a group, if coped with as a group, it becomes manageable. We continue to do everything we can to prevent loss of life, but I think as a species we have reached a mature group consensus that the risks involved are containable and worth taking.

I asked Fording what her best moment had been over the last ten years and what her worst future fear was.

Her answer was that the very first contact with Extra-terrestrials, on the very first mission, to Gliese 581g, while still just an understudy to Gene Vesberg, had been her best moment so far in terms of excitement and expectation. *You never get over your first time,* she winked.

My second question seemed to trouble her more, those famous steely blue eyes darkening with summer rain clouds, but I managed to coax a candid response from her before any strategy of safe diplomacy could cut in and tie her tongue. *The risk of an alien civilisation being intelligent and hostile enough, in equal measure, to somehow use our Entanglement technology to harm us.*

Is that possible? I asked

Probably not, she smiled, flashing her perfect white teeth. *The argument goes that anyone, any thing, smart enough to know how to use an Entanglement chamber would be smart enough to have built one themselves. And anyway, any hostile or unauthorised entity making its way to here would trigger an immediate quarantine of the Telepedrome complex, so nobody need be unduly concerned. It's just my job to lie awake at night sometimes and imagine the unimaginable. There are tastefully concealed airtight doors at the end of every corridor in this place. If they ever started coming down, the pyramid analogy, Raiders of the Lost Ark etcetera, would be horribly apt, believe me. But it will never happen.*

I asked Fording about her mentor Gene Vesberg, and I could see her becoming defensive, protective of him. She was dismissive of recent rumours in the media of stress and mental health problems, of a particular perennial rumour of a cover-up regarding the death of an early student participant in the first teleportation experiments. *Ridiculous,* she laughed, *do you see any electro-ghosts in this room?* She shrugged and looked around.

But perhaps I saw ghosts in her eyes. A week later I was granted access to Vesberg himself, now in semi-retirement from public life, but said still to provide intensive input and logistical support at the peak activity times of each mission, or the 'emergency' phase as he calls it.

The work is cyclical, he said, *or volcanic even, to use a terrestrial analogy. When a new set of astronauts dupliport out and begin relaying data back, things erupt here; teams of thousands, even hundreds of thousands of individuals, here and at other sites across the globe, out of necessity, roped into what we call "the war effort". But this is just the tip of the iceberg. At other times, less intensive but equally important work still goes on, years of analysing data from flora and fauna samples, trying to understand alien cultures, preparing strategies for possible return visits.*

I asked Vesberg his greatest hope for future missions. A large-set man of Scandinavian descent, Vesberg and his wife cut unlikely figures in the humdrum domestic life that seems to have become Vesberg's desired locus of operation in recent years. The stress got to him at times, he frowns candidly, his large thatch of Viking-red hair belying his advancing years. The pseudo-suburban bungalow bristles with astronomy and physics text books, and display cases of anthropological artefacts, not all of them terrestrial.

To have intelligent life forms join us in our travels, and be dupliported back here to meet the human race in person, he beamed, *now that would be something. I'm not sure that we've found any suitable candidates yet, but I'm quietly optimistic that perhaps in a future mission, perhaps in the not too distant future, we may find beings equal or more advanced than ourselves in technological terms, who may be able to assist us and further our aims of stellar exploration.*

Questions about Vesberg's private life and family history, he has a long track-record of expertly deflecting. The essential facts are well-documented, he assured me. Born in London to Danish parents, who then emigrated to

Houston. A brilliant early career back in Europe at the Large Hadron Collider. A Nobel prize shared with Charconnier and Leiphaltz for work on Graviton and String Theory.

He seemed more keen to talk about his protégé Hillary Fording and was dismayed that I had not dug deeper into her background, rather than his. *I'm just not very interesting,* he sighed, *but Hillary has two lovely children you know, one of whom is autistic. She is devoted to them both and is undertaking some very interesting research into the neural differences in autistic brains. She and her husband do a huge amount for charity you know... she really is one of the most compassionate and imaginative scientists of her generation...*

Distracting us from Vesberg's modesty at this point, his wife dropped a couple of glasses on the kitchen floor and screamed "a ghost, Gene!" as a weird light flashed in the next room, a minor short-circuit perhaps, then a power cut darkened the whole house.

We laughed as Vesberg led me to the door, and he slapped me on the back: We can send people to Alpha Centauri now, eh? But a reliable dishwasher is still beyond us!

(Next month we hope to interview some of the Entanglement Astronauts themselves – Ed.)

~

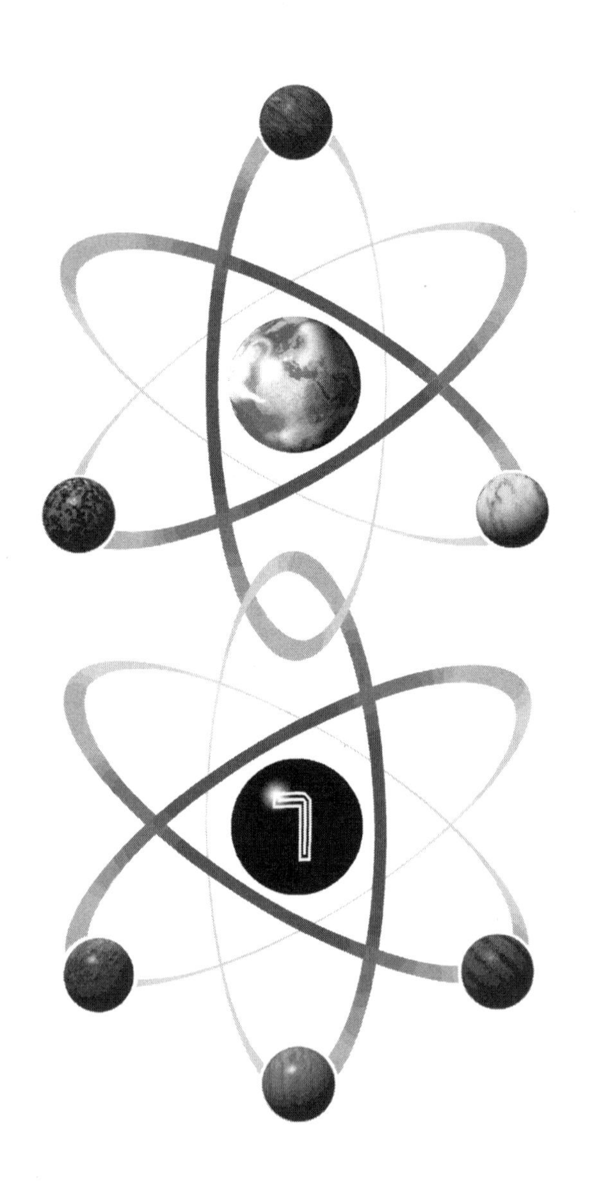
7

A TRIP TO THE ZOO

If the cosmic phone rings, don't answer it.

– Professor Simon Conway Morris

The two probe spores that landed on Zeta Reticuli 1c fed back images of a semi-arid world with possibly metallic city complexes scattered throughout its most fertile regions. Video of silver objects flying between the cities fuelled speculation that these were aerial vehicles with beings of advanced intelligence at the controls.
In view of the potential for a fruitful encounter with a civilisation equal or superior to our own, acting head of NASA Entanglement Doctor Hillary Fording took the unusual decision to dupliport four individuals at once, in two pairs, to two different sides of the planet, diverting Entanglement chambers for the purpose from the apparently barren neighbouring planet of Zeta 1b.
Our first report is from astronauts Gasson and Nelder…

Gasson: Not a bad little world. Bright, good weather. Another two-sunner, binary stars, good for TV sun tan. Deceptive though. Nasties in the atmosphere, arsenic, radon and lead dust in winds from the desert. Breathing apparatus essential.

Silver objects in the distance, like aerial motorways. Wonder why these guys haven't spotted us in their defence systems or radar yet. Looks like we're going to have to fire-up the surface-rover and head in their direction to try and introduce ourselves, try and flag down a silver taxi!

Nelder: What an unbelievable spectacle. After 15 hours rolling and bumping over the weird hard-baked blue dunes of Zeta (shale, lead and iridium-rich metamorphic rocks – a planet with signs of ancient extreme volcanism), the vegetation began to intensify: red trees like giant alpine sedum, succulents, with green seed-bubbles that are released from their trumpet-tops every time the wind blows.

Examining all these, marvelling, taking samples as we went, we finally arrived beneath the silver aerial 'motorway' and attempted to signal to it. Using our photovoltaic panels on the vehicle to flash up to them, by changing their orientation in one minute cycles – so far we haven't caught any fish. But truth be told, somehow we feel like minnows.

Gasson: Shit. A few of them spotted us, came half way down, circled, then moved on. Half an hour later another few swooped real low, circled again and left. Completely silver disks. A bit like old Earth fairy tales of 'flying saucers', very fast and neat. I took stills, and film, paused it, zoomed in. No apparent seams or chassis work. No obvious means of propulsion, i.e. wings, propellers or jet. Possibly highly advanced technology. Some kind of exotic-matter engine, harnessing matter to anti-matter reactions? Anybody's guess. These boys are way ahead of us by the looks of things. Starting to feel like dormice here, sniffing for cheese at the edge of somebody's big picnic. Can see glimmering silver spires of 'City Four' in the distance as Zeta 1 sets, while Zeta 2 prepares to rise behind us. Amazing light effects in the sky and clouds, rainbow mist we're calling it, but I'd need the spectrometer back at camp to identify precisely what constituent elements are in these amazing clouds.

Nelder: Gasson's dead. They took his suit off to see what he was, then cut him open to see why they'd killed him. They paralysed me with some kind of laser which scrambled my brain, my nervous system. Effects only wearing off now, hours later. Now I'm inside one of their craft I think. Strange smells. Like they're tinkering with the air in this compartment I'm being held in, to see what I can breathe or tolerate. Seamless silver walls, floors and ceilings. Mind-blowingly advanced. They're half our height, grey-blue skin, large black eyes. If they're speaking to each other, I can't hear it. Outside our audible range? But their faces, their mouths, don't suggest speech either. Maybe they have some sort of technology, like WiFi, wired into their brains. I saw them nodding to holographic screens that opened out of nowhere, even in the open air, on the blood-stained plain where they butchered Gasson. Oh God, I'm scared. These things are so beyond us. Cold, dispassionate, calculating. I feel... violated, powerless, weak. Where are they taking me?

*

Mission B: Soklov and Varinder.

Soklov: Your warning got to us too late, Earth. The silver sky-ships came for us and paralysed us with their beams. Now we are on board their ship being transported somewhere, but at least we have each other's company. We've tried flashing our universal signals of greeting at them, each projecting movies onto the walls from our suits when they come in to perform checks on us, but they seem completely uninterested in what we have to say for ourselves. One of them just put a silver probe up Varinder's anus and made him ejaculate into some kind of test tube. I am deeply disorientated and distressed.

Varinder: This doesn't feel good, the signs are bad, Nevada. Please relay my undying love to my wife Mariska and children Sanjay and Devan. Your daddy will always be with you in spirit, though far away, I will always be close, that is my promise, God willing. We never thought it would end like this. These creatures may be advanced, but I have a terrible sense of evil and foreboding from them. They do not love us, they are cold, colder than the stars and wiser than gods. I can't explain it, but it's what I feel. They seem to communicate by 'feel', they are messing with our brains somehow, putting ideas and images there remotely, to test us. God, get us out of here. They have no respect for us as intelligent beings. It is monstrous.

Soklov: Fortunately they have left our suits intact, including our radios and other portable equipment. They have also transported our lander module and put it here with us, in the middle of a large room with glass walls. There are other humans here, incredible to relate. Their English seems degenerate in some way, as if they are descendants of previous captives taken from Earth. Is that possible? Could the Zetans have been to Earth a century or so ago and taken these people's forebears back as subjects for study? What a hideous scenario.

The landscape and apparatus within this room are quite bizarre, I must break off this communication now and attempt further discussion with the other human captives.

Varinder: A reunion! Jack Nelder has just been let into the cage, via some kind of vertical white beam of light, astonishing! He seems in good condition physically but has just related to us the tragic and horrific circumstances of Gasson's death. He is deeply traumatised, his nerves shot. Shady figures, Zetans I think, are wandering around the outside of the glass, looking in at us. Sounds like sirens are going off, and lasers and water jets firing in to rouse our fellow humans. They seem to know what is expected of them, as if it is a daily ritual.

Nelder: Oh God. Soklov thinks this is a scientific study we're part of. But it seems plain to me that this is a zoo, nothing more or less. But a terrible and violent one.

In the far corner is an area of rain forest that other humans, in their torn military uniforms, are expected to fight over each day with machine guns and machetes. This is for real. Two have been shot in the chest and head, another one lost an arm and seems to be bleeding to death. All will be dead within hours, and no medical attention is being offered by our captors. The next stage, now in progress, seems to involve the burning of the forest and the setting off of explosions inside a kind of mock-up metal city they have in the other corner. People are being maimed, and women rounded up and raped. They've just taken Amanda Soklov and shaved all her hair off, ripped off her clothes. Varinder and I fought to protect her, but I got a rifle butt in my face for my trouble, four broken teeth, while Varinder has been shot in the leg. Oh this is Hell, Nevada. What is going on? Why is this happening? All the time, the aliens seem to be passing by beyond the glass, half-hidden in darkness, hundreds of thousands of them, sometimes I see their eyes glimmering, watching always watching, goading on this barbaric madness.

Soklov: It seems to be the next day. I am sore and tired, hideously bruised, but I have no memory of yesterday's events. Nelder and Varinder have just played me their diary tapes of yesterday and I am horrified and heart-sick. They too have had their memories blanked, so our video technology is all we have to go on. The people we saw killed yesterday, judging by our diaries, have now somehow been resurrected or repaired. Or could they be clones? The possibilities are monstrous and endless. That forest that was burned now appears magically intact again, and yet when I touch it, it appears completely lifelike and real. We are zoo animals, in the most sophisticated exhibit cage ever constructed, and our fate appears to be to wage war upon each other for alien amusement, ad infinitum, world without end.

Varinder: Just checked the diaries again. It's repeating every day, our memories erased at some imperceptible moment during the night. I tried to stay awake last night on guard, but I remember a strange smell. Perhaps they gas us to put us all out, or maybe something more subtle. I noticed a change in Nelder yesterday. He became more angry and aggressive around the same time as the other inmates. I think the aliens are able to affect our brains somehow, invisibly. Maybe it's hormones or some kind of waveform signals that affect our neural synapses. Their sophistication is formidable, and yet their moral scruples seem sickeningly negligible. How can they treat us like this? We are not savages! We are thinking, reasoning, intelligent beings, who created gothic cathedrals and exquisite oil paintings, Beethoven and Mozart. Well OK, we didn't create Beethoven and Mozart, they were individuals, but you know what I mean. Is there some way we could break this daily cycle within this cage? Start a guerrilla movement of art and culture and pacifism to win over and subdue the deranged mobs around us? Nelder just took a bullet in the eye, and Soklov is being made to perform oral sex on a regiment of mercenaries. Is that my answer?

Soklov: I made it out. I must have been so badly damaged yesterday that an on-site repair wouldn't suffice. Varinder told me it was something to do with my vagina and a machine-gun barrel. They thought I was still unconscious as they were hovering back down into the zoo complex, but I took my chances and ran for it.

The crowds must only come later in the day. I passed glass cage after cage, just like our own. If only I could have filmed it, oh the wonders I caught sight of! A dozen planets, weird aliens, incredible colours and shapes of vegetation, each only glimpsed for a second as I ran and ran, terrified, darting and diving, hiding in corners, looking for fissures, routes of escape, while the silver craft shot back and forth above, looking for me inside the darkness of some huge dome we must all be contained within.

When the sun came out, I understood the architecture I was part of. Great glazed shards of some metallic material, sloping overhead, a huge polygonal tent. A tent, yes, like a bloody circus tent! Oh my poor colleagues, Nelder and Varinder. When the Zetan visitors started coming in, during the first light of dawn, I waited for a quiet moment then darted outside.

Now I walk across their equivalent of a lush savannah, heading south towards their desert. I have a record in my diary in which Nelder states that the Zetans never found his and Gasson's lander module. I wrote down the digital coordinates as he told me them. There is hope. The silver ships stream by high overhead, but hopefully to them I am as insignificant as a fruit fly or an escaped lab rat. Why did we ever want to make ourselves known to other life, Nevada? Had you any idea of the dangers of that? I hope you have now.

I don't know if I'll make it. I've slept two nights in the open so far and escaped detection and recapture. The variations in temperatures are at the limits of my endurance and my oxygen is running low. If I make it to the module and it's undamaged then I may be able to return to Earth unscathed. Oh please, God. But I must mentally prepare for other outcomes. If I don't make it, but this recording gets through, then please relay my love to my mother and my boyfriend Steve. I've had a good life, I just wish I'd stayed on Earth and gone on enjoying it, without asking for more. What foolish greed. I would have married Steve and had babies, and made you proud, Mom. But it's nobody's fault all this, I must be brave now. So must we all. I did this for humanity, for the good of all of us, our knowledge of the universe and how God constructed us within it.

Prove to me that what the aliens see every day in that zoo is not really us. This is my challenge, my final statement, Soklov signing off. Prove to yourselves that we are better, that we are more compassionate than the Zetans, that knowledge is not everything, is nothing in fact, unless tempered with love.

~

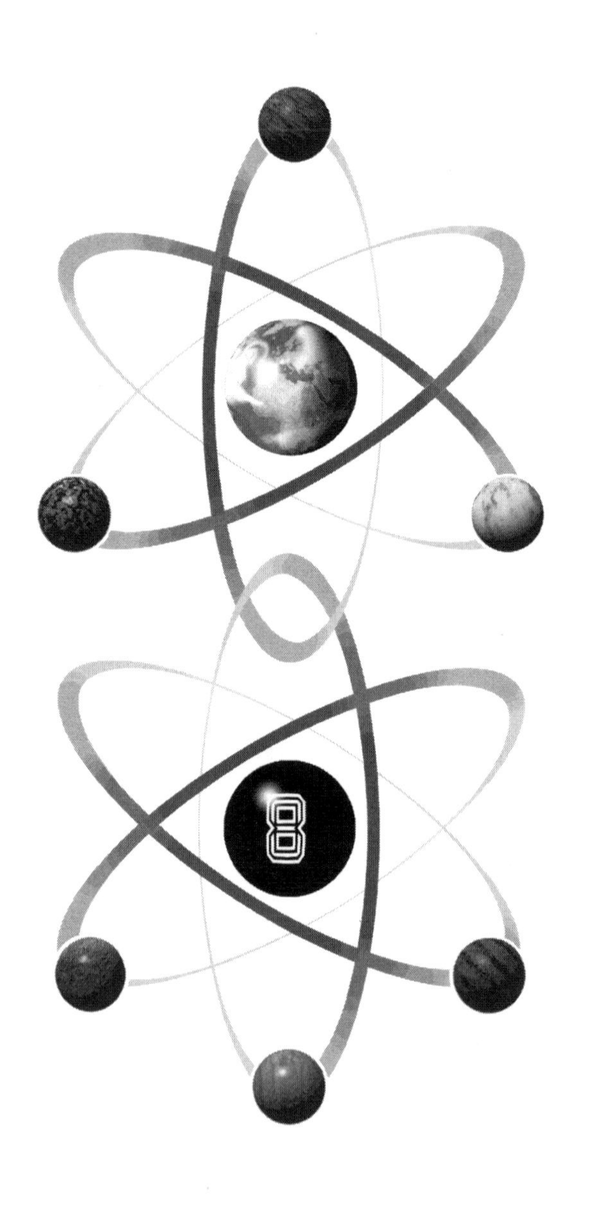

CENTAURI

No more? A monster then, a dream,
A discord. Dragons of the prime,
That tare each other in their slime,
Were mellow music match'd with him...

– Alfred, Lord Tennyson, *In Memoriam A.H.H.*

Alpha Centauri A g looked like it was going to be something of an enigma. After the unexpected complications and ambiguities of all the previous missions, Hillary Fording almost hoped that the hugely barren-looking surface of the planet might just be the whole story. But no matter how many times she replayed the aerial reconnaissance films she found the same inexplicable anomalies: cities, or at least some kind of massive structures, that could disappear completely from one day to the next.

It reminded her of sand castles on the beach, or the enigmatic games of her autistic son, Nathan. Playing with him that evening, laying out his toys on the living room rug, she told him about the strange things she was seeing on the planet she was about to commit explorers to, and his eyes uncharacteristically lit up. Usually these days it was only numbers and lists of colours and shapes that seemed to interest him, rather than this kind of direct conversational data.

Using his building blocks she even tried to recreate from memory some of the different ephemeral patterns and structures that had been observed from one day to the next. She had to be imagining it, but with real urgency, Nathan seemed to push the blocks towards their next configuration in the sequence, as if he somehow understood some underlying language, that all the computing power of NASA and the wider world had somehow missed.

Meanwhile, when she went to stand at the patio doors, she saw her other 'normal' son Peter engaged in make-believe war with the neighbours' children, dressed in his plastic Roman armour, brandishing a wooden sword, roaring like a little tyrant.

Boys... all born to kill... she whispered, *made by God, and yet we feel the guilt of it... why oh why if we are destined for the stars are we still equipped for the mud and blood of hell on Earth?*

She turned back with sad and loving eyes to gaze again at the self-absorbed and secret play of Nathan, strange changeling, born to be bullied by his fellow little savages, and cast aside by the strident march of time. Or was he?

*

Although Fording had no official second-in-command, her geology and biology lead-advisors, Melnikov and Serranto, one old, one young, tended to gain most of her attention and informally share the role. Fortunately there seemed to be little friction between them, although the younger was alarmingly keen to impress, and (although Fording did her best to hide the far-fetched possibility from herself) seemed to basically have a crush on her.

Such a syndrome had seemed common among young women after all, attracted to their professors, when she had been an astronomy student at UCLA, so why not the other way around now? The psychology usually went along the lines of offspring of divorced parents, looking for a missing parent figure. She hoped she would not find out this level of detail with Carlo Serranto. But then again, some hidden part of her wished the opposite.

Always immaculately dressed in masculine suits, with short silver hair, sometimes Fording still caught sight of herself in glass reflections in the Telepedrome or in the polished steel walls and doors there, and fancied she caught a glimpse in her silhouette of the pretty and precocious teenager she had once been.

At its best, her work still brought that out in her. The utter excitement of the countdown to landing on another world, ploughing through data and projections, she felt all the clothes of years fall away from her until she was like her little Nathan, lost in his own secretly marvellous world.

*

The astronauts would be two women this time. Something of an experiment and not, despite media speculation, Fording's idea. The full extent of the errors made on the 55 Cancri k mission had, after lengthy review (not yet made public), suggested that perhaps the intensity of shared experience on an alien world had provoked some kind of latent romantic bond between Bill Whitmore and Angela Sanchez, and even a sexual one, in response to danger. It was demeaning to think of the creators of interstellar technology as still so biologically primitive, but Fording thought of her high school science lessons and the microbes under the microscope reproducing like mad when threatened, and saw the logic in it.

Fiona Yung and Natalie Lapidaire said goodbye to their families and the watching world outside the silver doors, in the ever-blazing sunlight of the Nevada desert. The forecast had warned of a sandstorm near Las Vegas, but unlike the rocket launches at Cape Canaveral of a century before, such instances were of little relevance unless they clogged the Telepedrome's cooling vents. 'Launch' time was assured.

At 6pm, Pacific Standard Time, the silver 'plungers' began their work on live television, and Yung and Lapidaire, strapped down, were passed on their beds, slow and regal as dead queens lying in state, into the quantum-entangled matter chambers and thus dupliported onto Centauri A g. After a half hour of equipment checks and neurological scans, the probe doors were opened on the alien world and the two astronauts stepped out.

The ghostly apparition of two gas giants filled the beautiful daytime sky, the neighbouring planets named Centauri A c and A d, fabulous Jupiter-like jewels of swirling colourful gases. Their hues were currently muted through the deep indigo blue sky overhead, the drifting reddish clouds, an iron-rich atmosphere. Underfoot, the surface somewhat resembled what they had just left: a kind of sub-desert of reddish sand with small stunted cactus-like plants and clumps of grasses. From what aerial reconnaissance had told them, such was the measure of all of the surface of Centauri A g: an extraordinarily monotonous and boring world, save for its peculiar architectural ephemera.

Yung and Lapidaire walked for five miles, taking samples of the flora and fauna as they went: many peculiar insects that flitted ceaselessly between the desert flowers that were just beginning to open, apparently the start of spring in this latitude.

Back on Earth, Serranto ran back and forth excitedly as the information came through, relaying it to a pyramid of botanical experts scattered across the globe. Insects with twelve razor-thin legs like serrated fronds, others propelling themselves on fermented gases blown from their swollen thoraxes. Melnikov became restless that a landing site had been chosen so far from any of the planet's more volcanologically active zones. Fording sat astride them all at the helm in the control room, and smiled to herself at the joy of exploration, a sort of armchair Captain Kirk, as her husband had once described her.

Four hours into the mission, just at the point at which the astronauts would have needed to turn back, visual contact was made with large-scale anthropoid life, or perhaps it was arthropod or insectoid.

Erring on the side of caution, Yung and Lapidaire took up concealed positions behind some brown scrub grass, batting away clouds of red razor-flies and yellow puff-hops (nicknames being devised on the spur of the moment back in Nevada), and set up field telescopes with which to observe the larger scale life forms safely. Although apparently potentially intelligent, their physical appearance was alarming. The first impression, unfortunately, was of giant scorpions, being darkish brown with orange and red spots, six legs, two upper arms and large feathery antennae. Their eyes were large and bright red, with a peculiar diamond-like facetted structure to them, not unlike what would be the compound eye of a bee or fly on Earth.

The creatures were emerging from holes in the sand and coming together to communicate, touching their antennae together, which then produced green luminous sparks, which could be seen flickering across their eyes, then passing down through their bodies. Two individuals would meet, confer, break off, then another three meet, then five, seven, finally all breaking off, and so on. After half an hour, perhaps a hundred of them were meeting in a large circle of activity, and the green fire of communication was rippling across them all, but beginning to coalesce and co-ordinate itself into some coherent synchronised pattern. As if at some unseen and unheard signal, the entire group suddenly stopped and arranged itself into a perfect circle and began to pulse, their attention focussed on the centre, where a cloud of sand and dust began to rise.

What's happening? Lapidaire asked Yung.

Can you feel that? Yung replied.

What?

A vibration beneath us, and... fear...

Fear?

At that point, scarcely thirty feet in front of them, a 'scorpion' began to emerge from beneath the sand, then another to their right hand side. Instinctively panicking, not waiting for NASA's instructions, the astronauts stowed their telescopes and began running back in the direction of the landing site.

As they ran, like the stuff of nightmares, other scorpions began to emerge from the ground at various points around them, and once almost directly in front, each about twenty feet long, forcing the two women to run in different directions, heightening their alarm.

They're not approaching us... Yung screamed. *I'm not sure they can even see us! Stay calm!* she added, as much to herself as to Lapidaire.

Back on Earth, their families were greatly alarmed of course by the sight of their sleeping bodies thrashing around in their restraint straps, as if having the worst nightmares imaginable.

A sigh of relief went once around planet Earth, when they made it back to the landing probe and re-entered sleep state with the steel doors firmly shut. The comfort provided by their families that evening, albeit through walls of glass in quarantine, was decisive in renewing their morale and calming their life signs back to normal.

*

So we can't design that out from our equations then, eh? Vincent Hildegard, the mission psychologist, sighed as he sat with Fording and her advisors around the table that night, reviewing the mission progress.

It doesn't look like it, Serranto nodded, *we are organisms ourselves after all, and physiologically rather frail-looking compared to these things. The fear reflex is there to protect us. We're just lucky that they didn't seem to actually want to chase or attack our astronauts.*

I think you'll want to see this! a voice called, a head around the door. Colin Blakely, aerial recon supervisor, laid out some colour prints on the desk, activated the screen on the wall and tuned it to the channel from his desk. *Look! This is the site where we saw the dust rising. A new structure!*

Fascinating... Fording whispered.

Melnikov tensed up, his interest pricked. *Quite a structure, can we see it from the probe site also?*

Yes, in the distance, here, Blakely swapped the screen images across.

It's like a city... can we see movement inside it? Serranto marvelled.

Or a beehive, a crystal.... a snow drop, but more irregular, Venice from the air, a molecular maze... Melnikov mumbled.

Fear or no fear, we need to get our astronauts back over there tomorrow to look at this thing close up, before it disappears like all the others, Fording mused.

Do we really think these scorpions built this? How could they create such a structure in so short a time, any ideas? Melnikov asked.

Could be like a coral or a honeycomb, mineral-crystalline secretions from glands on their bodies somewhere... Serranto postulated.

Not from only a hundred of them, surely. We'd need to be seeing millions, and vigorously at work, not just sitting around thinking about it.

Interesting... Fording frowned. *Maybe you've hit the nail on the head there. Sitting around. We're sitting around every day, aren't we? And yet we do a lot of work, do we not?*

Of course! Blakely laughed, *or get the robots to do it. A full-time job either way.*

Well, maybe that's a sign of advanced intelligence at work, and technology. Vast amounts of work being accomplished, apparently effortlessly, by a small team of beings.

But they have no technology, none that we can see at least... Hildegard chipped in, frustrated. *Are you saying that these scorpions are telekinetic or something? That would be absurd.*

Fording sighed, and held her hands up. *Now, generally speaking, what have we learned more than anything so far, from all of these missions, over the last ten years, anyone, any answers?*

Everyone around the table laughed, a little uncomfortably, like they were back at nursery school, reluctant to take her pedantic bait.

How stupid we are? Hildegard asked dourly.

Close, very close, Vince... Fording smiled, *very close indeed. No, what we've learned is that nothing is absurd on an alien world. That absurd is a word best left behind on earth. Life itself is absurd if we think about it, its very existence in a vast and barren cosmos is absurd. Life on our own Earth is certainly absurd, from one day to the next, since we still wage wars do we not? – Still waste resources and squabble over them? Our own planet only seems non-absurd to us because we are used to it. But to a red-spotted giant telepathic scorpion from Centauri A g, I dare say Earth is as weird as a blue grapefruit. Open minds are what we need, and more field data. Lecture over. Everyone get some sleep now.*

*

Using the Ansibles, some additional body armour was dupliported out, and Yung and Lapidaire, showing extraordinary bravery, ventured out again the next day on Centauri A g. A Centauran day being equivalent to 52 earth hours, they were in fact thoroughly rested and prepared.

The most stressful thing, Lapidaire said aloud, as she walked across the Centauran desert, *is the spooky feeling that something might come out of this sand at any moment.*

Yeah, Yung chipped in. *I wouldn't go as far as to call it post-traumatic stress disorder, but we are still thoroughly freaked, Nevada, I have to be honest with you.*

Fording spoke to them directly via Ansible: *From our studies so far, this flurry of activity only occurs just prior to a structure being built. We believe that the site should be inert now, and empty. Also, the Centaurans have shown no aggression so far, remember, either to each other, or to you, or any other life forms. These known facts so far are reassuring... that armour of theirs may merely be to protect them from sunlight, or a vestige from their evolutionary past, like our monkey hair.*

I wish you were here to hold my hand, big sister... Yung laughed, and the control room followed suit, a release of tension.

Half an hour later, the tension had turned to awe as they approached the structure. *Earth, are you getting this? It's vast, beautiful. An incredible polygonal city, irrational angles and shafts and openings and vaults. It's totally nuts...*

Samples, samples... Melnikov cut in, at Fording's side,

tell them to find out what the hell it is made of.

Yung, can you sample the structure somehow? Get up close and touch it, cut it, just a tiny piece.

Tentatively, like an ant approaching the finger of a human hand, Yung walked forward then knelt down in the shadows at the base of the towering edifice.

Left behind thirty feet further out, Lapidaire turned and powered up her analysis equipment. Kneeling, she looked over her shoulder just in time to see several scorpions emerging from the structure and prodding at a screaming Yung. Clutching her sampling pot, Yung was gesticulating wildly and running back from the structure's base, as Fording shouted urgently into Lapidaire's ear: *The hailing signal, the greeting! Transmit it now! Please stay calm and transmit...*

Lapidaire fumbled frantically with the array of equipment in her backpack, laying it out on the sand in front of her, suppressing through a Herculean force of will all her urges to scream and run or help Yung. As she succeeded in setting the transmitter going, she found Yung holding onto her back like a child and turned around and embraced her, weeping and shivering. Around them, closely arraigned, an army of scorpions regarded them, hemming them in, removing all hope of escape. The crab-like clicking of their armour and the low guttural blips of their curious language now encircled them, along with strange heat and smells, the humming of a kind of electricity, sudden flashes from antennae and green pulses illuminating their shells.

Slowly, as time went by, Lapidaire felt her and Yung's heartbeats slowing, calming down. She was reminded of being a child again, looking after her kid sister back in Wyoming, and longed to be back at that moment, to escape the present. Gradually however, as the silence calmed, Nevada spoke into her ear: *What's happening?*

Well done. Is the signal working? It was a composite of some of their language we'd picked up from yesterday. Your life signs appear normal. Please report your condition...

Lapidaire forced herself to open her eyes and look about at the fearsome creatures surrounding her. Again, like a child, she somehow had thought that not looking would protect her, but in fact the imaginary objects of her fear had been worse than the actuality now in front of her. As she looked again, still stroking Yung's back, she found the scientist in her taking over. They were fascinating, complex, sophisticated. Of course they were, just as she was. Some God, some **something** after all, had made them both. How astonishing to bring two such diversities together under the same sun. It was like getting to meet God at last, a little bit of him at least, a glimpse of his insane genius, as much as she could bear. The limbs were jointed and armoured in elaborate ways, their evolutionary development entirely non-terrestrial. The red and orange markings on skin and shell were more beautiful and varied than they had appeared at a distance. The jaws were not dripping with hideous fluids as she had imagined them, but lined with many small black hairs. There were no fierce teeth or callipers on show. The eyes were astonishing. Insect-like, vastly different from human, yes, but the more she looked from one to the other, the more she began to see... something, feel something. One of them jerked back a little, the one she had stared at most. It gurgled and clicked, speaking perhaps. She turned and repeated the trick with another and yes, something responded, the creature twitched, retreated, calmed. Lapidaire thought of horses or cows, something gentle, curious, benign, the way they had come and gathered around her as a child. Incredibly, one of them came forward and lifted an arm towards her gently, tentatively, exploring. Lapidaire touched the arm softly and it withdrew, but when it came again she repeated the gesture, trying to stroke it.

It's OK, it's OK... she whispered to Yung. *I think it's OK, Fiona. You can look up now. I don't think they're hostile at all. We're going to be alright.*

Meanwhile Nevada was talking rapidly in Lapidaire's ear. Fording had Marc Dubceck at her side, head of the linguistics unit. *Listen to me, Natalie, we've been analysing their communication. Most of it is inaudible to you apart from the odd grunt, because it's in the ultrasound range, but we're going to start pitch-bending it for you and progressively translating. It will sound like gobbledegook to you at first. But I want you to start repeating the phrases and gestures that we've rehearsed before. The greeting protocols. Can you do that? As you speak, we will be translating and transmitting back into their language, or trying to. The more you do it, the longer it goes on, the more the process should evolve, with a bit of luck. Keep it simple at first, then slowly branch out, using gestures, remember. The sounds will come from the device on your chest, so make sure you angle it toward whoever you address and keep it clear of obstructions. You copy?*

Lapidaire and Yung now stood back-to-back and slowly rotated, facing the wall of brown armour and red glowing eyes. A babble of sound became audible, like insect clicks and whirrings, whistles, hoots, chatterings. *Greetings,* Yung forced herself to say, voice shaking. *We are peaceful, we present no harm to you. We have come to learn...*

A word came back, distorted, and Lapidaire nearly jumped: *What was that?!*

Don't whisper, Fiona, Fording cut in, *...everything will be translated. If you want to speak directly only to us for a moment, then press the com button on your left arm,* *remember? I know you're stressed, but you're doing very well...*

What origin? They are asking "what origin?" and "what destination?" Dubceck clarified the weird half words coming through for them.

Earth, Yung said stupidly, then realised the pointlessness of the word. *From the stars,* she pointed to the sky, and to her alarm then almost hysterical laughter, this sent the scorpions all moving back to look up and follow her pointing finger.

Oh my God, Lapidaire held down her com button, *They're responding! We're actually communicating!*

Stay calm, Fording intoned. *Concentrate on gestures. Use your arms.*

Arm, Yung said, pointing to her own, then reached forward to almost touch one of theirs. *Mouth,* she said, then repeated the technique, eyes, feet, trying to build a vocabulary. *We are from a star in your night sky.*

Too complicated, Lapidaire patched over to her. *Try shadow. Point to shadow, then sky, then say everything shadow, that might give us their word for night.*

Something changed. The scorpions began touching them gently, and vice versa. Yung found herself crying in relief and joy. The circle broke as the scorpions began leading them, escorting them to an aperture in their city, then they began to climb a steeply sloping ramp into its vast interior.

The sample... Melnikov whispered to Fording. *Get Yung to put her sample into the portable Ansible they have with them. We need to know what they're walking on, what the city's made of, if it's scheduled to disappear in 24 hours. It could be corrosive or radioactive. They could be in danger.*

Oxygen as well, Serranto added. *We need to keep monitoring the atmosphere inside these tunnels. Their breathing apparatus is filtering oxygen in from the*

Centauran atmosphere, if levels drop they will begin to use their own tanks up too quickly...

We feel safe... Yung said, as if in answer to all these overheard fears like ghosts in her head, and Melnikov frowned, and took the microphone from Fording:

Forget what you feel. Study, observe only. We need firm facts.

Annoyed at this breach of protocol, Fording took the mike back sharply and said: *Reverse that, both of you. Pay attention to what you feel, trust what you feel. Your subconscious can process data faster than your conscious minds, you're there to tell us things that robots can't. If anything feels wrong then stop and retreat.*

*

By the time night began to fall on Centauri A g, Lapidaire and Yung were seated at the centre of a vast irregularly shaped room at the heart of a bewilderingly complex structure. Above, below and behind them: scorpions moved, emerged from tunnels and entered new ones, meeting, greeting each other, discussing, exchanging information. The structure of the walls, they saw now, was partially translucent, so that the spectacle around them was growing more awe-inspiring by the second. They glimpsed corridor and chamber after chamber, layer upon complex layers, and up somewhere beyond it as a backdrop: the night sky, the stars, one of which, incredibly, they knew must be Sol and the Earth itself. Yung pointed to it and attempted to explain it to their hosts. Lapidaire opened a device on her backpack and showed the Centaurans their own planet from space, then Earth, and tried to explain the difference.

NASA's computers were making rapid progress on translation. Somewhere along the line, some *Rosetta Stone* of conversation had occurred between Centaurans discussing something the astronauts had said, and unlocked a cascade of meaning, and complete alphabets and dictionaries were being rapidly amassed and transmitted back to the Ansibles in real time.

What is that imagining? asked one of the Centaurans. They had asked his name and it had sounded like "Jarscallop", so this would have to do.

Why 'Imagining?' Yung asked, *have they no word for technology?*

How you do here come? So way long?

To find, to discover... answered Lapidaire, and stroked the side of Jarscallop's huge head. She had discovered that this was their sign of greeting and communication and, since she had no antennae, was probably over-using it as a conversational device.

Curiosity... we this understand. But said we how, you mis-altered wordings our, or your imagining did, the one your chest on ... Jarscallop's feelers were running over all the technological devices attached to the astronauts, caressing them like precious jewels.

How? Many centuries, tens of centuries of knowledge. We, our parents and parents of parents, studied and unlocked the secrets of the tiniest of things. Atoms and what make up atoms. The tiny building blocks of the universe, that revealed to us the rules of reality and how to use and bend those rules. We solved their mysteries then built clever machines that could carry us here. In thus simplifying her language, Lapidaire found herself somehow sounding like a stumbling alien herself, and struck by the strange vertigo of summarising human history and endeavour in so few sentences. *First we sent the probes, then we travelled instantly to the probes, by a kind of magic, quantum entanglement we call it, a profound understanding of the properties of matter exploited to our advantage.*

Yung shook her head. *No, they won't get that, you're losing them.* She addressed Jarscallop and "Sinthilluic" his apparent companion or queen, directly: *The things we call machines, you don't seem to have them. You call them imaginings. What are imaginings?*

Jarscallop gestured to everything and everywhere around him.

The whole world? Lapidaire looked confused.

No, I get it, Yung nodded her head. *They mean this structure. That's it, isn't it? How did you build this whole structure so quickly?*

By imagining it, came the simple reply.

Who, one of you? All of you?

It took all us of to this imagine, Sinthilluic said, *even but five with or six us of we imagine can something smaller.*

Like what? Please demonstrate.

Six or seven of their audience gathered into a circle and flashed their antennae furiously then watched as a pool of light began to glow at the centre of their circle. When they stopped, a scrub bush and a pile of rocks, complete with buzzing insects lay on the floor between them.

How often do you make things by imagining and why? Lapidaire gasped, shaking with wonder.

Average on, every about days eighty, the when people together come.

What is this structure? What does it mean? What is it for?

City this is model of thoughts everybody's, a crystallisation, a manifestation all of our minds of. We its explore corridors we as ourselves explore. This how is meet we choose and with partners which lay to eggs and create people new, children our. This how is where and enjoy we other each celebrate and life.

From space, the night sky above you, we have seen structures like this all over the planet. What are those?

Other colonies, Jarscallop said, *our cousins.*

Do you ever fight with them, have wars? Fight amongst yourselves?

Why you do this ask? Sinthilluic twitched, perhaps uncomfortably.

Because we had wars once, Lapidaire cut in, being selective with the truth, *for centuries, many died. A great sadness to us, but we learned to overcome it.* Yung looked at her uncertainly, nervous of these distortions.

Fording cut in at this point, a voice in their earpieces. *Be careful, Lapidaire. Dubceck is telling me that their word for war is illness, you are telling them that you are ill, diseased, or have been so in the past.*

Can catch disease this we? Jarscallop asked, his compound eyes flashing in its many segments, like fabulous diamonds.

No, no, Yung assured them, stroking their heads furiously. *Look at us! We are far too different from you for that. Can you catch diseases off the grasses or tiny insects of this world?*

Yes... came the ominous answer.

Bad call... Dubceck's voice could be heard lamenting in the background with Fording.

*

Somehow, Fording found herself having dinner in Reno after work with Carlo Serranto. Melnikov and Dubceck had been supposed to come along too, a winding-down drink on the way home, but through some sleight-of-hand and confusion she ended up in something horribly like a dinner date. Fortunately the lighting in the place was low, to hide her embarrassment. But was that fortunate?

Yung and Lapidaire had suddenly made it back out. Peacefully, if mysteriously, rejected, and were now making their way back across the desert to the landing site.

It seemed as if some kind of first stage of the mission, perhaps the mission in its entirety, was therefore nearly complete, subject to review of the data. Much had been learned, contact had been made. It seemed safe to clock off and leave old Gene Vesberg in charge, former director, back in for a night's excitement at the helm. The press would like that. Return of a familiar face.

Fording wanted to keep the subject firmly on work, but to her surprise Serranto started asking about her children, particularly Nathan, and she found herself disarmed, especially by Serranto's response when she mentioned Nathan's interest in the Centauran structures.

Damn, he was attractive. It was a cliché, but those dark brown Italian eyes... She nearly lost focus on what he was saying, which come to think of it, was actually pretty interesting:

I read a theory recently, a serious one, in New Scientist or The Lancet or something. Some research team in India. They said they thought they'd found evidence that autism was a kind of evolutionary leap. Everyone knows physical organisms can evolve, through natural selection, right? But the question no one's answered yet is whether consciousness can go on evolving. There simply hasn't been enough of it around for long enough on Earth for us to know. Advanced consciousness like ours, I mean. Maybe it's like a caterpillar and a chrysalis, waiting to find a way to turn into a butterfly. Maybe autistic kids, through the kind of intense electronic communication that the web makes possible, could be prototypes for a kind of human virtual brain, a mass-communication super-event. They're not good at traditional social interaction, because they're primed for something else, a whole horizon that we're just stumbling onto the edge of...

I thought you were a biologist and botanist, Carlo, not a Sci-Fi writer? Fording frowned.

Carlo laughed and shrugged his shoulders. *Hey, I'm having the night off, I'm allowed to be whatever I want sometimes, amn't I? Einstein was a patents clerk in his day job you know, hey wait...* Serranto was standing up, someone was entering the restaurant, a waiter going to meet him, some kind of emergency. It was Dubceck's secretary.

Mrs Fording, sorry to interrupt you, Professor Vesberg's orders. We have a major crisis unfolding back at the Telepedrome. A taxi is waiting outside.

*

When they made it back to Nevada just before midnight, Vesberg looked tired and worried, as if he had been left to baby-sit a child with rabies.

It's Yung and Lapidaire... we began to notice something odd in their conversation during the second hour after you left. They were repeating the same phrases over and over again, every ten minutes. They weren't even making sense anymore or listening to each other.

Why wasn't I told about this immediately? Fording barked, and Vesberg stepped back, visibly insulted.

Dubceck came back in and began analysing the data for the next hour, the conversation. We didn't think it meant anything serious or fatal.

Fatal? What's happened?

Before they even reached the landing site, they began to break up.

Break up?

Like radio static, interference. Holes appearing in them, right through them. I've never seen anything like it. Here, we'll play the film back for you. Then three minutes later, they became semi-transparent then they just disappeared. It's never happened before. Their original bodies are still alive next door, life signs completely normal. We've been reviewing records of the early experiments, dupliportation process malfunctions, asking ourselves if the entanglement could have been weakened and broken somehow.... that happened in some of the very first dupliportations last century you know.

Did it? I've never heard of that. But no. No, no, no.... that's not it at all. Fording ran her hands through her hair, agitated, struggling to think. *Their life signs, was there anything unusual in their life signs?*

Towards the end, yes, they began fading out, heart rate, breathing...

No. Further back, when they first left the structure.

Yes... Dubceck was poring over the data on screen now, *Look... Yung's heart rate and blood pressure went through the roof for a half hour, Lapidaire's pretty high too, even though they were just walking across the desert, talking calmly, inconsequentially to each other.*

No. That's it. We need to send a probe out into the desert again, back towards the structure. Don't you see? They're still there, inside it. The things we saw weren't Yung and Lapidaire at all, they were manifestations of them, imaginary visions of them, dreamt by the Centaurans.

But they were living, moving, real.

So was the city they built, right, Melnikov?

Silica and amino-acid, half and half. Particles of sand structured into living tissue, held together by some kind electromagnetic energy, the same as we saw in their bodies and antennae perhaps.

When is Centauran sunrise? Fording asked urgently. *How long will it take a probe to roll out there, a day and half, two?*

*

Lapidaire: Oh God, what a mistake we made. Were we safer not understanding each other? Or did we just not communicate enough?

As night came on, the city around us became gradually translucent, then transparent, so that more and more of the eerie moonlight from the two gas giants could filter down towards us, and behind that the stars, our distant home. It would have been beautiful if not for the fact that we were imprisoned now. The Centaurans shot out some kind of white silk from between their hind legs and wrapped us up like spider's prey. Yung screamed in terror, thinking we would be eaten, but I could not believe that the intelligence we had encountered could be capable of such barbarism. I was sure we merely misunderstood. They had thought that we were ill, carriers of infection, that was all, and so: chose to quarantine us. But who can say for sure?

They went back to their strange work. Above us and below us and all about: we could see their silhouetted forms moving backwards and forwards. A hundred thousand paths and rooms, overlaid across each other, no angle the same twice, the geometry infinitely irrational and complex, the internal structure of some vast ephemeral insectoid brain.

As the night progressed, the city's structure became progressively see-through, then brittle, then began to melt like ice, as the Centaurans all moved away, burrowing back into the desert sand. In the end, with the gas giants sinking in the west, we were left alone on the desert floor amid the last few ruins of ice, still tied-up back-to-back, looking up at the stars, the beautiful lonely stars in their deep ink-blue sea of night.

We were mortally cold by morning, but when the great yellow sun rose above the horizon we were rapidly warmed again, the life returning to us. The razor-flies and puff-hops came, sniffed us, all the little bugs and creepy-crawlies. But they didn't seem interested in us so much as in the weird white bindings around us. So shivering, beset with a thousand tiny bites and nips, we've sat as these little creatures very slowly gnaw away at our chains.

It's taking so long. We're still here and running out of oxygen and water in this daylight heat. We're burning up, and Yung has lost consciousness now. But I believe it's going to happen. Just like HG Wells had it in The War Of The Worlds: the little things, the overlooked and underfoot, they're going to save us, set us free again…

*

On Earth, Nathan Fording swept his little hands violently through the tower of plastic see-through bricks he had made on the living room carpet, and chuckled to himself heartily. His father came through from the kitchen to see what the noise was.

Hey, Nate! Mummy's coming home soon, another mission accomplished. Now does that sound good? We'll go to the park together. Hey, what you got there? Did you knock that whole palace down, the one daddy built with you?

Nathan pointed to the red cube, his favourite game, and swapped it around with his two inverted buckets, making his dad point to the one with the red brick under it, an old magician's trick. This time however, Mr Fording was genuinely astounded to find that his choice of bucket empty and the other one with both the red and a blue brick under it.

Now how the devil did you pull that off, Nate? He scratched his head.

Mummy not coming home tonight… Nathan mumbled, as if in answer.

~

9

INVESTIGATIONS

Leaving the Telepedrome administration block, Agent Downey found an attractive blonde girl leaning on his car, waiting for him. He had never seen her before in his life. Despite all logical and cautionary impulses, he felt excited. Then she opened her mouth.

Heading into Reno, Mister Downey? she asked.

And you are? He countered dryly, reaching defensively for his sunglasses.

Just a girl looking for a lift.

Who knows my name. How is that?

Oh word gets around, about you and Vesberg.

My ongoing case with Vesberg is confidential. My name is not given out to anyone as I enter and leave this building. So how do you know it?

You're assuming I work here.

Ahhh... now gossip has just escalated to security breach in my mental alarm system. Not good.

So what you gonna do? she laughed nonchalantly, tossing her hair back. *Arrest me on suspicion? Throw the cuffs on me? Bundle me into the back of your car?*

Why am I getting the feeling that you'd like that? Wouldn't catching a bus be easier for you? Downey looked around and thought he noticed a Venetian blind on the administration block twitching, someone watching them. He looked back again, but perhaps it was just the blazing sun reflecting off the steel and glass.

The girl sighed. *I guess you just never did flirting at school did you?*

I missed that class, can't have been paying attention. Wait! To his amazement, now that he had unlocked the doors, she was getting in on the passenger's side. *You can't just do that. I'm a federal agent!*

As he got in himself and sat down, he noticed some new expression on her face. *Shit, you didn't know that did you?*

Clever boy... she purred. *Neither I did. But I do now. You better escort this new security risk away from the site then eh?*

Downey sighed. It was true. Women had always seemed to get the better of him. He never understood what they wanted, and even when what they wanted turned out to be sex he didn't always understand that until he woke up naked with them, unlike every other guy he knew who always seemed to be in control. Or maybe that was just the way they told it. Maybe women found his diffidence attractive. Clueless, his ex-wife had called this trait, a cruel epithet for a detective. *Reno?*

She nodded and smiled, matter of fact, offering him some chewing gum.

As they reached the freeway, Downey tried to relax into the long drive. She looked harmless enough, whatever that was worth. *So... what do you want exactly?... I never did catch your name.*

Rebeccah. Friends call me Becky. Becky Lee Falconer. I'm a reporter.

Not heard of you, sorry.

Maybe you should have. I did an interview piece on Vesberg and Fording last year in International Geographic. You're interested in Vesberg, right, looking into him?

Downey frowned. *You're fishing for information from me I see. I'm helping Vesberg out... with some unusual problems he's been having, not investigating him per se. But I'm not sure why I should be telling you even that much.*

Maybe because you're not getting anywhere, and I've got some missing jigsaw pieces that will suddenly make a whole lot more sense of what you've been finding.

Interesting... Downey sighed, almost despite himself. He thought for a moment, eyes scanning the familiar desert, the scrub and rocks and cactus. *In return for what?*

Well, it's a gamble I know, but I was thinking... especially now that I know you're with the Feds, that maybe you have some pieces of my jigsaw puzzle too, only you don't realise it. We have pieces of each other's jigsaws and we're scratching our heads wondering why nothing fits.

Very pretty... Downey mused, *you make it sound like a marriage proposal.*

You wish, she smirked, *hey, when did you last get laid?*

Downey screwed up his face, and despite his best attempt at self-control, probably blushed. *What has that to do with anything, precisely?*

You mentioned marriage, don't blame me. Besides, you didn't laugh. If a guy doesn't laugh at that question then it's been ages.

You ask that a lot?

No actually, I just read that in a magazine. Listen, let's stop fucking about. I'll come clean right now. I have a document for you to read, a story. It was leaked to me by someone from within the Telepedrome complex, I have no idea who, but I do have a line of contact to them, convoluted, carefully anonymous. I can't give you a copy of this document, but I can let you read it once in my presence then I'll take it away with me. Pull in at the next motel, and you can read this thing then tell me in return everything you know about Vesberg.

Or you could read it aloud to me now, while I drive. What do you think I know?

These rumours about an early entanglement experiment having gone wrong, they've been doing the rounds on the web for decades now, right? Paranormal whackos getting off on it. But what if there's some scientific truth behind it, covered up by NASA? What if they're connected to Vesberg's early retirement due to stress? He's been seeing things, right? That's the word on the block. Except if he was seeing things it would be a psychologist was visiting him once a week, except it's not is it, it's you. Very strange. So I ask myself, what kind of apparitions can the FBI help a man stop seeing?

A name. Downey spoke slowly now, taking her seriously. *I need to hear a name, to know that you know what you're talking about.*

Lecaux. Guy Lecaux.

Downey showed no reaction, but that in itself told Becky something.

I scored a ten there, right? On to round two?

What else do you think you have?

His parents. I know, you think he didn't have any, brought up by ageing aunt and uncle, the perfect human guinea pig, but he had adoptive parents and he had a brother by birth, one he didn't even know about, but who's researched him since and has been looking for information. I've met all these people and interviewed them, along with old class mates and neighbours, even a few people who worked on the experiments.

At that Downey raised an eyebrow. She noticed.

They're all scared of course, all been sworn to silence. But something morally wrong went down there, all those years ago, and people don't get over stuff like that. It burns and burns inside them, until, usually near or after retirement, they find they need a metaphorical priest to confess to.

And then you step in... and ask them when they last got laid.

I ought to whack you... Becky snorted bitterly, *but not while you're driving.*

~

10

DISENTANGLEMENT

When the stars threw down their spears,
And watered heaven with their tears,
Did he smile his work to see?
Did he who made the Lamb make thee?

– William Blake, *The Tyger*

The mass rocket launches, the *Dandelion Year* as it would come to be called, were still five years off. When Earth would release its myriad 'probe-spores' of quantum-entangled matter chambers on their many separate trajectories to the stars. To do so, helium-3 would be required for the rockets' nuclear fusion engines, from its single most reliable and copious source: the Moon's surface.

Vesberg found himself living in New Athens, in among the white pueblo-style houses and streets under the vast geodesic biomes in The Sea Of Tranquillity. One-sixth terrestrial gravity. Earth's master architects had been shipped out to let their hair down at thc big hotel complexes: silica-concrete cantilevers a quarter-mile long (which tourists loved to picnic under when the sun was full-on), hundred-foot high lobbies that you could float down through, from your room to breakfast, by the simple trick of spreading your arms to reveal the cloth glider-wings between arm and back. Architects had always loved defying gravity, and here gravity was considerably easier to shout down.

Drinking was difficult (liquid in bouncing spheres), sex was pretty special, walking was weird, apt to a make a fellow run and leap, feel pretty great about himself, like an angel, an *Übermensch*. The old terrestrial problem of sea-legs was mild in comparison to moon-legs, and already, now that children were being born here, some returnees to Earth were complaining of aching limbs from its shockingly draconian gravity. Soon enough there would doubtless be true Lunans, products of evolutionary divergence; people with bones too weak to survive on Earth.

Vesberg was in New Athens incognito, under the name John Vanbrugh, and for good reason. Traumatised by the horrific Lecaux incident, he had resolved that NASA's next human guinea pig would be himself, under his own authority, in secret, no moral blow-back or shame. Hazel had been appalled at first obviously, but the sleep-inducement techniques had to be practised and mastered on someone. So at the Telepedrome in Nevada, NASA had fed Vesberg into the quantum-entangled matter chamber and watched his perfect semblance emerge simultaneously at the Mons Hadley facility on Luna.

Now by day on Earth, Vesberg lived his ostensibly normal scientific life as a NASA employee, returning home every evening for dinner with his wife, then would retire to a sterile stainless steel room in their mansion and go to sleep under computer supervision, only to find himself waking up alone in New Athens, in his comfortable luxury moonrock apartment, parting the curtains to see the blazing sun overhead in its counter-intuitive black sky, a beautiful crescent-Earth rising up on the horizon. From there he would set off on a full-day, supervising the helium-3 mining and refinement twenty miles out of town, and reviewing biological data on himself and other potential dupliport candidates.

Sometimes Hazel would let herself into his room on Earth, and watch him, strapped down for his own protection, his legs twitching (as he ran and bounced on Luna), his closed eyelids flickering and his face and arms turning (as he steered his moon-racer over wild terrain, whooping like a gleeful madman), his lips on Earth only emitting muted moans. Her husband was a man of two worlds now, the first ever perhaps, in secret, but doubtless not the last. Had all gone well, in a few years NASA would have gone public and proudly told the world(s) what Vesberg's self-experiment had taught them, but as it turned out, just as with the Lecaux mishaps, something unexpected intervened, that although it brought embarrassment, also offered tantalising clues to yet another dimly-lit plane of scientific knowledge that they had chanced upon.

After his vigorous day on Luna, Vesberg would come home, shower, eat a TV dinner, then fall asleep in a computer-monitored steel room identical to that on Earth, where a moment later he would find himself waking up to the smell of Hazel making breakfast, the sound of her soft contralto voice singing in the kitchen. It was theoretically a highly satisfactory arrangement, since both bodies on both worlds received their adequate allocation of rest. But like every astounding scientific breakthrough, and this was more astounding than most, the drawbacks were hidden at first, but serious. Where in this tight round-the-clock schedule was Vesberg, the disembodied mind of Vesberg, his intellectual nexus, getting the opportunity to dream? All his dreams were reality, quite literally.

Most ordinary citizens on Luna could only afford to

travel home to Earth once or twice a year on the scheduled rockets, Christmas and midsummer (a distinction lost on Australians) and, most employment being mining related, the wages were not as high as people had expected. The potential usefulness of the technology Vesberg was secretly test-driving was therefore obvious. If every man or woman working on Luna could gain their shore leave by the simple trick of sleep, then vast amounts of wasted energy, yearning, unhappiness (and psychological counselling for moon madness) could be averted overnight, so to speak. But the cost of every kilogram of quantum-entangled matter remained astronomical, astronomical being the key word, since outward to the stars was the top priority for which the stuff was being painstakingly manufactured and stockpiled.

That summer on Luna, Vesberg was invited to a reception in the Selenis Hotel, designed by Hank Leitbau, the expressionist master architect. The thing resembled some kind of alien spider, an intersection of hanging shards and mandibles that seemed poised to fall over at any second but nonchalantly refused to do so: white gleaming mooncrete, curving picture windows, lacelike anthropomorphic structural vaults overhead like spider webs. Everyone seemed sure it was beautiful.

Somewhere during the evening he was introduced to Clara Marquez, and immediately captivated. Vivacious and scholarly, they were engaged in frenetic conversation for only a few minutes before they took each other's arms and jumped off the balcony. On Earth, that last sentence would have signified something quite shocking of course, some suicidal gesture, impossibly romantic. But their armpit wings fanned out and the two of them floated gracefully down to the ground floor hall together, low-g spheres of champagne blowing around them like soap bubbles or confetti.

Clara was a theoretical physicist with a background in geology, fascinated by the quantum mechanical possibilities on Luna with its helium-3, the potential to turn nuclear fusion to new uses, to build bases on Europa and Titan. She was, in short, Vesberg's kind of girl.

He had to be careful. He maintained his cover as John Vanbrugh with a ridiculous (but convincing) stick-on moustache for the next four months as they began dating. Although a senior figure with NASA back in Nevada, he didn't yet have much of a public profile, but it was nonetheless possible that Clara might realise his real identity.

Her own background gave her good reason to travel to the mining sites with Vesberg, and he even appointed her to assist at the Mons Hadley facility, fast-tracking her security clearance.

Of an afternoon, the bulk of their work done, the two of them would sometimes leave together for protracted moon-racer excursions, hurtling at high speed over the craters, thrilling and spilling, sometimes saved by silica-foam bags, once taking a thirty-six hour hike to the far side, looking for archaeological sites, the disputed Zetan ruins and so forth.

Back on Earth, when Vesberg woke up each day to his other, original life, Hazel became increasingly suspicious. A woman knows her own husband. And while the laws of entanglement did not allow that the scent of perfume on his neck on Luna would leave any trace on his neck on Earth, the impact of that perfume on his demeanour, his heart and mind and soul, was quite another matter.

Some nights in late August, Hazel would arise in the middle of the night after some vaguely disconcerting dream, afraid to remember its symbols, and go to stand at her curtains overlooking their carefully maintained garden, its desert palms gleaming in the moonlight. And there it was, rising up over the trees: the moon, where her husband was, where he went each night, unknowable and unreachable, his dark side made manifest. Since time immemorial, the moon has governed human bodies, women particularly. The great unseen oceans of the Earth and the secret blood of every living thing: heave and sigh in awe of that fickle lantern, beholden to it. Hapless slaves, like the creations of God unable to question their obscure master. Wolves, dogs, madmen everywhere: stare through the bars of their convulsive prisons at this enigma, their tormentor. And now people actually lived on it, were born there. What could that mean?

Hazel heard a soft moan from her husband as she passed by outside his room. Pressing her ear to the door to listen… she heard another moan, then rising louder. She turned the door handle and went inside, and thought at first that moonlight filled this room also, then realised it was only the eerie light of the monitoring computers reflected by the stainless steel walls.

Fascinated and vaguely guilty in trepidation, unsure if she was allowed to venture this close, Hazel looked in awe to see that her husband had an erection under the blankets and body-straps, and that his breaths were quickening, his lips occasionally flattened as if by contact with some unseen object… or person. His chest heaved as he approached orgasm, and she swore she could see the sheets flinch and darken for a second. A wet dream? But he was awake, somewhere else, betraying Hazel, betraying himself with his own body which he was powerless to hide.

Meanwhile on Luna, getting his breath back, their lovemaking over, Vesberg stood up and went to join Clara at her hotel window. Her room was on the top storey at the highest point at the centre of the main biome, the suburbs of New Athens visible far below. He draped a thin white blanket over her shoulder and kissed her neck as she pressed a button and turned the electro-blinds to clear. *Sometimes it reminds me of Andalusia,* she sighed, *the hill towns of southern Spain, Ronda la Vieja, where I grew up.*

Do you miss Earth? he asked her.

Oh sure. Six months is a long time to wait for a train home. Don't you?

Vesberg laughed, unable to help himself, the low-g, the *Übermensch* effect, getting hold of him. *Nope... I go there every night in my dreams.*

Are dreams enough though? Hey John, she got excited, pushing him back onto the bed, *I read an article about that last week, the NASA exploration programme. They say that's exactly how they're going to use that teleportation thing, quantum entanglement, except they're calling it dupliportation now. They say the astronauts will go to Alpha Centauri by being duplicated, then come home in sleep, in their dreams.*

Vesberg smiled nervously, caught off guard. *Yes, I know...* he said, *I've worked on that programme.*

She played with the hairs on his chest and smiled darkly at him. *You're not just a mining specialist are you, John? I've seen the way the security men at the hotels watch your back.* She stroked his cheek now, watching his eyes carefully. *When were you really last home on Earth, John?*

Vesberg stood up, shivered and returned to the window again, as if to close the blinds, then looked off to the east and caught sight of a full Earth rising up from behind the far horizon, like a great blue eye, complex, virile, all-knowing, watchful. *Last December, like I told you before...* Vesberg said to the window glass.

No, I don't think so... Clara sighed. *You know what I think? I think you went there last night, John.*

I have to be leaving soon... he said, turning quickly, looking for his clothes.

And why is that, John? Why do you always have to scuttle off home to that luxury pueblo of yours? I know you've not got a wife, not on this world at least. How come you can never bring yourself to spend the night here, to fall asleep here in my arms?

It's... it's complicated, he stammered, avoiding her eyes, straightening his hair in the mirror. *I have to take some medication and stuff, sleep-therapy tapes. I snore...*

Clara's Mediterranean temper flared and she stood up and grabbed his scrotum in her hands and kissed him viciously, biting his lip. *Don't you lie or cheat on me now, John, don't you ever...*

Back on Earth, in the eerie electric light of the silver room, Hazel Vesberg gasped as she looked on at her husband's sleeping body, his chest tensing and freezing, his breath sharply drawn in. Blood appeared on his lip and trickled down his chin.

As if to answer it with her own love and fear, a tear came from her eye and ran across her cheek.

*

The following week, Hazel Vesberg took her own revenge of sorts. Having heard her husband lie when he woke up each morning on Earth, she waited until midnight Earth-time then stole into the computer room and slipped her hand under the covers and began to massage his flaccid penis.

At work on Luna, in the middle of giving a briefing to a Chinese delegation on particle physics, he had to suffer the embarrassment and indignity of a raging hard-on in tight trousers, followed by a violent ejaculation as he staggered and stumbled across the room, heading for the toilet.

The terrestrial NASA entanglement monitoring system was alerted and a team sent out to the Vesberg home in Reno, and Hazel tried to maintain it was just a software glitch until confronted with the CCTV footage.

*

Helium-3 comes from the sun, the greatest nuclear reactor of all, in endless but varying waves of solar wind, deflected by Earth's atmosphere, but embedded copiously in the soil of Luna. But this flypaper status is a two-sided coin. The greatest of hazards on the lunar mining colonies were solar flares, gamma-ray bursts, and meteor showers, for which an elaborate system of satellite warning stations had been set up, together with lead-shielded underground bunkers beneath every major building, where citizens could retreat upon hearing the sirens.

Clara and Vesberg were out on 'safari', on the fateful afternoon of November 15th, half way up the slopes of Mons Huygens, stepping out of a moon-racer, about to unlock the door of a remote geodesic 'bothy', where they doubtless planned to make love and wine bubbles. The combined Leonid meteor shower and Gamma-ray burst was of a scale and ferocity which proved the costly inadequacy of the Lunar Orbital Warning System and devastated the colonies of New Athens and Nuevo Rio, and the resort of Shangri Lhasa, claiming 3058 lives in total and causing damage which took a decade to repair. Inadvertently, the tragedy sealed the fate of the supporters of manned spaceflight and decisively boosted the hands of what would soon become known as the Telepedrome Dupliportation Programme. The proponents of unmanned spaceflight would rely on quantum teleportation to place human consciousness, in much greater comparative safety, onto the surface of aliens worlds deemed likely to harbour life.

Being too distant from civilisation at the time, and having switched off their in-suit datacoms for privacy, Vesberg and Clara Marquez had received no warnings and took the full dosage of debris, particles and plasma. The radiation killed Clara almost instantly, being briefly of an intensity half that at the epicentre of Hiroshima.

What happened to Vesberg however, was more complex and unexpected. Quantum *dis*entanglement had been performed on sub-atomic matter since the late twentieth century, but never on a large, complex, living organism. Indeed, to this day it remains as banned and outlawed as human cloning and nuclear fission, the results being too unpredictable to be conscionable. Whatever the contents of the Leonid shower, some of the particles effected a change on Vesberg's state which has not been identified or replicated in lab conditions since: they severed the quantum entanglement between Vesberg's lunar semblance and his own original body on earth, that is to say: between Gene Vesberg and John Vanbrugh.

Terrified of losing both their top scientist and the guinea pig of a very expensive experiment, NASA took over the Vesberg's home in Reno in the critical hour of warning they had before the shower hit home, and fearing the worst without lunar radio contact with Vesberg, they bombarded the pores on the skin of his terrestrial body with a high-energy spray of lead atoms for the fifteen minutes of probable meteor impact that their calculations pointed to, while pumping the inside of his body with potassium iodide, sodium bicarbonate, and magnesium chloride.

Übermensch again, saved by the boffins of his nearby home-world, Gene Vesberg knelt on the cold white wastes of Luna and wept, holding the dying body of Clara Marquez in his arms. By then the black sky was alight with icy blue and silver streaks, a million cruel spears of mortality raining down on a world without water or tears.

By the time he returned to the ruins of New Athens with Clara's body, he would find that he could no longer sleep, or rather that when he dreamt he could no longer return his consciousness to Earth and to his wife and home in Nevada.

Vesberg hailed Nevada from the only vid screen still working, in a police bunker on Kennedy Boulevard. On Earth, weeping and terrified, Hazel, helped by the NASA technicians, brought the original Gene Vesberg to the screen to confront his counterpart, and John and Gene, Vanbrugh and Vesberg, looked at each other in mutual horror and wonder. Both were sentient, both were awake, violating the known laws of physics and biology. Vanbrugh tore off his false moustache with a howl of involuntary pain, while Vesberg remained impassive. Vanbrughs's forehead was bleeding from meteorite debris, while Vesberg on Earth put his hand to his face and found nothing. They were no longer the same person from this point forward. They were free.

Gene Vesberg went on of course, to become the famous lead scientist of the Telepedrome programme, the Einstein of his day. But a small number of very studious biographers and historians have since noticed a very peculiar anomaly in his profile, and mostly dismissed it as clerical error: Gene Vesberg is 140 years old.

Despite recent advances in telomere manipulation technology, and judging by his still youthful looks: this is entirely impossible. Except by one means only: in the Dandelion Year, NASA concealed John Vanbrugh, at his request, inside the Proxima Centauri Long Orbital probe, with sufficient oxygen and food to survive the fifty year journey, a fusion rocket travelling the 10 light-year round trip at constantly accelerating velocities approaching light speed. Due to the effects of relativity and time dilation, he only aged one year inside the rocket for every five on Earth, and returned in time to secretly take over from his own ageing original.

They could have put him to sleep for the outward trip, to

relieve the boredom of the terrible blackness of interstellar space before reaching the Centauri system, but at his own request he remained conscious for the entire journey. He said he wanted time to reflect on the death of Clara Marquez, for which he somehow blamed himself.

Thus in the end did Hazel Vesberg obtain a second husband, a younger man, just as he had betrayed her with a younger woman, the strange symmetry complete, half a century later. It's not known how Hazel received the new Gene Vesberg, the replacement spouse that NASA thoughtfully provided for her, a few hours after the original's death from cancer. But at least he'd had a long time to work on his apology.

~

Can't you see something wrong in that story? Becky Lee Falconer asked Agent Downey, leaning over him with a cup of coffee, allowing him to look recklessly down her exposed cleavage with an expression of incredulity in his eyes.

Wrong? Downey puzzled.

The wrong man died of cancer... think about it. I reckon Vanburgh and Vesberg met secretly after Marquez's death and agreed to swap places. That way it makes more sense...

11

ESCALADORE

I falter where I firmly trod,
And falling with my weight of cares
Upon the great world's altar-stairs
That slope thro' darkness up to God...

– Alfred, Lord Tennyson, *In Memoriam A.H.H.*

There seemed little doubt that the planet of Sigma Draconis d contained life. Even to enter its atmosphere, the probe-spores had had to push their way through a bobbing aerial sea of white fleshy balloons that encircled the upper stratosphere. On the rocky surface however, the probes encountered an impenetrable fog that ebbed and flowed, thickened and intensified with the days and seasons, but never really lifted visibility to beyond sixty feet.

With safe robotic mobility limited to a few square miles within the corrosive ammonia-rich atmosphere, the mission thus awaited the arrival of its dupliported human components to shed light on the potential inhabitants of Sigma Draconis d.

Brenda Jeffries and Raj Ghalli emerged from the dupliportation chamber into the midday sun, when the fog was its brightest, glowing throughout its depths from a rainbow corona overhead where it tried in vain to penetrate the grey murk.

After travelling west for two days, through apparently unchanging surroundings, they reached the edge of a silver nitrate sea, lapping against shores of lush viridian vegetation. Humid, drinking in the fog, the leafy plant life turned towards them as if sentient, and fired barbed tendrils out to explore their suits, which were fortunately densely woven.

Launching infra-red camera probes overhead, the astronauts identified an alien city on the far shore, twenty miles distant. On a second pass, the probes established that the ocean was never more than four feet deep in this latitude, and being without tides or winds (Sigma Draconis d having neither moons nor active volcanology), they resolved to amend their kit and suits accordingly and proceed to cross the ocean on foot.

The silver nitrate sea lapped around them, clung to their limbs, as they waded slowly forward. They felt as if they were turning into metal, or were people of metal already, futuristic golems, shining, emerging from the primordial swamp of their re-birth.

Halfway across, Raj panicked, as some sort of octopus-like creature wrapped itself around his legs. But the NASA probes accompanying them dipped below the surface and gave it some sharp electric shocks for its trouble, while getting intriguing footage of a creature that the astronauts could not delineate.

Reaching the city at last on the second day, they crouched on the grey shingle shore in astonishment.

The Sigmans communicated through their foggy atmosphere by pulsing lights, a kind of Morse code emanating from antennae on their chests. Their city seemed to be an almost infinite series of doors, carved one against the other, in countless terraces, beautiful and chaotic, leading up over the cliffs into endless space overhead, fading out into fog. Cave-dwellers, the Sigmans were dull grey with brown stripes, their skin snakelike but translucent. Internal organs were just visible: glowing beneath their skins.

Jeffries and Ghalli watched in awe as one of their fishing ships came in to shore: carved from the red shell of some sea monster, and bolstered with a rigging of bamboo-like wood from the nearby forests. The lines of the boat were both delicate and wave-like, jagged and graceful, dressed with thin gossamer sails of some sort of pale blue silk, woven from plant fibre, perhaps.

The Sigmans coming ashore, and others greeting them, now noticed the astronauts and began to approach them. As well as the language of light, they also emitted strange moans and croaks for emotional emphasis, which while the NASA computers struggled to decipher the light pulses, Jeffries and Ghalli found surprisingly helpful, and their best clues as to the tone of this interaction.

Trying in vain to use human speech and bowing with hands open in a passive greeting, the astronauts found the Sigmans more interested in the flashing lights on the sensors of their equipment. Picking some of these devices up in their large three-fingered hands, someone dropped one and the probes went into emergency-mode, approximating to god-only-knows-what incoherent profanity in the obscure language of light.

I'm getting scared, Nevada! Jeffries called out. *This situation is feeling out of control...*

Alarmed by the lights, more Sigmans were emerging from their myriad doorways, armed with spears of the same bamboo-like wood as the astronauts had seen on the ship rigging, but enhanced with what looked like violet-coloured shards of glass, dripping with crimson liquid: poison perhaps.

Their emotional grunts and wheezes were now agitated and terrifying, their antennae all flashing rapidly in panicked gossip. Three of the strongest-looking lunged forward and one thrust a spear tip into Ghalli's side. The NASA aerial probes, each the size of a soccer ball, administered electric-shocks to the assailants, but to little apparent effect. In fury and despair, Jeffries cried out and took a spear out of the hands of one of the Sigmans, who seemed too stunned by this boldness to react. She slashed the tip of the spear across what resembled a throat, then swung the other end with maximum force across the faces of another two, who howled in agony and wheeled away.

Jeffries knelt, tearful, over the supine body of Ghalli: *Raj, talk to me, how badly are you hurt?*

Flesh wound... it's the oxygen loss and temperature drop... my suit's compromised..... he gasped, then louder: *Nevada, is the auto-patch working? I have a suit puncture here, possible contamination. My circulation feels weird...*

Jeffries noticed Ghalli staring over her shoulder and spun around expecting to see a return of the aggressive Sigmans, but instead saw that something strange was happening to the Sigman who she had felled.

Apparently dying now, its head was turning paler and paler until white, its features disappearing, its three eyes and twin nose-ear organs wilting away. Like an expanding balloon, its head finally popped free of its body, and with a tiny yellow light inside it like a Chinese lantern, the head floated off and upwards, rising into the sky, disappearing into the fog.

What the hell? Jeffries stood up and took a few steps forward into the fog. A few more Sigmans were lying on the ground, injured in their stampede away from the scene of the misunderstanding. These bodies too, one after the other, now followed the same sequence, their heads growing pale and featureless then gently detaching, glowing, and rising up into the sky.

Nevada, we need help. They may be massing for a counter-attack. How can we get out of here? What do you advise?

In the Telepedrome on Earth, NASA director Hillary Fording glanced around at her advisors. Lana Anders, on linguistics, was beginning to decode the light language, while Pignatelli on biology was concluding that the chemical composition of the poison in Ghalli's leg appeared harmless to humans. Salgado on logistics and robotics was calculating escape strategies, relative to the original lander sites on Sigma (where the dupliportation chambers resided) and coming up with timescales of days rather than hours. It was Fording's call.

Stay calm, Brenda. She hadn't intended to use her first name, a breach of protocol, but found her emotions taking over, her scientific side in abeyance. *Stay absolutely calm. Panic is the biggest danger you face, and the potential for more misunderstandings. We think we'll have the basics of their language cracked in a few minutes. Ghalli's injury appears superficial. Can you apply the skin patch over his wound from compartment 3a on your backpack please? That will close over automatically and meta-weave to his suit fabric. Then we'll want to reconfigure your technology for light projection. I'll have full instructions to you in under ten minutes. In the meantime, we're going to play you back some of the emotional noises the aliens made during your encounter. The initial ones sounded curious and the later ones aggressive. Do you think you can mimic the passive noises?*

Fifteen minutes later, the astronauts began beaming a rapid succession of light pulses into the fog, raking across the doorways in front of them. They swung their equipment back and forth, up and down over the cliff faces above them, the light patterns bouncing down the walls of the many corridors into which the Sigmans had each retreated.

Additionally, using a microphone, Jeffries began making whale-like sounds, three different kinds, borrowed from the replays in her left ear. Just when she had concluded that all this was pointless and was about to prompt NASA for an escape plan instead, she heard Ghalli whisper at her feet: *Oh shit... it's working...*

The pulsing lights were turning the fog an uncanny pink colour now, and the cliff of carved doors above them bristled with thousands of grey-brown legs and arms and heads, emerging slowly in fascination, peering with luminous red eyes down at the extraordinary aliens who had washed up on their shores.

Their legs were jointed quite differently from humans, Jeffries saw, as they began to descend the cliff face, moving more like spiders or beetles than terrestrial bipeds. Something in their feet enabled them to grip vertical surfaces with incredible purchase.

What the devil are we saying to them? Ghalli asked incredulously, stumbling to his feet, leaning on Jeffries.

Nevada, did you read that? Are you seeing this? What message are the lights conveying to them, can you begin translating into English for us?

Nothing all that fancy, Jeffries. Just that we are visitors, coming in peace, in friendship, that we are from very far away, from the sky. Stay calm please, like I said, and don't lift any weapons unless we say so.

Gradually the Sigmans returned and gathered around Jeffries and Ghalli, and tentatively began to engage in some sort of conversation, while the unseen boffins on Earth battled to expand their vocabulary of the language of light with every passing minute.

*

The astronauts were led, in time, up into one of the largest and most ornately decorated of the cliff doorways, and from there into the mountainside then downwards, further and further, by way of ever more complicated networks of steep staircases. Indeed, beyond its façade of doors, this was a city of stairs it seemed. *We should call it Escalapolis or Escaladore...* Raj Ghalli joked, *their word for the planet seems to mean nothing coherent anyway, just sounds or rather not sounds but flashes and colours of light. How can we ever have a translation unless it is made of recognisable terms from other sentences?*

Escaladore it is then, duly christened... Jeffries whispered, as she followed behind him through the hallowed dark, the dimly lit passages, mindful of her footholds. The Sigmans were furrowing their brows at this chatter, and so Jeffries then translated it for them, the equipment on her chest now firing out beams and pulses of light, while her own voice in her ears said: *I was just saying to my friend that we shall call this place The City Of Stairs.*

After a brief pause for translation, the answer came: *What is your city called?*

Jeffries laughed and paused, trying to translate backwards through the ancient tongues of her ancestors to find a literal meaning. *The Dear Green Place,* she said smiling.

Sigmans couldn't laugh or smile of course, but she noticed curious puckering of a vertical fin on their foreheads at this point, accompanied by a passive grunting sound, and felt instinctively that this was good. *Perhaps you should travel less far and often, and you won't get so homesick,* they replied.

The countless passages and staircases, endlessly descending, were not lit by flames or electrical current but by the glowing bodies of the Sigmans themselves. And gradually as the passages widened, all the staircases began to meet and coalesce until at last they opened out into one vast polygonal staircase in the round, which is to say of course: an arena.

As they climbed downwards in awe of the cavernous hall through which they moved, their Sigman guides asked: *You said you came from the sky. Did you see our dead there?*

Your dead? Jeffries paused, nervous of this reference, in case it referred back to the unhappily fatal nature of their initial confrontation and misunderstanding.

The Sigman leader, whose name they translated as *Kemsarv*, pointed to a white glowing balloon floating by, and Jeffries suddenly understood with a start. *Yes, when our technology descended through the sky, we went through a huge sea of white spheres like these. Were those all parts of the bodies of your dead? Do they decay eventually?*

Kemsarv looked puzzled and the translation began to break down. Words came through scrambled, light pulses were projected that left the Sigmans confused. But they continued to lead the astronauts down towards the base and centre of the arena, with renewed haste if anything, as if the answer to these mysteries could only be revealed from this point.

At the bottom of the arena was a pool of silver nitrate, on which hundreds of white spheres floated. These were being offloaded by Sigmans, in red shell galleons, who carried them out as cargo from some obscure source. Kemsarv pointed into the far distance, indicating how the pool narrowed into a canal, at one point, which stretched off into a darkened cave mouth. There boats could dimly be seen coming and going.

Around the pool, falling over their feet, and scattering everywhere like tadpoles, the astronauts now saw to their astonishment that there were trillions of tiny Sigmans, hatching from the white glowing eggs. The spheres emitted the wriggling young through their south and north poles (as it were) then wilted away to nothing afterwards, leaking a yellow milk and yoke, sustenance perhaps, that had fed the young through the period of their gestation.

Ghalli, a Hindu by upbringing, suddenly became alarmed and distressed at the thought of standing on the tiny young, then noticed to his confusion and horror that the Sigmans themselves seemed unafraid to trample them too, treating them just as humans would react to frogspawn.

Aren't you afraid to kill your own young? Ghalli asked and the physically obscure alien faces grimaced and emitted a snort and a puff of gas, glowing red then blue. *There are more of them than there are pebbles on the shore or stars in the sky...* he said. *It would be madness to care too much.*

Looking around about now, the astronauts could see how the tiny glowing Sigman spawn were climbing up the stairs and crawling into little beehive-shaped cells and fissures under every step, which every few minutes an adult Sigman would walk past and paint with a kind of yellow ooze, food perhaps, from an ornate shell-pot, carried under its arm.

This is indeed a strange world, Jeffries marvelled, smiling. *How long do your young take to reach adulthood?*

The Sigman leader pointed to the roof of the cave overhead and rotated his (or her) arm. *Twice the fingers on my hand, six circuits of the sun.*

But wait a minute... Ghalli struggled to think, as the Sigmans began to lead them to a boat, apparently intent on leading them to see some other new wonder. *How do you know about the sun, when your world is so bound in fog?*

Yeah, hang on... Jeffries interrupted. *You mentioned the stars a minute ago. How can you know about the stars in the night sky? We didn't think the fog ever cleared here on your world...*

The answer to this and to all your other questions is at the end of your next journey. We will show you. Please step into this boat. It is quite safe I promise you... Kemsarv answered.

The shell boat sailed through the canal for a further hour, through dark caves and passageways, leaving the relative brightness of the arena behind, for a world illumined only by their companions' bodies, their pulsing internal organs, which now seemed to grow curiously dimmer.

What's happening? Jeffries asked them in their language of light.

This is a very sacred journey for us, please do not talk again, in our language, for a while... they said politely.

It had been nearly night time on Sigma Draconis d when they were last outside. But when they finally emerged from the cave mouth, they saw that it was day again and that they had passed through an entire mountain and were now on a low flat plain across which the silver river meandered at its leisure. Visibility in the fog now expanded to about a hundred feet, but still the astronauts observed no clues as to how their guides could have an understanding of astronomy.

The vegetation on the plain grew more virile and bluish-green around them and at last they came to a large circular sea, perhaps a mile across. The rising convection currents from the surface of the lake were cutting a hole through the fog, an astounding pillar of light that seemed to lead up into heaven.

This is our most sacred religious site, Kemsarv said, *our place of birth and regeneration.*

Looking closer as they approached, Jeffries and Ghalli now saw that white spheres were floating down from the sky through this funnel of light, gradually dropping in great clusters, like bunches of grapes from the gods themselves, onto the silver surface of the radiant lake. The Sigman shell-boats with their picturesque sails circled and looped, picking up the spheres, harvesting them like fish, the sailors all the while chanting in a manner which seemed reverent and religious, even to human senses.

What brings them down? Atmospheric pressure, exhaustion of some gas inside them? Ghalli asked, half to himself, half to the Sigmans.

It is their time, their time to fall, and so fall they must. And from this are we born... Kemsarv answered, *...and now it is time to rise, to see the stars and the sun. Will you come with me?*

Jeffries and Ghalli looked at each other puzzled at this, wondering to what the Sigman leader referred. Drawing a pink glass cutlass from his ceremonial robes, he gathered six of his most loyal subjects about him in the boat, bid them to kneel, and then with swift and terrifying strokes: severed each of their heads, one after the other without sound or protest.

Holding the heads together in one hand like party balloons, as they whitened and expanded, he looked at the astronauts one last time and waved, ironically the first human gesture he had learned, then glided upwards into the sky many miles overhead.

He had tossed the cutlass at the astronauts' feet as he left, and now several of his remaining companions came and knelt before them, bowing their heads in supplication. Perhaps Kemsarv had also expected Jeffries to cut Ghalli's head off, not realising the horror and sin that murder represented to people from Earth.

We've seen the sky already... Jeffries smiled incredulously to Ghalli. *Do you think he'll be insulted if we just stay put?*

Ghalli laughed nervously, shaken, looking at the decapitated bodies left at the stern of the boat, staining it with their turquoise blood. *What are we missing here? When death is birth, is murder still a sin? Is death even sad at all here?*

Brenda Jeffries looked up into the sky and wiped a tear from her eye, remembering the death on Earth of her beloved father, while Raj Ghalli found some oars and rowed the boat to shore.

The Sigmans they had spared, seeing their ethereal phase had been postponed, merely boarded another ship and resumed their work of fishing and of harvest, undisturbed and ungrateful, blissfully uncomprehending of the obscure taboos of an alien race.

~

12

THE JUNGLE OF EYES

Fording had any mother's normal suspicion regarding an outsider showing interest in her son. Carlo Serranto had been adamant that she and he should travel together to San Diego with Nathan to have him assessed by a controversial new physician there, called Doctor Olbert Duisberg. *His theories on autism are ground-breaking...* Serranto told her. *I've already told him about some of Nathan's extraordinary abilities.*

You've done what? Fording exclaimed, indignant, nearly swerving the hire car they were taking to the airport. *This is my son we're talking about, what would my husband say if he knew you were doing things like that?*

What d'you mean? I mean I'm sorry, but it's not like we're having an affair for Christ's sake... The silence that then ensued contained a certain frisson for both of them.

In the back seat, Nathan sang quietly to himself and drummed his feet on the floor. Half-closing his eyes, he made the freeway lights distort into fabulous stars that rotated and distorted.

*

Ross 128 d was a planet covered in vegetation so dense that little could be gleaned about it from the usual aerial reconnaissance, but with life apparently so abundant, intelligent life had to be a reasonable bet down there.

Astronauts Milliken and Okra elected to take the plunge and were strapped in at beehive cell number 152 at the Telepedrome. An hour later they stepped out into the mother of all jungles.

Wheeled or even tracked probes would have been useless here... Okra said, clambering over roots and dense bushes. Giant thick-trunked trees vaguely similar to terrestrial baobabs, stretched hundreds of feet into the air. The intense sunlight of the world above was filtered here to a dim twilight, even at noon.

Keep your eyes open for spoor, footprints, hoof prints of any kind, droppings. We're not hearing much so far... nothing like birdsong or insect noise...

Their compasses were essential but even with this, the astronauts felt compelled to tie yellow tapes around every tenth tree they passed, to ensure, Ariadne-like, that they would return to their base successfully without getting lost.

Needless to say, Okra took to singing "Tie a yellow ribbon 'round the old oak tree..." until Milliken thought she saw something moving in the distance and told him to shush.

*

Doctor Duisberg had finished the usual preliminary examination of Nathan Fording – the light in the eyes, the heart-rate – and was now showing him shapes and colours.

Fording wondered to herself if the initial checks were just some form of sly hypnosis that all doctors used. A subliminal conditioning to make the patient accept the physician as high-priest, chief shaman, magician for the evening. Duisberg the Dramatic, she was thinking to herself, the Dread Duisberg, when he unexpectedly addressed her directly, one strangely independent eye rotating to focus on her, beneath his densely frizzed hair: *The father wished to stay outside...?*

Fording frowned. *He's not the father... or my husband. Just a colleague actually.* She had insisted that Carlo sit outside to avoid exactly such a misconception, but now she was suffering it anyway. Doctors were still the worst old chauvinists on the planet; probably always would be.

Your son has some remarkable abilities, Mrs Fording, did you know that?

Well, of course, he's got a great memory for maths and all the names and numbers of things...

Duisberg nodded and smiled in a way that seemed to suggest he was talking to an idiot. Perhaps it was his work that made that a habit, she thought to herself uncharitably. *Allow me to demonstrate something, if I may. Nathan?*

As ever, Nathan didn't seem to particularly respond to his name. Only the oblique approach seemed to get through to him.

What is the square root of 496? 872?

Duisberg passed a pocket calculator to Fording, to confirm the answers.

And how many light years distant is Zeta Reticuli, Gliese 581? And from Gliese, can you draw how the stars of our own area of space appear, the configuration they form?

Duisberg took an atlas of stars from the desk and passed this to Fording, who struggled to keep up. *What is this?* she rasped in a hoarse whisper, almost angry. *Is this some kind of stunt? Have you and Carlo cooked this up in advance?*

Carlo?

My colleague, friend, outside.

Mrs Fording, I've never met you or your son or your Carlo before tonight, I swear it on my mother's life.

She found this turn of phrase a trifle over-dramatic; very

much the stage magician.

Then how can you possibly have known that my son would know these things? Carlo must have emailed you about them.

Not at all, Mrs Fording. You're missing the point, with respect.

Funny how when people use that phrase about respect, one felt immediately insulted. *Which is?* she asked frostily, folding her arms.

They both turned to look at Nathan where he continued to draw stars and maths equations happily on the white board on the floor.

He is not the first you see. I have found twelve of these cases this year alone, and they are on the rise. The abilities are similar, the symptoms the same.

But what could that mean? Fording gasped.

Duisberg scratched his head. *Now this may sound silly, Mrs Fording, but considering your profession, I was rather hoping you might be able to tell me...*

*

The first thing they saw were beetles. Two or three of them, giants compared to anything on Earth, each one about two feet long, black shells, multiple legs and antennae.

Just as Okra began filming them, the spiders came down. The astronauts were deafened by ultra-high frequency screams of panic emitted by the beetles. The undergrowth erupted with hundreds more of the beetles who had been lying concealed. Okra and Milliken fell to their knees, covering their ears in pain. Each about seven feet across, the spiders were camouflaged by an appearance similar to the mossy green tree trunks: their nine legs were densely covered in dark fur. Their bodies rose into central hubs from where nine black shining spherical eyes looked out.

On their undersides, a central beak-like mouth was protected by leathery folds.

The spiders moved much faster than their prey, and carried woven rope nets that they deployed with great dexterity. Their own chatter was of a lower register, seeming to consist of co-ordinating commands to focus the hunt. Huge numbers of the beetles were expertly bundled into the dangling nets, then the spiders moved on, crawling between tree trunks, twenty feet overhead.

The relief as the screaming of the beetles faded into the distance was enormous, and Milliken and Okra stood up from where they had been crouching in the undergrowth.

But their relief quickly turned to horror: what they thought was undergrowth either side of them now came to life and stood up with sickening, lurching movements and regarded them with multiple eyes. Two spiders had been lying in wait, observing them. They tried to run in opposite directions but the nets exploded over them and they found themselves bundled together as the black furry limbs advanced upon them, the spiders chattering excitedly to each other in unintelligible clicks and croaks.

*

Outside, in reception, Fording found Serranto playing with a patient's dog, pointing a strange silver gadget at it, while the animal growled and whined playfully back at him.

Eventually he noticed Fording standing looking at him, holding Nathan's hand. *What are you doing, Carlo?* she asked, tired, puzzled.

He hurriedly put the device back inside his inside jacket pocket and looked around to see if anyone had been noticing him. *Oh... nothing...*

What do you mean, nothing? Fording frowned.

Earth aliens... Nathan said. Both adults stopped dead and looked at him, then brought their gazes back up to look at each other querulously.

Smart kid. In a way he's right.

Fording shrugged and shook her head. *You can tell me what on earth you're on about on the way to the car. Let's get out of here.*

Linguistics... Carlo said, as they exited into the car park, the full moon risen now into the twilit sky. *Dubceck and I had a crazy idea last month, over a couple of beers, and we agreed to test it. In fact we've put a little bit of money on it, a small bet, just for fun, a private game.*

Go on... Fording sighed, unimpressed.

We wondered what would happen if we turned all our latest translation technology, all the stuff we've developed for dealing with aliens, onto terrestrial species, like dolphins, whales, monkeys, elephants.

And dogs... she opened the car door and fixed him with a pointed stare. *You're crazy. Now aren't you going to ask me how I got on with Nathan?*

I was waiting for you to volunteer that, trying to know my place, as you told me earlier, not freak you out in an already freaky situation.

Do you know what that man actually asked me, Carlo? she frowned, starting the engine.

Go on, horrify me, Carlo sighed, grasping the mood of the moment.

Whether Nathan or I had ever been abducted by aliens.

You're kidding? He's never discussed any crack-pot stuff like that with me. Look, I'm sorry, Hillary. Did he really phrase it like that?

Well, UFO experience, he coyly worded it, but I knew what he meant. Was he trying to be funny, ironic, you think?

Oh, I see what you mean now. You being a famous woman who abducts aliens, as it were. Did he know who you were? I never told him, you know.

Of course, he might have, he knew I was an astronomer at least. Abducted by aliens!

After ten minutes silence on the freeway looking out at the darkness all around, with Nathan sound asleep on the back seat, Carlo finally asked: *Well, have you?*

*

These days the computers didn't even have to be asked to analyse alien language. All on-planet sound was recorded from the astronauts' suits and automatically scanned for patterns akin to speech and hypothetical alphabets postulated to recreate them.

Three hours after the entire human element of the control room back on Earth had descended into abject despair, a computer announced with a small bell like a microwave pizza finishing, that a language program for the Rossian aliens had now been successfully extrapolated.

Contact had been lost, but if the astronauts' suits remained intact then there was a chance those could still be used to project language remotely.

Okra and Milliken jumped right out of their skins, as did the Rossian spiders grouped around them, when their suits began projecting greeting messages outwards.

World which star you say from travel.... The words began breaking through intermittently, communication taking hold both ways.

The Rossians had now dropped the complicated looking metal equipment with which they had been examining the astronauts, and when they began to recognise the repeated phrase "please untie us", they reached forward and released their human captives from where they had been strapped down for their own safety.

We are not hostile! Okra exclaimed, jumping around excitedly. *This is a peaceful mission of scientific exploration. What were you doing to us?*

We too are scientists and peaceful, the answer came back from one of the largest of the spiders. It was disconcerting and disturbing to try to make and maintain eye contact with a nine-eyed monster, but they gave it their best shot. *We were trying to examine you, to establish your biology and place of origin.*

Another Rossian, perhaps his lead advisor, stepped (or scuttled) forward: *Which star have you travelled from? What distance? Your name for it is meaningless to us of course, but you could draw a map...*

Parchment and charcoal were hurriedly provided and Milliken sketched and annotated for them.

We were frightened that you were going to eat us like those beetles... Okra said nervously.

The Rossians muttered and conferred at this, then replied: *Those creatures, Distelambricans, we do not eat them, we employ them as livestock to weave materials for our city.*

But they were screaming out in terror and distress.

Really? We cannot hear those sounds. Perhaps your ears are different from ours, if you are truly from so different a world. Can you teach us more about yourselves and your home star? Can we travel there in return?

Yes, we can show you films, moving images of our world and teach you vast amounts of knowledge about it, we will be honoured to. But for you to travel there will be impossible. You are too large to fit inside our Entanglement chambers.

Milliken nudged Okra in warning, to stop from saying anything regrettable in the midst of his flow of euphoria.

Where is this vehicle that you travelled here in?

It is back in the jungle now, where you found us, but it is not a vehicle as you might understand it. It copies us instantly between places.

Shall we go and bring it here for you?

Please, please do not, or even attempt it. The technology

is potentially extremely dangerous if not handled correctly. You might damage yourselves and prevent us from returning.

You have sent something dangerous to our world, without permission? they asked, with impeccable logic. *What if more of you start appearing through this device? What if you try to invade and overrun us?*

Milliken was becoming alarmed by the escalating fears of the Rossians and raised her hands to try to calm them. *Please, do not be afraid. What you fear is quite impossible, we promise you. Only we can be transported through the chamber, only the two of us. More cannot be sent after us, we pose no threat!*

*

Stepping down from the plane back at Los Angeles, Fording and Serranto were alarmed to encounter a small band of paparazzi calling out their names. How could they have got word of this entirely private business, a tip-off from the airline? Enquiries and complaints would have to be made when they got home.

Fording hated the multiple camera lenses, the clickings and whirrings, the flashes startling and upsetting Nathan. Serranto made to punch one of the photographers, narrowly missed, and the image made the front pages the next day, coupled with allegations about their private lives. Soon they were being accused of having an affair without ever having had one.

*

The Rossians took Okra and Milliken to meet their queen. Perhaps the astronauts expected another spider with a fancy robe on, but they were confounded, not to say dumbfounded.

The Rossian ‘city’ was a vast semi-aerial construction,

woven by the captive Distelambrican beetles out of sticks and mud and excretions from their glands. It was an apparently chaotic but beautiful maze (in the manner of Venice) of corridors and chambers, spun between giant trees and across gullies and streams, through which Rossians constantly moved like the commuters on the streets of New York or Tokyo.

The city had many 'windows', on its upper faces, through which Rossians might emerge and set off clambering into the surrounding forest or across the roof of the city, which seemed to serve as a kind of open-air plaza.

The design of the city was that of a vast spiral, and the Rossians led Okra and Milliken through this rapidly, using many adept shortcuts so as to approach the sacred heart of this ancient construction. As they neared their goal, the temperature began to rise and more and more 'checkpoints' had to be passed, heavily guarded by particularly fierce looking Rossians.

Their queen, when finally revealed, turned out to be an enormous white amorphous slug, perhaps two hundred feet long by forty feet diameter. Like the queen at the centre of a terrestrial beehive, she was attended by numerous spiders scuttling back and forth to cater for her every need of sustenance or defecation, and (the Rossians explained) reproduction. All Rossians were born from this single mother, who they reported was of an age that the astronauts translated as equivalent to over four Earth centuries.

Her skin glowed periodically with strange electrical activity inside and something resembling wires which seemed to be conveying her thoughts and words into some elaborate machinery on the wall, from which the spiders took readings. The Rossians had metals and various forms of machinery, even steam power apparently. Though direct comparison was difficult, the astronauts assessed what they saw as closest to Late Victorian on Earth; on the edge of an industrial revolution.

The scientific Rossian who had been doing most of the talking to them, was called Perfnak, and he bid the humans and the rest of his Rossian entourage be silent while he crouched his limbs into a form of kneeling and seemed to pray before the great slug mother. Some sort of priest came and connected tubes inside a kind of steam-age crown which he lowered onto Perfnak's head (above his nine eyes) and a rapid series of electrical pulses seemed to pass to and fro between him and the Great Mother.

After about ten minutes the session ended, and Perfnak addressed the astronauts and the other spiders to relay the orders he had received.

The Great Mother welcomes you, Perfnak said, *to our city of Jostan. We are only one of 87 colonies in the known world. Your visitation will give us good luck and power over our adversaries. To forge our friendship, alliance, and cultural exchange, you must send back one of our new-born larvae to your world, using your machine. Our race must start to live on your world and begin a new colony.*

Okra and Milliken looked at each other in horror. *But no! We have already explained that this is not possible. You are too large to fit in our Entanglement chambers.*

No, Perfnak responded, lifting one of his nine legs in the air to indicate a chamber off to his right from where a small wriggling larva, an infant spider, was already being prepared. *The Great Mother heard all my thoughts and my memories of the words you first spoke to us. You said size was a difficulty, but we have solved that by this suggestion.*

But I also explained, Milliken panicked, sweating, *that our technology can only send two people, the two of us. You don't understand the vast complexity of this device, and I have scarcely begun explaining it to you. The two chambers can only be used for us, unless one of us dies.*

We are twinned forever now on two separate worlds, this one and our home planet. To send your larva would be to kill one of us, an act of murder.

Okra cut in: *Then there's also the problem of contamination. Your offspring would be immediately quarantined on Earth. It would never escape the confinement that would be imposed on it there, never breathe the air or see the daylight of our planet.*

Also... Milliken stammered, *to kill one of us now would be an act of murderous aggression against our species, our race. Our brethren might then attack you. They would certainly kill the larva that you sent.*

And yet... Perfnak mused, *you have sent yourselves here and potentially contaminated us.*

We are wearing suits and breathing apparatus. Milliken answered desperately, hoping this half-answer would conceal the misdemeanour the Rossian had so shrewdly deduced.

And you have told us you are male and female, you could raise your kind here and colonise us.

No, it is forbidden. Our great mother, our democracy, our group brain, has forbidden this. We will never defile or populate your world. We come only as peaceful observers and will leave you and your world unharmed. We will return there now and leave you in peace if you so wish. Please do not harm either of us. Do you not believe in the sanctity of life?

We do, Perfnak answered, *but we have many enemies who threaten us. You speak of your power to harm us in retribution for an ill we have not yet contemplated. Such power could be of use to us. Can you show me such power? Otherwise, how am I to dissuade the Great Mother from her idea of sending a larva to your world and risking your anger?*

Reluctantly, shaking, the astronauts set up the broadcast

equipment incorporated in their suits, and showed the Rossians images of World War Two, the atomic bombs landing on Hiroshima and Nagasaki, the devastation afterwards, the piles of bodies in the death camps after the fall of Nazi Germany.

Afterwards, Milliken was connected up to the tubes so as to hear the Great Mother's reaction, who had been watching the images also: *You spoke of sanctity of life? – And yet you have done this to your own kind? When Perfnak spoke of threats from our neighbours he meant only skirmishes and displays, injuries, theft of resources. No one and nothing on this planet is capable of the evil of which you are guilty. Your weaponry appalls us. We are very afraid. Please leave this world and promise never to return. Please take away your vehicle or destroy it afterwards, however it works. We mean you no harm but we can never trust you who have done such things. Leave us forever. To us, you are unnatural.*

*

John Fording was furious. *I hear about some quack doctor examining our son... I hear about it through some trashy newspaper, before I hear about it from you? And it's all got something to do with pretty boy Carlo Serranto? It all starts to make sense, this last year... "Carlo" this, "Carlo" that... "he's so funny, so attentive..."*

No, stop, John! Fording held her face in her hands. *You've got this completely wrong. Is that really how I've spoken about him? Is that what you think?*

What am I supposed to think? John shouted, holding the newspaper front page aloft, *...When I find stuff like this on sale on every street corner?*

Trust, John, you have to trust me. That's just newspaper tittle tattle, extrapolation, made up to sell papers. It's not the truth. Can't you trust me, trust what I tell you? How did you ever get to the stage of feeling like this towards me, hostile, distrustful? When did this happen?

So it's my problem now. I see. Great. Very clever. You've turned it all around. You have a public affair with a colleague and get photographed taking a holiday with him and our son. Our son! While I think you're just working late... and you tell me I've got a problem? I've got explaining to do? How on earth do you manage to turn it all around like that? That's perverse genius!

John, I can't talk to you when you're like this. It's pointless. I'm sorry.

Yeah, so am I.

I need to go, somewhere, anywhere. I'll be back tomorrow... once you've cooled off and you're ready to listen and be rational.

Off to your pretty boy then!

No. Away to think, on my own. Can you look after the children?

They both spun around to see Nathan standing in the kitchen with his jacket on and his suitcase packed.

*

The spiders carefully but respectfully escorted the astronauts through the complicated twisting streets of their labyrinthine spiral city, seeking to lead them further and further away from all they loved and held dear.

But as they reached the edge of their suspended city and prepared to venture out into the surrounding trees again, they saw that the flood season had begun and that this seemed to greatly distress their human guests, who chattered excitedly between themselves and to the strange disembodied voices that often sounded from within their suits themselves.

Nevada, do you know what's happening? Is the landing unit safe from this inundation we're seeing?

Our instruments show that the lander has sealed itself against the water but that it is now on the move. Could the flood be carrying top soil and vegetation with it as it goes? The lander appears to be accelerating and losing altitude, slipping downhill in other words.

Shit, shit! Okra slapped at his own head to the alarm of the Rossians. *Now we know why their city is built in the air... we should have asked that question.*

Will your vehicle be damaged by the flood season? asked Perfnak.

You say "season"? Milliken frowned. *It has automatically shut itself down into its protective shell. It should survive anything, but how long is this season?*

Half an orbit of the sun... came the answer. Nevada translated: *that's an equivalent of three Earth months approximately.*

Can you help us? Can we pursue our lander and make it secure, take it out of the waters?

In what direction is it drifting and at what speed? asked Perfnak's most astute scientific advisor.

Okra put the question to Nevada, who provided an answer to which the Rossian replied: *in three days at that speed, if it doesn't get caught up in roots and debris then it will enter the territory of the Shalbayrakans, our neighbours and enemies, from where we could not retrieve it for you.*

If you were to go after it and fall into the hands of the Shalbayrakans, then how do we know that they would not seek to use your power against us? Perfnak asked.

The probe lander cannot be entered by anyone other than us. Even a thousand years of drilling and cutting would not gain you access to the interior, with the level of technology you appear to possess.

Then the only issue is yourselves. To return home, you would have to endanger our security by leaving our territory and we cannot allow that. You must stay here and live among us for the rest of your lives, or we must kill you, and we will not permit ourselves to commit such a sin as that. You must stay as our guests.

Your prisoners you mean?

That will be a question of perception and inclination on your part of course. We will treat you well.

Okra and Milliken looked at each other, while back on Earth in the control room at Nevada, Fording and Serranto did likewise.

We're wasting valuable time, Milliken said. *Please. We could travel on your backs. We could set out together and find our drifting lander, with our monitoring technology to fix its location, and your nets to catch the probe and lift it up.*

The floods are dangerous, Perfnak replied. *Why would we risk the lives of our strongest and bravest people to assist you? People from another planet, who so frighten us with stories of evil you have done to each other?*

Milliken thought for a second then took a decision that sent Nevada (eleven light years away) reeling in unheeded protest and alarm: *If you help us do this and we succeed then one of you, indeed a larva as the only way possible, may travel to our world and learn our customs there. It would not be allowed to breed or colonise our world, but one of you would be visiting our world, as we have visited yours, as benign observers.*

Dubceck yelled aloud: *What the devil is she saying! Has she gone made? How could we do such a thing? Keep such a promise? Has she any idea of the implications?*

Fording nodded her head in agreement, but was also conscious of the cost of mission failure, of the failure to return the astronauts safely. *It's a gamble... I see why she's saying it. We'd need a lot of preparation, special facilities, international agreements, but it's not impossible.*

It could be done.

Well, they're not waiting for our consent by the sound of things, are they? Serranto countered. *So much for staying in control, your iron grip, your supremely professional leadership!*

Fording and several of the other senior advisors around the control room now spun around and looked at Serranto in horror at these blatant indiscretions.

Serranto, my room! Fording hissed, *Dubceck, take over.*

*

In her private office, Fording slapped Serranto's face and demanded an apology and explanation for his outrageous outburst in front of their colleagues. His answer was one of stuttering incoherence.

She spat in his face. He wiped his cheek then kissed her passionately on the lips. For a moment their embrace was a struggle, a wrestle, then somehow antagonism bled seamlessly into empathy and attraction then passion.

They unbuttoned each other's clothes and made love violently on top of her desk. They came together in less than a minute, as if releasing something that had been brewing all day, all week. Silently, shamefaced afterwards, they merely returned to the central control room together, as if nothing had transpired other than a sound talking-to and a rapid re-establishment of professional discipline.

*

The torrents blasted past the tangled roots. The smooth black hull of the lander unit could be seen just protruding above the top of a vast tangle of leaves and moss and debris. The spiders climbed down as the astronauts shouted instructions relayed through readings from Nevada, nets were thrown, the lander partially captured, the stockade of branches split up and sent down river. But one of the nets was torn at its upper edge, the probe teetering on the cusp of escape. Okra climbed heroically down off Perfnak's back and tried to pull the net over the edge of the probe, even as Nevada protested violently regarding the dangers involved. The flood surged, several trees snapped, the probe tipped and rotated, crushing Okra's leg then slipping out of the net, dragging him with it. He vanished, screaming, into the churning tide of muddy water and the probe continued on before wedging itself behind a further stockade of debris.

Dubceck, in command at this moment, forced Milliken to keep going and not focus on her grief and shock. Undeterred and with the help of the Rossians, the probe was then successfully retrieved, and with the aid of several hundred reinforcements to help with its excessive weight, was finally hauled back into Rossian territory and thereafter back to the spiral city itself where it and Milliken could be guarded and prized by the Rossian nation.

*

As far as anyone knew, Nathan Fording didn't watch television, and his mother made no direct systematic effort to describe to him the details of the various Telepedrome missions in which she took part.

Nonetheless, he took to incessantly drawing spider's webs around this time, or they could have been fishing nets, woven to a spiral pattern.

His father, increasingly anxious to please on the alternate weekends he had with his children, took to buying Nathan toy rubber spiders about the size of a hand. Nathan never tired of them and kept asking for more. John wondered what he was doing with them after a while, and could see no explanation.

At the rented apartment soon to be shared by Hillary Fording and Carlo Serranto, Nathan took to placing these spiders in various inaccessible and partially concealed corners in each room, where they would make his mother or the cleaning staff scream every time they found one or one tumbled out onto the carpet.

Hillary Fording had been terrified of spiders as a child. Nathan had meticulously altered each of these, using red felt tip markers with indelible ink, so as to have nine red lurid eyes around their heads, watching, always watching.

*

The tragic death of Okra had one unexpected implication however, that was in time duly acted upon. His drowned body on Earth was removed from the dupliportation chamber and given a hero's funeral. After two years of technical modifications and the teleportation of additional machinery by Ansible, the spare Entanglement chamber was used to dupliport a Rossian larva, carefully produced and selected by the Great Mother to be an emissary to Earth. There it was kept in a specially built mobile annexe of the Telepedrome where it could view Earth's scenery and interact with human envoys attired in suitably sterile overalls. The larva duly grew into a giant spider called Zurtinth who learned much of terrestrial science which it could recount to its fellows each time it went to sleep on Earth. In return, Earth gained a deeper understanding of an alien culture and physiology than any it had hitherto achieved.

Within twenty years however, the Rossians attacked and overwhelmed their neighbours and began an expansionist empire, the first their planet had ever witnessed, which went on to claim three quarters of their planet's inhabitable land in the succeeding decades. Every request made by the Rossians for the secrets of human nuclear technology have so far been refused.

~

13

CHAN'S LEG

This new adventure engaged them more deeply than ever in philosophical disputations

– Voltaire, *Candide*
(translated by Tobias Smollett)

The second strangest of all worlds was perhaps Tau Ceti f. A planet orbiting an orange star surrounded by dangerous and unpredictable belts of debris that would frequently impact upon the planet's surface, endangering life there. Terrestrial scientists had predicted that this constant interruption would have prohibited the evolution of life. But they had overlooked one bizarre means by which consciousness could sidestep even these formidable difficulties.

On 'landing' on Tau Ceti, astronauts Bruchert and Chan were immediately met by a welcoming delegation who knew their names and their planet of origin. This was very peculiar, because the probes had attempted no prior contact with the aliens, and the exact time of 'launch' due to various unexpected delays, had in effect been unknown to the astronauts themselves.

The TauCetians, tall and enormously slender white creatures, after making the humans welcome, then immediately engaged in a 'Rosetta Stone' of conversation between themselves, perfectly calculated to give the human computers the data they needed in order to decipher their language in the shortest time.

With such apparent signs of high intelligence, Chan and Bruchert expected to be led to a city of enormous size and futuristic sophistication but this was not the case. The TauCetians built their humble homes mostly out of timber and appeared to have a level of technology no higher evolved than late medieval European.

On the way towards their capital city, called Eedphyaorsu, they were led along a winding road across a great plain dotted with many lakes of emerald-green water. As they walked, no less than nine meteor strikes took place nearby, and each time, miraculously, the TauCetians seemed to know a few minutes in advance where the meteorite would land and took appropriate evasive action, changing their route, taking a detour across a field or around the far side of a lake.

But this is astounding! Lee Chan exclaimed (now that the terrestrial translation software was up to speed). *You seem to know the very future itself, before it happens. Or do you have satellite warning systems that we haven't noticed yet? How can you know the trajectory of each impact so precisely and react to it so calmly?*

Sati-what? Ghyhoort, their lead emissary responded. *What are those? Of course we see the future. Do you mean to suggest that you cannot?*

Ridiculous, Claudia Bruchert chipped in. *Seeing into the future is impossible. Prophecy is superstitious nonsense. Every rational being knows that, don't they?*

But we are perfectly rational I can assure you, dear visitor. And perfectly alive. We would however be perfectly dead, as would you probably, were we not able to see the future just so perfectly. If you are incapable of such basic life skill, then it is just as well that you have us with you today as your expert guides.

As they reached the outskirts of the town, they found a happy race of people about their business, building, trading, cultivating and conversing. Every so often a wooden building somewhere would go on fire, struck by interstellar debris, but always a small team of TauCetians would be waiting beside it with vats of water, ready to extinguish the flames with great efficiency before the flames spread further than a matter of feet. Building materials to make repairs, perfectly calculated, were also at the ready, and the repairs or rebuilding accomplished in scarcely more than an hour.

At the centre of this industrious city, a royal palace stood on a system of elaborate wheels, ready to be moved around by a few feet or several miles at short notice, whatever the occasion demanded.

In there, the astronauts were introduced to the city's ruler Reculhtra, a very old and wise TauCetian attended by many learned scribes and scholars.

Ahh, there you are, the people from the sky who cannot see forward! he exclaimed. Such blindness! How do you survive on your star? Do you not die each day by the accidental million?

Chan and Bruchert looked at each other. *Well, not quite millions, but I suppose we do. Do you not have any accidents on this world? How far can everyone see into the future?*

Why, we all have different abilities. All citizens, even new-born babies can see a few hundred heartbeats into the future. More intelligent citizens further, and so on, until one comes to me of course. I have been elected leader because I can see into the future for about four and a half orbits of the red sun (equivalent of three Earth years), *the greatest ability so far known on our world, save for that of old Helbernytchu, who died over a thousand orbits ago, and may have been exaggerated legend.*

But wait a minute, Chan thought out loud, *doesn't this mean that you have a chance to change the future?*

I don't understand, Reculhtra replied. *We foresee a meteor landing and our moving things out of its way, we then move things out of its way, there is no changing taking place.*

But what about some truly unforeseen calamity?

Nothing is unforeseen in this world, by me at least, nor by all of us, working together. Each of us specialises in the period of the future we see clearest and shares it with our fellows. Together, we are truly safe and forewarned, guarded against disaster.

But what if... Bruchert struggled to find an appropriate example, *begging your royal pardon, but if you foresaw your wife falling in love with someone else and having a child by him. Wouldn't you be tempted to send that man to the other side of the world or even to kill him?*

What perverse ideas and fantasies you harbour, my poor blind friends! Knowing that all is foreseen by someone and all knowledge shared, who would dare to hide such a thing from his fellows? Also we know the profoundest truth of all, which I am beginning to grasp that you do not. The future cannot be altered. If I foresaw that my wife should cease loving me, I would simply privately mourn and prepare for the loss and make the very best of my time with her in the interim period.

I think I get it, Chan mused. *On a planet where everyone sees the future, everyone must also accept it. But what of the man who foresees his own death by an incurable disease, his plans blighted in mid-stream, how can he keep on living, knowing that all his efforts will come to nothing?*

What impractical and vainglorious beings you must be

on your world. What plan or dream could be so grand that another good man might not carry it forward in your stead? Such a man, again, would make the best of the time he had left and make peace with his friends and family. Sound advice at the best of times anyway.

OK, I've got it now, Chan exclaimed. *Neither I nor my colleague Bruchert can see into the future and you know that now. That introduces a new factor never before seen in this world.*

Careful... Bruchert cautioned him.

What if you foresaw some accident that was going to befall one of us and told us about it. We do not share your stoicism and our technology is highly evolved. We could take on your future vision and prevent it, and stop it happening. Of course we could.

Reculhtra laughed aloud, a curious gurgling sound, accompanied by pink steam firing sideways out of his large leaf-like ears that quivered in the breeze. *How ridiculous. You mean of course the night after next, when you run out of your quarters in the middle of the night and get your leg torn off by a sefarcul... I assumed you knew about that. You survive of course and get magically sent back to your own world using that bewildering technology of yours. How does that work by the way? Surely it makes seeing into the future look puny in comparison.*

Never mind that! I don't want my leg torn off by a... what did you call it?

Reculhtra drew a picture on the sandy floor, accompanied by a verbal description, but after the fifth or sixth mention of teeth and claws Chan found he was losing focus.

I wish you hadn't told us that. Bruchert wept, dismayed. *No, no, I mean I wish you'd told us sooner I mean. We need to prevent it!*

Make your mind up. But it really makes no difference under the circumstances. Of course the accident only happens because you leave your quarters alone. Such a thing would never happen to one of us because we would foresee the sefarcul being out there and feeling so hungry... the poor thing.

The poor thing my arse, my leg! Chan spat. *No one and nothing is going to disarticulate me on this planet, and that's final.*

Greatly apprehensive and out of sorts, Chan and Bruchert found it very hard to focus on their cultural studies and biological data gathering for the next two days. Chan was granted extra 'shore leave' with his family and with a NASA psychologist to try to calm him down. Of course, as dictated by the rules of Entanglement, once dupliported no one could take his place except in the event of his death, which they knew at least had not been predicted. And surely some other explanation than second-sight must be at play on Tau Ceti f to account for the aliens' daily good luck and preparedness.

*

Despite their apprehension, the astronauts enjoyed a good day on Tau Ceti f the afternoon before the fateful evening. NASA had reassured Bruchert and Chan that the rules of cause and effect and space-time must hold good on Tau Ceti f as elsewhere in the universe and that if they just 'sat tight' in their quarters in the palace whilst armed to the teeth, then nothing dangerous could possibly befall them. The future (supposedly) would be altered and the ridiculous supernatural beliefs of the TauCetians would be spectacularly disproved. They might even be hailed as gods after that, or certainly as the scientifically superior beings they surely were on such a world.

During the day, at the risk of interrupting more important cultural discussion regarding history, geography and botany, a sweating Chan had kept asking questions about sefarculs, their body size and solitary hunting habits, easiest ways to kill them and so forth. The TauCetians had answered all these indiscreet questions patiently with a sad look in their eyes, occasionally patting him on his left leg as if bidding it a sombre farewell.

In the middle of the very dark TauCetian night (a planet with no moons and frequently dense cloud cover) Bruchert heard animal noises outside, then loud beatings and thrashes against the external doors and windows, and became concerned that the TauCetian defences weren't effective enough and some beast might actually fight its way into their quarters. Perhaps, she told herself, their predictions were not so accurate as they maintained, and Chan was to be attacked indoors or driven out into the darkness to escape. It was useless asking the TauCetian guards to increase their numbers or defences, their stoicism and defeatism in the face of an immutable future was truly enraging to behold.

While Chan was in the corridor arguing with the guards about the need for more barricades and shutters, Bruchert lost her temper and threw open the external door for a moment in order to direct a quick and massive flamethrower blast in the direction that her radar sensors told her the beast was located. After all, it was not her who was predicted to fall prey to the animal, so surely she would be immune to its attacks on a brief sortie. But of course sefarculs, more or less like all creatures on Tau Ceti f, can anticipate the future.

Drawn by Bruchert's blood curdling screams, Chan realised in a flash that all humans look alike to TauCetians. Of course. It was Bruchert that they had seen being attacked by the sefarcul, not him. Also of course, this meant that he would not be injured by the animal. Filled suddenly with anger, confidence, exhilaration and determination, he burst out into the yard after Bruchert, his firearm blazing, screaming like a commando, ready to save her sadly maimed body from certain death.

Sefarculs are vicious, but seldom over-eat. Having swallowed Bruchert, it had really only room for Chan's leg.

The TauCetians had shrewdly observed how badly human beings take knowledge of impending ill-fortune, how little Bruchert had desired such knowledge. By staying silent, they had granted her a pleasant last two days of her life, thus showing a rapid grasp of an alien psychology in exactly the way that the humans had not.

On Tau Ceti f at least, the future cannot be altered.

~

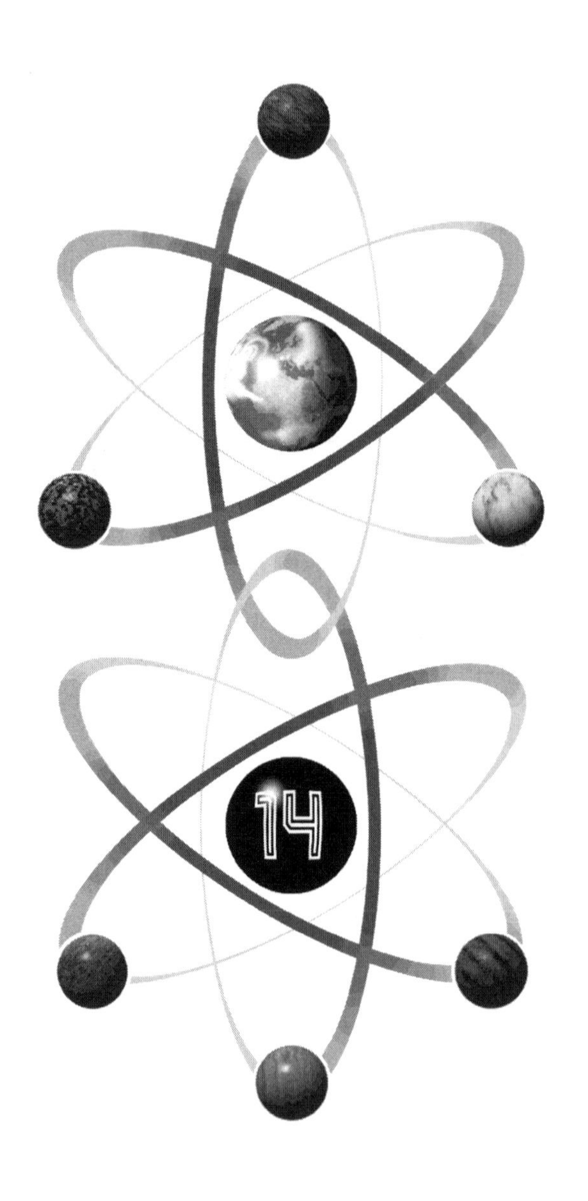
14

VIRAGO

Was it just coincidence that Hillary Fording's relationship with Carlo Serranto first began to falter around the same time as the mission to 41 G. Arae d, soon to be nicknamed Virago? The Telepedrome 'voyages' had each revealed surprising variants on the principles of reproduction on alien worlds, but none so much as Virago would. The astronauts assigned to the mission were Jacques Filimore and Gwen Macdonell, a male and a female, perhaps an unfortunate choice in retrospect.

Virago's most intelligent species were amphibious, as befits a planet 80% under liquid CO_2. Their bodies were about 1.5 times human size, resembling loose brown stomach bags, which palpitated like disembodied human hearts as they swam in liquid or walked about on land. Their limbs were somewhere between arms and fins, in our terms, with long prehensile tails which gave them speed of movement underwater, and enabled them to stand themselves upright on land.

The sea level on Virago rose and fell annually due to the disruptive presence of three massive moons, so their coral cities, like the people, were viable in both environments, emerging strewn with brown weed in Spring, disappearing beneath the waves again, littered by fallen leathery 'leaves' in Autumn.

The faces of Viragans were not dissimilar to humans, with two vertical slit eyes to the front, but their mouths and noses were combined into curious protuberances, which most closely resembled penises and vaginas, and were deployed for pretty much the same purpose, and with alarming frequency.

*

Filimore: Orbital reconnaissance had suggested that Virago was an intensely populated world, a city for every fifty square miles on average, and now we see why.

Our first contact occurred underwater. We chanced upon what we would later realise was a school party: an elderly teacher imparting wisdom to about forty or so juveniles.

Our camera probes had already warned us of the Viragan physiology (and physiognomy) since examples of their species were within easy reach of the initial landing sites on such a populous world.

The pupils were lining up in front of their teacher as we approached, as if handing in their homework, except that on closer inspection we were disgusted to see that the teacher was inserting his... Macdonell is prompting me to be less judgemental and more tolerant of so alien a culture, and to refer to these reproductive organs only as 'nose' and 'pouch'. Perhaps this is not all so crazy as it looks to us. After all, we reproduce using organs extremely close to, or integrated with, those with which we excrete waste. Surely that is a high risk strategy, in terms of hygiene, compared to Viragans, who use noses and mouths.

When the class saw us approaching, panic broke out and the Viragans formed themselves into a defensive ring, like a huge forty-part jellyfish, then beat a hasty retreat towards shore. But even this behaviour was not without its unsavoury aspects. Our advanced landing probes had only ever filmed one-to-one copulation, but to our astonishment we saw that the juveniles and teachers were forming their ring by use of an organ on the back of their heads, whose existence had hitherto been unknown to us. A kind of reverse vagina into which the 'nose' of a partner could be inserted from behind. Thus, the fleeing ring of pupils and teacher were simultaneously defending themselves, fleeing, and having sex.

Of course, our preliminary studies had suggested that juveniles of this age could not reproduce, but what if this kind of 'mass orgy' (Macdonell is cautioning me again concerning my terms of reference) occurs in adults? And what of parenting generally among Viragans? Do children know who conceives them, and are they brought up and protected by those individuals? We have much to learn.

Macdonell: A crowd gathering on the shore gave our computers a helpful boost on de-encryption. The Viragan language is apparently quite simple, even having things we might call nouns and verbs. Give me a few weeks and I might attempt some of these noises myself.

Their soldiers encircled us then led us to a secure chamber inside their coral city, one of the largest we think, perhaps a capital. Eventually, after many hours, we were questioned by one of their wise men, called Zsychra, and we showed him videos and told him about our home world, much of which astounded him. Eventually he held his head in his hands and asked me to stop, saying that the quantity of knowledge was overwhelming him. He then knocked on our cell door, had one of his assistants come in with whom he then copulated in front of us.

I must say, we found the spectacle even more disgusting close up and on dry land. The way his great fleshy belly contracted and puffed as he thrust his 'nose' into the pouch of his subordinate resembled the most sordid of human intercourse, and indeed almost parodied it, making us feel ashamed and embarrassed for ourselves as much as him.

He seemed puzzled by our disgust however, as his assistant retreated, Viragan semen oozing down his face. I took a risk and decided to show him a film about human sexuality and tried to explain it to him.

After an hour of head scratching (yes, Viragans share that rather endearing trait with us), he burst out laughing (another trait shared – although at first I thought he was taking a fit and choking to death).

No wonder you do it so seldom and are so ashamed! he exclaimed, *considering you have to do it with your excreting parts. I feel truly sorry for you. That is utterly disgusting. I take it you won't be attempting this unnatural practice with any of our citizens? Indeed, I must insist right now that you promise not to!*

*

Filimore: I think we bonded with Zsychra after last night's session. Today he took us out as free people to show us his city, in disguise at first so as not to alarm people with our alien appearance, but later unveiled us at a few public squares where he had arranged in advance for what he called "the most enlightened and educated citizens of Telezjic" (the city's name) to meet us and ask questions.

Their city is not really carved of coral, but from

harvested shells from the many sea creatures of the planet, which they bind together into a kind of concrete using lanthanum sand as mortar. Their architecture is colourful and highly evolved, drawing much of its inspiration from the abstract geometrical forms that occur naturally on the seashells themselves.

Everywhere we walked, through streets and squares, glimpsing into public buildings and private houses, we saw Viragans copulating, panting and humping, crying out in carnal excess, shooting semen into each other in a variety of horrifying ways. We asked Zsychra, who had been a little cagey on the topic the night before, to explain to us how Viragan children were born and raised. *We don't even really know if you are male or female yet,* I laughed. He looked very puzzled then took us to their equivalent of a maternity ward where he promised that all would be revealed.

At least then, I presumed, there would be no copulation, and a welcome break from the constant sound of coupling going on around us.

*

Macdonell: There are no sexes, or rather: only one. Zsychra, like all Viragans, can both sire and carry children if he so chooses. The choice is down to strength and domination, and thus the indecent little circle of panic we witnessed yesterday was a demonstration of the pecking-order among the class of infants. And yet, the last one, the omega male so to speak, has the right, and indeed obligation in a ring, to penetrate the leader's head from behind.

God, this is mind-blowing. I am both nauseous and in awe simultaneously. The constant copulation in Telezjic is how people establish a chain of command, a social sliding scale, a hierarchy. The copulation goes on so that strengths and weaknesses can be constantly tested. Although making love, they are also in a sense fighting, wrestling, their social order constantly shifting.

But how do children get born? I wanted to know. *I suppose only your king or queen, your supreme leader at the top of the tree, can have the privilege to penetrate alone and never have to receive somebody else's 'nose' thrust and discharged into the back of his head? Where is your leader or leaders? Can we meet them soon?*

Again, Zsychra looked puzzled. Our word for leader, we could not translate for him, approximating it only with 'teacher' or 'wise man', of which he was only one. *Children? Born?* he responded, holding up his hand which seemed strangely swollen. I thought he was pointing to something but then he added: *as it happens I am due today, I will precipitate a birth for you.*

Entering the hospital ward he then, to our horror, held his arm out over a trough of transparent shell, and struck his own left hand off with a metal blade. Falling into the water below, the hand began crying and writhing about, and as he bandaged his stump we watched the midwives rush over and attend to the severed hand, which we now saw to our astonishment was indeed a miniature little Viragan, complete with legs, arms, head and tail. I made Zsychra show me his good hand close-up, and indeed now that I looked for it, I could see the likeness, its latent potential to grow into an infant Viragan.

But what about your hand...? How will you cope? I don't understand... I stammered.

It will grow back within twelve hours, a little longer the older I get, he answered calmly.

But wasn't that painful? I asked.

Agony, he said, *until we invented painkillers. I've been doped up for days, which is why everyone thought me ideal to come and meet you... so calm I wouldn't be alarmed by you. Noseless people are the stuff of nightmares to us.*

But this is astonishing! Filimore exclaimed. *Your children are your own severed hands!*

Zsychra chuckled, and went a colour which I think might have been a Viragan blush. *And yours are your shit, formed next to your shit and excreted like shit, as far as I can see!* he responded in matching incredulity.

Will you have contact with your hand... I mean your son, daughter, offspring I mean, issue? Will you bring him, it, up?

The midwives do that of course. Do you each hold onto your still-warm excreta-children on your world? Do they not smell? Hanging onto your own effluent does not sound very healthy to us. Should I be scared of catching diseases from you, your unclean customs?

I was about to ask him whether he didn't love his left hand, when he turned a midwife around and began penetrating her.

What about your leaders, don't you have a parliament, a debating chamber? Macdonell asked, having noticed that Viragans didn't mind continuing conversations whilst engaged in sex acts.

We have no leaders, he assured us again (we could not translate for him our words for king and queen), *the top of our chain changes every day, but each day that person only receives as his reward the honour of being penetrated from behind by the most lowly and weak citizen of our entire city (a role which also changes from day to day, incidentally).*

Then what is the purpose of all this hierarchy? This constant conflict or sex or whatever it is?

What is its purpose on your world? he countered.

Evolution, I answered. *Survival of the fittest. The*

passing on of beneficial characteristics, discarding of bad, the genetic improvement of our species through competition and selection.

Then we are not so different, Zsychra smiled, except that his smile was a movement of his penis (I mean nose, sorry) that I find difficult to describe.

But everyone gets to reproduce on your planet, from what we can see, without exception. In our world, those who are unattractive or undesirable are denied this privilege, and so are removed from the gene pool.

Really? What savage and cruel people you must be then... Zsychra frowned, wiping his nose, as the nurse returned to her station. *How can you have combined such barbarism with the skill and knowledge to travel to the stars?*

How indeed... a voice inside me mused, thinking of our wars and massacres and famines, everything we had tried to tactfully omit from the films we had shown him. But Zsychra was perceptive.

Surely yours is an evil world, Zsychra continued, *torn with suffering and sadness, where children are excreted and only the beautiful reproduce? I am very sad for you. And you say that you have two sex types?* (he had no word for 'gender' which we could not translate for him) *that you are each split in two? Everyone must feel so incomplete, so unhappy all the time on your world. Maybe this is why they are so restless and cruel to each other, in anger and spite against their unkind God who made them thus.*

*

Finally Zsychra proudly took us to his parliament. It had no prime minister, president, king or queen. Just row after row of circular galleries, a vast auditorium in the round, where great rings of wise citizens engaged in the daily privilege of group sex, running and rotating, penetrating and being penetrated, crying out in ecstasy, moaning and puffing in exertion, firing semen into each other's heads, while occasionally talking over the din, turning over the odd idea or two, debating and contemplating their city's future, how to solve its problems and rise to its challenges.

But those philosophising words were just pretty noises, amid the gasps of sex, the grunts of wrestling. They were wistful lovers' talk, idle sighs, the cluckings of doves, sweet little nothings.

*

Hillary Fording woke up with a start, in the bed of Carlo Serranto, and quietly headed for the shower, hoping not to wake him. She had been having nightmares again about the Virago mission, and seeing the same counsellors who were still seeing Macdonell and Filimore every week, six months on. Just as well Fording had had the foresight to cancel live public transmission of the Ansible footage. In the end, the Viragans had insisted that the two astronauts copulate in front of them, for educational purposes, before they could leave, and the ensuing spectacle had left them both traumatised with self-loathing, akin to that of rape victims, and emotionally estranged from their own families. To this day, Fording found she would sometimes have to keep eyes closed during sex and avoid looking at Carlo naked. She had abandoned sex altogether with her husband. For his part, although he had never admitted it, Carlo seemed incapable of letting her go on top any more, having become fixated on the insidious notion that this was an encoded power statement signifying her professional superiority.

She heard a noise behind her, and looked up to see Carlo's sleepy face regarding her in the mirror, standing at the open bathroom door. *Sex nightmares again?* he sighed running his hand through his dishevelled hair.

Human beings, we're all nutcases, Carlo, never more so than when we're fucking. I never realised it before. Sex is a healing pantomime for the disturbed, the lack of clothes regressing us to a childlike state.

Yeah... Carlo answered, joining her at the wash basin to use his mouthwash, *I've had the same uncomfortable thought recently, particularly when I find my mouth on your nipples... and as for oral-*

Don't! She put her hand on his lips, then kissed him. *Let's not go there...*

...Ever again, he finished her sentence gladly for her, then they smiled and shook hands on it.

She was reminded of an old joke she'd seen years ago in a newspaper cartoon of two dinosaurs shaking hands and one saying to the other "can we just be friends?" with a caption underneath of "Dinosaurs died out during the platonic period". One unforeseen hazard of the insights of the Telepedrome exploration programme, it suddenly occurred to her, might be that humans could die out, in a self-conscious period.

~

15

THE CHEAP GODS

I want you to meet someone... Becky Lee Falconer said, taking Agent Downey's hand across the table in the downtown restaurant that had become their habitual rendezvous these last six months. The interior was remarkable for its unremarkableness. Notionally Italian, faded tricolour stripes seemed to have bled their way into every menu and curtain, like the buntings of some decades-old civic celebration forgotten by time, that concept of lethargy creating an air of relaxation that effectively counteracted the grime.

Downey nearly joking, said *Who? Your parents?* then remembered she had told him that they were both dead. Instead he merely raised an eyebrow, preparing to settle the bill.

Lecaux... you believe me now, about Vesberg having been behind the cover-up?

Maybe... Downey countered, pouting his lips and tilting his head equivocally.

Well, I have an eye-witness, first-hand testimony, willing to testify before a grand jury... potentially, although she'd need protection, anonymity, a new identity even. Becky's eyes drifted up to the television playing with its sound down, on the wall above them. Catching the interest in her eyes, Downey turned around also. On screen, Fording and Dubceck were giving a press conference, showing images of a new world about to be conquered.

I'll bet that bitch has protected him over the years, you know... she could be in on the whole conspiracy.

Fording? Surely not, Downey grimaced. *She's a different generation isn't she? – Even more so in light of that whacky stuff you maintain about his date of birth. I thought it was only men felt threatened by a powerful woman in a trouser suit? You jealous?*

Becky laughed and threw her hair back, catching the yellow winter light in her hair. *Don't you believe it. She threatens me too...*

*

51 Pegasi e was a world of perpetually falling methane snow and drifting nitrogen fog. Dave Watkins and Wei Lee Meng were dupliported out to the side of an extinct volcano from which, in the occasional moments when the fog cleared, they could see farming settlements laid out in the flat fertile plains below.

This time considerable progress had been made in advance with establishing contact via the robotic probes sent out from the landing site, and the Pegasin language had been partially deciphered, a welcoming committee promised on their arrival.

As they walked down the mountainside, a small crowd of hand-picked Pegasin dignitaries advanced towards the astronauts, then fell to their knees in front of them, calling out:

Hail the star people! The angels of the dawn, your time of coming has long been prophesied! You have come to purge our world of sin and light us the way to the final harvest!

Meng and Watkins looked at each other in confusion and

disgust, then made their first use of their translation software:

Please listen carefully, this is the truth... we are neither gods nor angels. We are humble mortal beings as you are, travelled from a humble planet like this one, but far away in your night sky. We have no answers to your problems, whatever they might be. You cannot possibly have prophesied our coming here. That must simply be coincidence, superstition and self-delusion. We have come only to learn about you and your world and to tell you about ours, if you would wish to know...

To this the leader of the Pegasins cried out: *But if you have travelled from beyond our skies, you must be gods. You must have met the gods up there, or passed them on your way here. What did they look like?*

Again Meng and Watkins conferred and agonised a little over how to proceed. Dubceck at NASA advised them to tell only the truth. This time Meng took over:

We saw no Gods, because there are no Gods beyond your skies. Out there is only black and empty space, among which are only trillions of stars, each of which are distant suns just like your own sun. You are immensely tiny and only one of many thousands of other worlds with life forms on them similar to you. No gods preside over your lives or events here, neither to punish nor reward. You are no better or worse than the animals which you keep as livestock here, or the wild animals which you have not yet tamed. The only difference is your intelligence, and your peculiar curiosity and facility for confabulation. We speak from experience, because in our own past on our world we were like you and thought like you. But when we learned more and became more advanced we gradually realised what we know now, the gist of which we have just told you. Belief in gods will only hold you back, muddy your thoughts and make you fight amongst yourselves. Seek facts instead, shun superstition, and you will progress as we have.

Gods who are not gods? Gods who have died? Who come here to announce to us their own cessation of existence!? What a calamity! How have we angered the gods that they thus annihilate themselves in sorrow for us? How can we repent, and bring back their favour?

Again Meng and Watkins regarded each other in despair, seeing too late their hopeless predicament.

*

Hillary Fording returned to the apartment to find Carlo Serranto and Nathan on the doorstep 'talking' to the neighbours' dog. *Who's been a good boy then?* Serranto was asking while an electronic device in his coat pocket translated back: *What? What do you want? What pup? Are you injured? Do you want to be my friend? Can I play chase with your pup?*

Honestly, Carlo... Fording sighed, slipping past with the shopping bags. *Do you really expect Nathan or indeed myself to believe that ridiculous little party trick?*

Believe what you like, Hillary, but Nate and I have been talking Mutt all morning, parliamo doggiano, muttlish, canineze... We'll be speaking it fluently in another week. Problem is that Tibbles from next door has nothing on his mind but balls and biscuits...

I grew up with a few girls like that in Illinois...

Hey, steady on old girl... Carlo laughed, covering Nathan's ears, then making them stand up like a canine's.

Woof woof, Nathan shouted, and Carlo ruffled his hair and sent him running across the living room to return to his games in the corner.

Carlo... Fording sighed, pouring them both coffee and sitting at her favourite window overlooking downtown Los Angeles. *Nathan is fourteen years old now... you're starting to sound more childish than him.*

Hillary, Hillary... he sighed. *What's up? Where's your inner child got to today? Lost in the woods?*

See any woods around here? she shrugged, looking around her, over her shoulder to the desert beyond.

Forests of the mind, Hillary, you know what I mean, work troubling you?

Fording produced some photographs from her handbag and laid them out on the table. *51 Pegasi.. a pretty name... and a pretty pickle.*

How so? Serranto frowned.

Because they keep worshipping us. We're changing the very thing we're trying to study, ergo study invalidated. And it's dangerous too. They could start some kind of 'rapture' soon and begin topping themselves because they think we're angels of their apocalypse.

Reminds me of the Aztecs and Cortez, Quetzalcoatl, the coming race, all that jazz.

Yes, history repeating, mirrors within mirrors, except that this time we're in charge.

You sure of that? Serranto scratched his head. We were in charge back then too, or thought we were.

Meaning?

Ideas, bad ideas, people can get over. It's physical contamination that did for the indigenous Americans... and for the Martians in the War Of The Worlds come to think about it.

Wrong way around. That's the conquerors getting it in the neck.

Mmmm... I know. I chose my words carefully. But have they, our astronauts I mean, chosen their words carefully? Statements of non-divinity are hard to retract once you've issued them.

You think we should have played God and not shattered their illusions?

My father once said something very interesting, Hillary. Well, he said many interesting things, but he said this one with great emphasis, although I never found out what experience in real life it was that had precipitated it. He said never shatter a man's illusions without first providing him with an alternative.

We've told them how their solar system is configured relative to the rest of space, shown them movies and pictures.

Hillary, Carlo put his hand on hers to stop her for a moment. *You've been talking to Dubceck too much. Facts and figures aren't enough for sentient beings. It was myths and legends and religions that spurred us on across the centuries, created our greatest works of art. Think of religions as bedtime stories that inspired us all when humanity was young. Not literal truth, but inspiring, useful ways of seeing. Do you read Nathan physics equations at bedtime?*

But we're scientists, not artists, Carlo.

Oh, that old chestnut. I disagree. I think that the mathematics and physics equations that have made Entanglement possible are so beautiful that they are art, they are music. What we've done with them certainly is. In the end, at the real high-end, which is what we're engaged in now, I'm not sure there's any difference anymore. Art and science might have split apart some time in the eighteenth century, to keep out of each other's way, but I'd say they're growing back together now, approaching a reunion, and that's a good thing, and a signal of attainment. And besides, we have to be polymaths in this job, Hillary, sociologist and psychologist and philosopher, we mustn't compartmentalise and limit ourselves.

You should be preaching on Pegasi, Carlo, that's quite an ecstatic vision you're working yourself up to there.

Serranto laughed. *I'd be better for them than Dubceck,*

that's for sure. He always reminds me of a limerick I heard years ago.

Go on, Fording smiled over her coffee cup.

He proceeded in a whisper:

A mathematician named Hall
Had a dodecahedronal ball
The sum of its weight
Times his pecker plus eight
Was seven and two thirds of fuck all.

*

Meng and Watkins were led down the cultivated avenues, while the Pegasin peasants all fell on their knees by the wayside, beating their chests and wailing adulatory and self-emolliatory self-flagellatory incantations.

The Pegasins were predominately blue in colour with four legs and four arms, and yet somehow despite these major differences, surprisingly human in appearance. They stood upright (when they weren't praying) and the top and back of their heads carried curious reddish-brown plume-like crests somewhere between hair, skin and feathers, whose function seemed largely for display (pending detailed medical examination). Their eyes were green with black cat-like irises and pupils, their mouths circular, ears apparently non-existent (… did the plumes perform this function instead?) and yet all this, once one had grown accustomed to it, seemed to convey recognisable emotions in a way similar to the human face.

Their fields of crops were largely yellow trumpet-shaped plants of various varieties, brown leaf creeper and red cabbages full of black grape-like spheres which were made into wine and jam after careful distillation.

The Pegasins, suitably over-awed, took it as a great honour to explain and describe these facets of their flora and fauna to their living gods. Fauna? Birds and insects took the form of a small range of bat-like creatures, all red in colour, some with yellow spots, the smaller of which were pests that fed on their crops, the larger of which (a foot long with three foot wing span) were a treasured delicacy when roasted.

Their apparent leader turned to Meng and asked:

Will you address our people at our central market today, our place of worship? Will you explain to them how they have sinned and brought such shame upon the gods that they have wilted and fallen from their gilded palace in the sky?

Dubceck, getting more and more tired of this, and chided by sociological concerns being raised in the media over previous days, prompted Meng: *Just say yes, it's simpler that way... but when the time comes you can tell them something else, like the truth for instance...*

Smiling, wondering if they understood this gesture, Meng and Watkins merely nodded their heads and assented.

*

Becky Lee led Jack Downey into a darkened hotel room, with its curtains still closed. It was 2pm now, and Downey found the darkness odd and unsettling.

This is Amy Weston, Jack, she was Guy Lecaux's girlfriend, fiancée, before the experiment.

Downey offered his hand as his eyes tried to adjust to the darkness, but the figure sitting on the bed did not offer her hand in return. He took this to be some gesture of contempt towards the FBI or the American nation in general. To his surprise, she spoke with an English accent and was wearing, of all things, a veil. This creeped him out, and he struggled to control an involuntary shiver.

Guy was a French student studying in London, we met there, just after he had failed his second year exams. He needed the money for his re-sits, which was why he applied to the NASA programme. He wasn't expecting to be accepted. Do you know some of this stuff already?

Sure... Downey answered. *But please go on.*

Fifteen other students applied, we heard later, but all were rejected, on health grounds we were told. But we saw later how that must have been a lie. Guy was no athlete, and some of the people rejected were. They were interested in his background, his family.

Or lack of it... Becky chipped in.

The veiled face turned towards Becky and took her hand. In the darkness, Downey thought he noticed something deformed about the fingers. *Yes, precisely...* she continued. *The first few times he came home he was fine. They were just doing preliminary trials on him. Then he started becoming pale and shaky. After three weeks, the experiments culminated and I got a phone call asking me to come to the research centre.*

Where was that?

A military hospital near RAF Brize Norton. Thing was though, when I got there, they wouldn't let me in.

Why not?

They said they hadn't called me. And they were right. It was Guy himself who had called me, his tone of voice all strange, except that when I told them that they said it was impossible. They kept me there for hours questioning me and made me sign the Official Secrets Act, various legal disclaimers, promised me Guy would be home in a few days. They sent me home, but I never saw Guy, or any of them, every again.

No explanations?

Silence, phone numbers gone dead, discontinued. Then threats, visits from various shady figures.

Amy, Miss Weston... Downey cleared his throat. *May I ask what happened to you, your face, your hands?*

She turned to look at Becky again, and Becky nodded

and produced some photographs from her handbag and laid them out on a small table between them. *Do you recognise any of these men, Amy? And can you confirm to Jack that this is the first time I have ever shown you any photographs of these people or any others?*

Amy nodded. *Sure. That's true. I've never seen these before...* She held her breath then pointed that oddly shaped index finger again towards one of the plates. *But this, this one, this man is the last one who came to visit me. He seemed like some kind of bigwig.*

Becky had picked up the plate now and showed it to Downey. It was Gene Vesberg, a younger version, although not much, the man was notoriously ageless.

What did he say to you, Amy?

*

Being a tidally-locked world, the passage of a year made little difference to Pegasins, since their sun always appeared at more or less the same point in the sky. Of much more dramatic impact on their lives was the rotation of their vast and colourful moon Protos, a gas giant with a rotating storm on its face, a great 'eye of God' as Pegasins thought of it, perpetually watching and judging them.

As with Earth's moon, the passage of Protos across the sky seemed to have profound effects on the Pegasins, both physical and mental, all of them mysterious and surprising.

Before Meng and Watkins could even address the people from their ceremonial temple at the heart of their agricultural market city, another transit of Protos was suddenly completed and a festival thrown, after which everyone seemed re-booted, persuaded of entirely different viewpoints and outlooks.

The astronauts' initial guide, who they now recognised as some kind of priest or spiritual leader seemed to capture the mood perfectly by declaring that a new kind of red bat-bird, blown in from the west on a methane storm, was now clearly the incarnation of the gods and angels who secretly governed their lives. The astronauts suddenly found themselves politely ignored and neglected, as all the people of the vast settlement set about capturing a red bat bird for themselves that they could each worship every night and implore with devout prayers and lamentations, that it deliver them from evil and boost their future crop yield.

The upshot of this was that NASA's erstwhile copious flow of information from the co-operative natives was suddenly completely curtailed, as everyone became too busy with the study and worship of bat birds. This was most inconvenient to NASA who had been doing so well.

*

In the darkened hotel room, Amy Weston continued her disclosure to Agent Downey:

He showed me photographs and films of Guy, pieces of him, weird stuff, 'artefacts' he kept calling them, as if that word had some different meaning for him. He was a scientist alright, spoke in gobbledegook all the time. He said Guy was dead, but that instead of his ashes being scattered, somehow his image was scattered... his "after image" he called it, his "temporal shadow". Then he said he had died for one of the greatest secrets in the history of humanity, a scientific breakthrough, something I would find out about eventually when it became public, but in the meantime I must never talk about Guy's role within...

Entanglement... Downey ventured.

He never used that word. But I figured that must have been what he meant, decades later, when the breakthroughs were announced.

Did he threaten you, Amy? Offer you money to stay quiet?

Compensation he called it.

How much? Downey pressed her.

She looked at Becky before she answered. *Half a million Dollars.*

Cheap at the price, Downey thought, but said nothing. *So you took it.*

Yes, Amy whispered, nodding her head, *...but it wasn't just the money, he gave me something else...* she nodded to Becky who produced an unmarked cardboard box and passed it to Amy who carefully opened it up on her lap. What she lifted out of it was about a foot square, made of stainless steel, but badly burnt and buckled. Obscure vent-like structures on its sides were twisted into fantastical shapes, the ruptured fabric of the metal itself showing through in a few places, like a kind of weave. It looked like meta-materials, cutting-edge NASA technology designed to heal and re-form itself, but irrevocably damaged or altered at the atomic level. Downey wished he'd brought a Geiger counter. It was probably still buzzing. It looked hot to the touch although it couldn't possibly be.

That man...

Vesberg... Becky interjected.

He told me it was Guy's last remains and that I could have it in return for my silence along with the compensation on the one condition that I buried it in a grave and never tried to open it.

You didn't bury it... Downey observed the obvious.

She shook her head. *No. I opened it.*

Becky stood up. *Shall I open the curtains, Amy, let some light in now?*

She nodded her head and lifted a hand towards the veil. *It exploded when I opened it, Mr Downey. Burnt half my house down before the fire brigade got there, but it was no ordinary explosion. I can't explain it. Ghosts were released into the room, and screams that weren't mine. I was...* she faltered now, words failing her, overcome with emotion. *I was altered...*

When Becky lifted Amy's veil, Downey wished he hadn't stayed. He thought he could handle it, but the months and years of disrupted sleep he would suffer afterwards suggested otherwise.

One half of Amy Weston, her left half, remained intact and normal, but the other had been imploded somehow, inverted and remoulded so that it showed the imprint of another human being who had collided with or embraced her, with supernatural force. Ribs and skull, everything impossible to reshape without fracture had somehow nonetheless been reshaped at the molecular level, while the host went on living. Amy Weston was half her self and half the three-dimensional shadow of her doomed lover, Guy Lecaux. It was impossible to say if the dark eye on that right side, inverted, still fully functioning, was a window to the soul of Amy or to some other plane of existence from which it looked back, watchful, horrified, reproachful.

*

Every attempt to regain the attention of the Pegasins, even to the extent of picking up red bat birds and threatening to do something profane to them, were of no avail in relieving NASA's predicament.

Dubceck and Melnikov puzzled over matters, but after two weeks the next transit of Protos approached and hopes were raised that at this point attention would return to the human guests.

But this time, as the vast gas giant sank smouldering into the distant misty mountains, *Shapurnal*, as they now knew the high priest was called, sent his eyes into his head and spoke in tongues then declared that now everyone in the settlement must worship blue volcanic pebbles, which he had decided were fragments of the eyes of Nassos, their great father god who had sailed the skies at the birth of the world before being withered by the terrible star of Protos.

Thus had the human race overestimated the potential extent of its influence on the culture of 51 Pegasi e. Dubceck was both frustrated at the sudden curtailment of data and relieved that he had not, as insinuated by the media, irrevocably damaged an alien culture.

As Meng and Watkins gave up their mission and retraced their steps back up the mountain, they passed the disinterested faces of the Pegasins, going about their daily business, heavily enthralled in their latest religious project of worshipping a refuse collector from one of their eastern provinces who had last week been declared a demi-god. Now the piles of previously-worshipped blue pebbles were being used as garden ballast at the bottom of their irrigation trenches.

Maybe the answer was in the perpetually falling methane snow (a subtle off-white shade of green) that had not halted once in all the time of their stay upon the planet. For a moment all the religious shenanigans made them recall the three wise men of the New Testament, minus one. But hadn't the explorer Ernest Shackleton and his men, near to death at the Antarctic, reported the presence of an extra figure in peripheral vision, sensed by all, implied to be Christ? There would be no nativity this time, just a revelation discontinued, but at least a homecoming, cold or otherwise.

Watkins turned to look back upon the world they were leaving and shouted out: *Your gods are dead!*

Meng laughed. The words, whether in English or the language of aliens, was equally lost upon the wind at this altitude. Where their footsteps had progressed through the snow, they saw now that they were being erased within minutes. Then they understood that in this world, as perhaps in every other, they had been ephemeral, kings for a day, then doomed to be forgotten.

~

16

URSA MAJOR

...We are all falling. This hand also falls.
Look at the rest: it is in all of them.
And yet there is still One who catches all that falls
With unerring tenderness in His own hands.

– Rainer Maria Rilke, *Autumn*
(translated by Nina Allan)

Everything seemed to be happening at once by the time of the Ursa Major mission. The reporter Becky Lee Falconer had at last broken the story of Gene Vesberg's cover-up of the Guy Lecaux case. Her newspaper, the Evening Tribune, had stood by her claims of confidentiality of sources, but when called before a congressional committee she would be compelled under oath to name federal agent, Jack Downey, who would then come under scrutiny for treasonous disclosure of secrets of national security importance.

Meanwhile, some other keen and ambitious reporter from a rival newspaper would soon break the story of Hillary Fording's extra-marital affair with Carlo Serranto, and his supposed demotion within NASA when the affair ended. The relationship had stemmed from the amount of time that Fording had spent out of hours with Serranto working with her son, whom Serranto believed to be the 'herald' of a new evolutionary leap in human consciousness.

Rather than focus on this benign and compassionate aspect of Serranto's interest, the media had somehow conjured up spurious and unfounded images of Fording and Serranto making whoopee in hospital corridors and broom cupboards within earshot of Fording's autistic son. Nathan was not technically 'retarded' or 'disabled' nor indeed any longer legally a child by the time of these supposed dalliances, which at any rate he had not overheard or seen. But since time immemorial, truth has never been allowed to pollute the refreshing waves of a good scandal. Once a lip-smackingly unsavoury image has made its indelible mark on the public consciousness, no amount of retractions, legal actions or apologies, are ever able to quite wipe clean the retina of the world's watchful eye. In short, mud sticks.

In such a context, one might be grateful to be autistic and thus overlooked, side-tracked by the madness of mainstream humanity, a moment of dead-calm at the eye of the hurricane. And such was Nathan Fording on the evening of April 14th 2206, as he sat at home, poring over his mother's reconnaissance photographs as had now become their tacit arrangement.

Ursa Major 6f was a lush world of turquoise jungles, pink skies and amber and purple oceans. Its many large cities were built of metal and stone to such precision as to obviously be the work of an advanced civilisation. That civilisation however, appeared to be entirely missing. Furthermore, the geometry of these abandoned cities defied all logical analysis. Streets led nowhere, buildings opened and closed with no coherent regard for normal rules of shelter or enclosure, the cities were, it seemed, the work of madmen.

But did we say deserted? The cities had seemed so at

first, but when astronauts Dean Weninger and Juan Sagrado made the first journey of exploration through one, weird changing ghost shapes had appeared around them in an astounding sequence of forms, a film of which Nathan was now analysing.

*

Nathan could hear his mother and Carlo Serranto fighting in the next room. He had been taken around the Telepedrome today as a special treat for his sixteenth birthday, on condition that he touched nothing, particularly not any computers, with his worryingly whizzing fingers. He had taken to spending hours online recently, soaking up knowledge, searching forums and notice boards for teenagers of similar disposition to himself, like-minds. His mother spoke darkly of a condition, but to him his difference from others was a source of joy in his loneliness, if that wasn't a paradox. He was fascinating company for himself.

Now he had solved the puzzle. It was obvious. He remembered his mother's NASA password even though she changed it weekly and thought he never watched her fingers on the keyboard. But of course she had to look down at the precise moment when he looked to where her fingers went.

The mathematical algorithms were sound, the geometry irrefutable. He sent his message to Dubceck and ordered it to be broadcast to the astronauts' suits at the same time. Dubceck was bound to obey an email from Fording herself.

His mother burst into the room a second later and screamed in horror: *Who let you in here? Carlo said you were waiting in the visitor's lounge! What do you think you're playing at? Have you any idea what you're doing!?* She hit the red alarm by the door and triggered a complete lock-down of the facility, then dragged Nathan away by the head and shoulders, slapping him across the face. He was too old for a spanking.

It's over, Carlo! Fording spat at Serranto a few minutes later, heading for the control room. *You're fired and dumped, all in one! Don't ever expose my son to danger and don't ever desert your post and expose this facility to unauthorised access. Your security clearance is hereby withdrawn. Please leave the building by the civilian exit!*

He tried to protest and explain and apologise, cover for Nathan, but she ripped his name-tag from his lapel and slammed the door in his face.

*

Dubceck was late in arriving at the emergency meeting Fording had thrown and finally came in excitedly, carrying a laptop with him.

Fording, close to tears, was about to explain and apologise for her grotesque dereliction of duty in allowing her son to infiltrate and potentially damage a Telepedrome computer, but before she could speak, Dubceck congratulated her, incredulously, on the extraordinary series of equations he thought she had just sent him.

How could I not see it!? Of course, it's incredible to contemplate, but these beings are 4-dimensional. We can only view them as 3-dimensional shadows, but if we build the right visual translation software, we could speak to them using light projections of 3-dimensional shadows, postulate shapes and ideas that we believe would signify alien intelligence to them. It's mind-blowing, but the maths is sound, everything points to it. It should work!

The whole room, the fourteen scientists around the table turned to look at Hillary Fording with startled expressions, but hers was more startled still. *I... I... I don't know what to say. I mean... what equations? Show me. Show us all, get them up on screen.*

Now, said Dubceck, *before you ask, I've already got a team running all the data we have so far through these equations in order to try to reconstruct the appearance of these alien beings, if that is what they are, although of course we will only be able to view diagrammatic approximations of their appearance, 3-dimensional versions of them if you will. Kind of like the way a drawing of a complex abstract object might take the form of a sketch on a flat piece of paper, but only through looking at a dozen of such sketches depicting it from different angles might we be able in our minds to build an actual sculpture of the actual 3-dimensional shape... Just think, this has never been done before, if it works! Will we be able to make sense of what we see? – The first images of 4-dimensional aliens. Well done, Doctor Fording. I never knew your maths was so good. What other talents have you been hiding?*

*

That night when she got home and let the housekeeper go, Fording took up her print-outs of the UrsaMajorans to show Nathan, but when she entered his room she found he was already building models of them out of green Plasticine.

Contrite, she sat down quietly beside him at his desk, and looked on as he kept working. After a while she ran her fingers through his hair and tears came to her eyes, rolling silently down her cheeks.

Nathan paused, then turned and hugged her, stroking her back. *It's OK, Mom. It's OK...* he said.

Uncle Carlo won't be coming here again, Nathan... you know that?

Yes... he nodded his head. *It wasn't his fault, Mom. I asked him to give me a NASA door code so I could go to the toilet. It was a lie. He's a good man. You two were good together. I'm sorry for what I caused.*

She pulled back and looked at him astounded. It was the most direct social interaction she had ever achieved with him in sixteen years. Then he blinked, muttered some obscure maths then turned back to his sculptures.

I didn't think... Fording stammered, *I never thought you understood people, or cared about emotions much. And all this time I've been wrong, you've been listening and understanding. What else do you have the answers to?*

What's to understand? He sniggered to himself. *People are embarrassing, vexatious. Simpler being a machine, staying below radar cover. You're getting too old for all this excitement, Mom. You need a boring boyfriend, boring like Dad, or Dad himself for that matter, he's got boredom trademarked.*

He looked at her again, dead in the eye, the way he almost never had before this strange symbolic day at the threshold… of something.

Fording suddenly sobbed and laughed at the same time, then embraced Nathan again, shaking, the tension pouring out of her in long waves.

*

Of course, parts of what the computer simulations and Nathan's sculptures depicted could not be defined or understood by 3-dimensional brains. A long protuberance at the back of the head had to be denoted as infinite in length (Nathan curtailed it at three feet for artistic licence), and two holes near the ankles represented a wormhole which joined together via the navel, but such a convolution could only be thought, not depicted. The spines down the back changed length depending on the angle of view, from ten inches long to ten miles, this on a creature apparently twenty feet tall.

But all of the foregoing, it must be remembered, was visual translation and approximation, via Nathan Fording's equations.

All that the astronauts and any other human would ever see unaided of these beings were spheres, ellipsoids and rhomboids of continuously changing shapes, as their limbs and torsos intersected in and out of 3-dimensional space.

What the humans looked like to the aliens could only be guessed at. Smudges on wallpaper? Rainwater stains on pavement slabs?

New headsets and inter-dimensional translation software (the first in human history) were Ansibled out to Weninger and Sagrado two weeks later and a new attempt made at gaining the attention of the UrsaMajorans.

Entering the city a second time by the same streets, the astronauts found they could make more sense of the buildings and avenues than before, although much of them remained physically inaccessible.

Suddenly amorphous shapes began appearing next to Weninger, an UrsaMajoran walking past them. With their headsets on they could make out a figure of the kind that the simulations had trained them to recognise. Walking across the street to talk to another one.

Prompted by Fording, Sagrado began 'loudly' projecting their specially prepared 4-dimensional greeting message.

After a few minutes of confusion and uncertainty, a bewildering cacophony of 4-dimensional shapes, Sagrado found himself lifted up into the air by a shifting miasma of blobs (a hand and forearm, when viewed through a headset).

Sagrado repeated the greeting signal and looked up expectantly into the empty space above him which his headset told him held the face of a higher-dimensional being.

Of course, over and beyond the spatial translation, there

was still the question of what language the UrsaMajorans spoke, but Nevada was hoping that such advanced beings would be able to decipher human English within minutes.

Fording asked Weninger to project his greeting message too at this point, but he stalled for time, nearly refused, while looking up at his suspended colleague and still pondering in fear what his fate might be.

As Sagrado was moved away through space, afraid to lose contact, Weninger finally complied.

The alien creature and its companion then brought Sagrado back and knelt over the two human curiosities to examine them, discussing in some bizarre patterns of sound and light which have not been deciphered since.

It was Dubceck, in a fit of uncharacteristic creativity, who would later draw the analogy with two fastidious but humane housekeepers who had discovered two spiders on their prize crockery or polished floorboards.

Weninger and Sagrado were taken to some kind of sorting area for dividing into stones and tree debris, charcoal and leaf litter. Placed among bark and dirt balls for a few minutes, they were then jettisoned at high velocity through 4-dimensional vacuum tubes to a disused quarry on the other side of the planet. It took them six months to return on foot to within range of the lander probes, re-enter the Entanglement chambers and return to Earth.

Whether the UrsaMajorans had failed to understand the human race or understood them all too well, remains an open question. Ten years on, computers are still trying to decipher the data gathered during that brief interaction. This great curiosity and endeavour on the part of humanity, is yet to be reciprocated it seems, by the UrsaMajorans.

~

SEVERANCE

Fording's last command, under siege from a hostile media, was the planet of 36 Ophiuchi k, which became known as Severus. No one had thought life possible on a planet with such an unusual orbit. Severus wove a path of startling geometric complexity around three suns, which in turn orbited each other, a tertiary star system. The result of this was that Severus was bathed in light and heat for twenty years at a time and then suddenly 'slingshot' out into the cold blackness of space for an interval of two years before returning to the fold. The probe-spores and Ansibles arrived just before the start of the slingshot and astronauts Hakim and Beringsdottir dupliported out to observe whatever would happen next. What they found astounded them. The planet was full of life, but that life would be 'flash frozen' at incredible speed as the planet changed orbital phase.

Mohammad Hakim was from Egypt, one of the hottest and most arid countries on Earth, while Britta Beringsdottir hailed from Iceland, one of the coldest and darkest. Perhaps their differing perspectives would prove insightful.

The Entanglement chambers dupliported them to the outskirts of a city of enormous vibrancy, bursting with sound and colour. The probes had already partially deciphered the indigenous language from their radio broadcasts, and now began using this knowledge to project greetings messages outwards from the landing site.

The level of technology in evidence seemed to approximate to early twentieth century human, but the physiology of the beings did not. There was a superficial resemblance to elephants, except that these beings had three stubby legs and four 'trunks' or suction tentacles and one large central eye in their heads that glittered with deep and compassionate intelligence. Two flapping 'ears' sprouted from either side of their heads also, which may have had other sensory functions than their basic one of sound detection, perhaps sensitive to infra-red and electromagnetic field fluctuations.

They sent out what looked like soldiers at first, uniformed personnel with weapons that resembled long fishing-rods with some kind of dangerous electrical charge at their tip. But these were merely to protect one of their dignitaries, perhaps a president, who shuffled forward from their midst and formed his (or her) tentacles into a curious star formation, which the astronauts later learned was a sign of peaceful welcome. No doubt the open palms and bows of the humans were equally perplexing to the Severans.

This dignitary in fine robes, called Salsurt, took the human visitors to meet Oradlup, the leader of the city, which was called Sabveltyja, which they explained meant 'perpetual carnival' in their strange language of hoots and roars, which the human computers now quickly mastered.

The meeting took place in a particularly fine palace hall of beautiful stone floors and very elaborately decorated walls and roofs (of timber and bone – the Severans carved the bones of their own ancestors into artefacts of great beauty, believing this to give the dead immortality). Their figure of speech "an uncarved bone" meant 'wasted opportunity' or 'tragic loss'. The astronauts were greeted with great warmth and fascination. The Severans had some understanding of astronomy and seemed to grasp the human explanation of which solar system the visitors originated from and where both the star systems sat within the Milky Way galaxy. When the astronauts tried to discuss the orbit of Severus itself however, they ran into difficulty. An important official who they would later understand to be a high priest, raised his tentacles in protestation and called for silence followed by two minutes of prayer (to pray, Severans intertwined their tentacles into a curious knotting formation and emitted a sound like muted trombones).

After a respectful silence, Beringsdottir attempted again to tell the Severans about the impending slingshot orbit and to enquire as to how this civilisation had coped with the event some twenty years earlier.

But again the high priest protested, Oradlup became agitated, and another period of prayer had to be entered into. This time, the astronauts were taken aside afterwards and politely asked never to raise the subject again. This was disturbing of course, but Beringsdottir and Hakim were advised by Fording to comply so as not to cause offence and go on learning as much as possible about the alien culture.

This policy paid dividends. A great celebration ensued. Hakim and Beringsdottir were shown dancing and costumes, food they could not eat (although its appearance delighted them) and music that sounded like hell (although the elaborate instruments of wood, bone and tellurium were visually stunning).

Then they were led through the streets to meet many ordinary Severans and enter their homes, their places of work and entertainment. This was a city of overwhelming complexity and exuberance, of constant joy and celebration. Multi-coloured decorative garlands hung everywhere between the eaves of the magnificently carved architecture. By night lights came on and smells, images and sounds intensified; everywhere there was rhythm, excitement, exuberance. The city was a living heart, beating like a drum or the throat of a joyous worshipper, vibrating, bubbling with song, ululation, exultation.

In a quiet moment with one of their most renowned poets and singers, Hakim dared again to whisper the forbidden question regarding their planet's orbit: *Do you know your world is about to end? To be plunged into dark and cold? Should you not be preparing for such a terrifying eventuality? Has it not happened before?*

The poet did not invoke the intercession of the priest nor strike Hakim down for blasphemy, but merely shrugged and said: *It is the will of God.* Hakim could not help but smile, recognising this modest stoicism as resonant with the oft-repeated "Insha'Allah" of his own dear faith. And yet, he remained alarmed. His faith was allied with rationality and science, but here, it seemed to him, were lemmings running gladly towards the edge of a cliff.

The astronauts enjoyed the extraordinary hospitality of the Severans for three more days and saw every wondrous sight and sound they could and came to understand much of the aliens' biology and cultural customs. Severans mated and had children much as humans did, recorded and respected their past and each held high hopes for their future despite the fact that as the humans saw it: that future was forfeit.

On the fourth night, Beringsdottir and Hakim knew the planet was entering its final phase of darkness, that no sun would shine again for two years, and yet as they walked the streets (having been generously granted freedom of the city by Oradlup) they still saw no sign of preparation, lament, or farewell.

In the morning, the Severans rose to go about their daily duties, attend their places of work, but no sun, only the light of their two barren silver moons (Ytranglas and Bezalam) fell across the streets, weaving a spell of foreboding of death, to which the citizens seemed immune or were determined to ignore.

The temperature fell by ten degrees an hour, then twenty, then thirty, forty. As the astronauts looked on aghast, protected by their own survival suits, they saw waves of ice shiver and shimmer across the world and freeze the city dead as it passed, each living being reduced from nonchalant vibrancy to deathly stasis within seconds.

The commuters on a wooden carriage with bone wheels, were frozen stiff, the driver slumped over its controls, the latecomer running to catch up frozen with his tentacle raised in the air, another clutching his basket, a trader with his wares. The carriage progressively shrouded in ice until it was an iceberg, a phantom, frosted white, unrecognisable.

The leader in conversation with his ministers was frozen at the table in the middle of discussing affairs of state, the ice a white shadow that had passed across the room in less than half a minute.

The musician in a café, froze stiff, his tentacles halfway through a phrase on his bone violin.

The builders toiling on the city of Sabveltyja's latest tall building, stopped in mid-manoeuvre, their tentacles clutching the great tree trunks and bone pins they were carrying, while the unfinished masterpiece turned white as if bewitched by a spell. The building was turned into a wedding cake, a palace of icicles under a falling dust of castor sugar.

The sportsman, leaping across a trough of burning coals at the centre of an arena of three thousand spectators, turned to ice in mid-flight and landed on the other side as a bouncing splinter, an obscure crystal accretion, surrounded suddenly by an audience of blank eyes, unmoving white faces like painted scenery who could neither applaud nor disapprove.

The 'Vraitchirtal' birds, Severan symbols of hope and freedom, froze in mid-air where they flew, high above the ceremonial square in front of the presidential palace, and fell numbly to the ground, mute as stones at the feet of the passers-by: a thousand white statues, the crowded dead.

Incredulous, Beringsdottir and Hakim walked through this spectacle for many hours as the ice accumulated and multiplied and everything so recently warm and alive became at last unrecognisable, abstract, mere patterns of frost, a fading memory.

They took samples. Hacked out a few specimens of smaller animals and Ansibled them back to Earth for analysis. They had all been flash frozen, heart stopped, killed without a moment's warning. Or so they thought.

*

Two years later the astronauts returned and watched a wave of life move across the planet just as quickly as they thought a wave of death had done, as the slingshot orbit returned Severus again to the life-giving warmth of its triple suns. But so fast had the freezing process been that all life had been preserved, suspended, miraculously intact.

The carriage driver found he had inexplicably crashed, the sportsman that he had broken his ankle, the politician that he had forgotten the point of his sentence halfway through its convoluted progress. The builders dropped the beam they had been carrying, the musician made a mess of the tune he had played half his life, and put it down to impending senility. The Vraitchirtal birds rolled and squawked on the moist pavement then fluttered upwards again to resume their symbolic flight and show the world their magnificently coloured feathers.

Nobody bothered to ask anyone else if they had felt that strange shiver too, if that momentary feeling of being lost or haunted might be significant of something larger and universally shared. Such talk would be silly superstition.

Only the visitors from outer space knew otherwise, and perhaps the Severan priests, who if they knew, somehow *knew without knowing*, had been taught to encode some ancient knowledge, an intimation given to their forefathers. What did it matter after all, if things were not really the way they appeared to most people; if things were more terrible and wonderful than anyone guessed, provided life always went on, or appeared to go on, so very much as usual?

~

18

RELATIVITY

Hillary Fording should have phoned first, found herself a reliable spy perhaps among Vesberg's house staff to tell her who was coming and going. As it was, she ran into Marc Dubceck exactly when she least wanted to, in Vesberg's living room, him leaving, her arriving, under the diffident eyes of the security and medical personnel.

Hillary, err... he looked as discomfited as her for a moment. *Look, can we go outside and talk? You got a minute?*

She hesitated, grappling for some ludicrous excuse, but rushing to see an incapacitated Vesberg just didn't seem credible enough to wash with a man of the towering logic of Dubceck.

Him? He pointed over his shoulder with a desultory thumb. *He'll keep. He's getting medication. It's all mental stuff, he's strong as an ox physically.*

Out of earshot of his staff, among the dense hedgerows of Vesberg's back garden, they managed to unburden themselves.

I heard you split up with Carlo, I'm sorry.

Fording raised her eyebrows. This caught her off guard. They had never even publicly acknowledged any relationship in front of him. But then again, she had to keep reminding herself, it was all over the papers now. Wrong-footed, she even found herself divulging *I'm not going back to John.*

Perversely, irritatingly perhaps, Dubceck now changed the subject: *You should have come and seen Gene when Hazel died, Hillary, you know that... he mentioned it to me, in there just now, it mattered to him.*

I sent flowers to the funeral... she muttered, embarrassed, found herself reaching for a caffeine stick in desperation. To her surprise, Dubceck shielded her hands for her, lit her up, and accepted one too, apparently without judgement.

Desperate times, desperate measures, he whispered, then added suddenly: *Not good enough.*

What isn't? she asked, strolling to the garden end, gazing back at the house's white shiplap façade under the cloudless blue.

Sending flowers. He was devastated by her death, and now this, his mind's collapsed under the pressure, temporarily.

The press are saying it's a ruse, to head-off the trial, get himself off scot-free, certified unfit for trial.

Bollocks. He's genuinely bonkers right now. You'll see for yourself in a minute. But I don't doubt that he'll recover with the right care. He's just a broken man. But fixable.

You ever been bonkers, Marc? Fording allowed herself a sad smile, which Dubceck's eyes answered with dry sardonicism.

No, shucks. Boring old me, Hills. So sorry for being rock solid. Smoked some marijuana as a student but never inhaled. Sucked a few cocks but never swallowed. I didn't testify against you by the way, let's stop beating around the bush.

To the internal affairs guys?

To the police, the FBI. Not just about this shit. You and

Serranto too. It's all mixed in together in their heads right now.

It shouldn't be. There's no connection.

Well it is. They've never been the cleverest of people in my experience. Generally the kids that failed their science grades and majored in sport and racism instead.

Marc, you made a joke, congratulations. Fording smirked, stubbing out her caffeine stick.

Really, he smiled at last. *Was it a boy or a girl?*

Still born I think. Miscarried.

Too bad. You better get in there and read Little Bo Peep to the old Viking. I just wanted you to know I never said a word against you. Even if we've not always seen eye to eye, I respect you enormously.

Quite suddenly, there were tears on both their cheeks and, choked, embarrassed, Dubceck was gone before Fording could thank him. She had wanted to ask him whether he thought she would ever be allowed to resume command. She was afraid of what the answer might be from a man who never lied.

*

The curtains were drawn in Gene Vesberg's room and a nurse and psychiatrist were in attendance. Fording hoped they would leave so that she might persuade Vesberg to let the light in.

Hillary... is everything OK? Who's running the show, who's at the wheel... Dubceck was just here...

I know, I ran into him. I'm sorry I never came to see you when Hazel died, Gene, I know how much she meant to you. There, out of the way. Now she hoped she could relax, all plain sailing.

Vesberg looked at her oddly. Then to her surprise he reached out a hand and stroked her hair and cheek. The medical staff were leaving now, taking a hint, maybe the wrong one.

You're a sweet girl, Hillary. There's nothing to forgive.

I'm fifty-eight... she smiled ironically.

Vesberg snorted. *And I'm heavily sedated. Conveniently lost count of my age.*

What's wrong with you, Gene? They told me the trial's been halted. Not like you to shy away from a good fight.

It's not a fight anymore, Hillary. I killed that young man, all those years ago.

Nonsense. It was an accident. NASA, the whole government are responsible. Compensation, reparation, apology, repentance, the world moves on.

Does it, Hillary? And can I? The survivors of Auschwitz never moved on. Why not? Because ghosts haunted them. People don't just die, they change state. They torment the living.

Is this you talking, Gene? What superstitious mumbo jumbo. Talk like that belongs in the nineteenth century.

You've never been tormented by demons, Hillary, you don't know what it's like. The dead can be as alive as us, maybe more so.

Fording shook her head, and wiped a tear from her eye. *You've lost it, Gene. You're not thinking clearly. Drugs, therapy will straighten you out. Even Dubceck thinks so. If you didn't freak him then you won't freak me.*

Vesberg straightened his pillows sluggishly and sat up in his bed. *Hillary, I've been realising something recently, these weird dreams I've been having. Haven't you ever wondered if your entire life is a dream?*

Fording laughed. *Not since I was a dreamy little schoolgirl, reading Edgar Allan Poe.*

Have you ever had any near-death experiences? Close-calls, near-misses?

Fording frowned. *Nearly electrocuted myself once when I was about ten. Stuck a pen-knife into a lamp socket. My elder sister slept in the bunk bed above. She'd left her light on so I tried to switch it off the quick way. Ka-boom. If I'd been standing on the floor with wet feet I'd have been toasted.*

Exactly... Vesberg gasped, rubbing his eyes. *You see? What if you did die? What if all this since is just a dream after death?*

That's crazy talk. You mean you don't exist? You're just a figment of my imagination?

Not exactly. Maybe it's like planets, stars in the night sky. How Gliese 581 looks from Earth, compared to how Earth looks from Gliese 581. I mean we're both real, Hillary, but we're both dreaming and separated by our dreams, light-years apart. How is your son?

You mean Nathan? What's he got to do with it? Nobody ever asks about Justin. I do have two children you know.

You told me once that Nathan could draw how stars appeared to each other, the patterns of inverted constellations, hundreds of combinations, without ever having been taught.

Yes, he can, she said quietly.

You get the analogy, the irony?

No.

Autism. He's not supposed to be good at seeing the viewpoints of other human beings, and yet he can do exactly that with stars. He's woken up, Hillary, and only the likes of us, everyone else, the supposedly normal ones, are left behind, sleeping. It's all about levels, waking up. He's gone to the next level.

Carlo used to say wild stuff like that. I seem to be surrounded by more and more nutcases the older I get, Fording sighed.

Vesberg took Fording's hand suddenly, as if choking, eyes widening, staring at something behind her. *He's here again, Lecaux, coming through the wall for me, look!*

Fording turned her head but could see nothing, unsurprisingly, but when she turned back Vesberg was shaking uncontrollably with a weird white light across his face.

Nurse! Nurse! Doctor! She stood up and cried out, pressed the buzzer by his bedside. *He seems to be having some kind of fit.*

Two orderlies hurried in and held him down, followed by a doctor who sedated him with a needle to the arm.

What's wrong with him, Doctor, really? she asked, while Vesberg foamed at the mouth.

Nothing physical I can find, Mrs Fording. Just this obsession with ghosts. Guilt I suppose. Repressed material. I wish we could have analysed him thirty years ago before he started pushing all this into his subconscious.

No, no... Vesberg was speaking again and gesturing to Fording to come closer so he could whisper into her ears. *Lecaux is the key... Lecaux is dreaming all of us. He is each of us, our premature deaths...*

Not waiting for anyone's permission, tired of all this claustrophobic madness, Fording pulled herself away as Vesberg fell back onto his pillow exhausted. She paced over to the windows and drew the curtains open.

As the sunlight crossed the room like a tidal wave, an unearthly cry gurgled in Vesberg's throat and some weird white apparition writhed and separated from him then fled into the blinding whiteness of the sudden daylight.

The medical equipment, the ECG, the light and power all spiked, fused and blew, leaving everyone dazed. *What the hell was that?* Fording stammered.

Power cut, just a power surge... the doctor muttered, white as a sheet. *The fifth one today. The electrics in this house must be medieval, I've ordered a temporary generator already. I know I should have insisted he was moved to my clinic or the city hospital.*

Is he alright? Fording asked, of a nurse now taking Vesberg's pulse and heart-rate.

Oh, he's fine, just sleeping now.

God, Fording gasped, *I'm not sure if I will.* She put her hand to her forehead and found a fine spray of black dust all over it.

~

19

THE TRANSLUCENT SKY

Now Dubceck was in charge, Fording forced into suspension on full pay pending investigation, soon to be early retirement. Had he hoped for something humdrum and practical for his first command, then he was to be disappointed.

The surface of 82 Eridani b, similar to Jupiter's Europa, was a perfect sphere of ice, a half mile thick. But in landing, the probe spores had inadvertently broken through this layer and landed roughly on an entirely different world concealed within.

When we say 'landed', we must of course correct ourselves immediately. The hidden inner sphere of 82 Eridani b was an ocean world, teeming with life to whom the underside of their omnipresent ice sheet was the sky and their sun only a dim glow which rolled slowly across it. They looked up through rippling water, the thin oxygenated atmosphere above it, and the opaque ice layer above that.

Like Europa, the planet's outer layer was criss-crossed by a thousand cryptic patterns, where ice had cracked and thawed and re-formed progressively over millennia, and meteors impacted and scoured across it on oblique trajectories.

The chosen astronauts, Mashimoto and Breitlung, had trained for six months in underwater environments on Earth. A floating probe spore module had been specially adapted to be their base, providing an opportunity for respite for them in the oxygen layer above the endless waves and storms.

As they slowly drifted, diving down towards the Eridanian underwater city they had named Eridanopolis, they found themselves passing through lanes of fast-moving 'traffic'. The Eridanians appeared to travel in underwater cars between their great city and its outlying suburbs. The city itself was a seemingly endless ring of vertical stacks of grey tube-like structures, a kind of Manhattan made of enormous metal straws, perforated everywhere with circular doors and windows through which these vehicles were entering and exiting with alarming speed. The oddest thing of all was the way that none of these vehicles seemed to be taking the slightest heed of their alien visitors.

Eventually, Breitlung decided to place herself directly in the way of an oncoming vehicle to force some kind of confrontation, but the vehicle merely corrected its trajectory, with smooth expertise, to effortlessly avoid her position. Such was the speed and manoeuvrability of these vehicles that the team at NASA began to discuss the bizarre possibility of some kind of differential time-field being in play.

Dubceck called in a theoretical physicist to offer advice on the option. Theodore Gottleib of Geneva University flew in the following day and joined Dubceck in the control room.

Well, Gottleib began, *looking at the size and density of this planet, it is enormous you know, ten times the Earth's diameter, and within its liquid zone, a mile down, a vast dense core of rock exists, itself eight times the Earth's size.*

Don't you see? Einstein stated that space-time was only a product of distortion in the gravitational field. We've never really properly understood that apparently brilliant assertion, or had a chance to test it out until now. This world makes a larger dent in the fabric of space-time than our own and therefore time passes quicker here. We may even appear almost static to the inhabitants.

But why would we even be aware of that? Surely any creature passing into the sphere of influence of such a massive planet would simply begin to move and think and age faster, at the same rate as the locals in fact? – The effect should be subjectively undetectable.

Yes, perhaps, except that maybe that's where Entanglement comes in. The consciousness of our astronauts is still bound to Earth's gravity and therefore to Earth's quality of space-time.

But what about non-subjective elements, our instrumentation? The probe spores?

We read and access their data with consciousness bound to terrestrial gravity, therefore the same effect applies.

Are you catching any of this, Mashimoto? Dubceck drawled, leaning back in his chair and pressing the Ansible hailing button.

Mashimoto and Breitlung were currently asleep, on top of their hi-tech inflatable lily-pad island, floating in the grey oceans of 82 Eridani b. *What? What?* Mashimoto mumbled, sitting up abruptly, disorientated, glancing at the sickening waves and feeling the now all-too-familiar lurching in his stomach, thankful that he came from a long line of seafarers.

Could you construct some sort of technology to counteract this time differential, or at least to test or prove whether such an effect is truly in play here...? Dubceck asked Gottleib, putting him on the spot.

Here, look at this, he said, elevating a display screen

from the centre of the table. *This is film of yesterday afternoon.*

The Eridanian vehicles were a huge variety of sizes, large and small, but as Breitlung and Mashimoto vigorously darted about, they comically failed even to catch one, even the very smallest, in their specially adapted nets.

Gottleib laughed heartily, then wiped a tear from his eye, catching sight of Dubceck's disappointed expression. *Not much of a welcoming committee after 20 light years, is it? Reminds you of trying to catch flies, don't you think, giant flies?*

Yes, Gottlieb mused, *stroking his beard, that analogy may be instructive, and yes, of course we could construct a device to do what you ask, to put the probes into an accelerated space-time state. How many robotic devices could you spare, small enough for Ansible transport, that we could work on here before sending them out?*

*

Breitlung: The probes did it for us, but that doesn't make me feel any less guilty. Darting around at dazzling speed, they trapped an Eridanian car, quite a large one actually, and we took it back up to the surface to open up and try to talk to its occupant. This we did in a little water-filled chamber beneath our flotation island. It took half an hour of tapping and prising, then cutting and wrenching. The stench was appalling, but after an hour's work of removing outer shells and inner shells we realised that there was nothing inside, that in fact we had just murdered an Eridanian by dissecting him alive, and throwing aside all the various pieces of him in the fruitless search for his non-existent centre. God this is awful, how could Mission Control be so stupid and direct us so ineptly on this one? How can we hope to communicate with this civilisation now when our first contact has been such a grotesque act of barbaric slaughter?

Mashimoto: What now? Have we misunderstood everything we've seen so far, trapped by our own terrestrial assumptions? We must try to find their central command, their leaders, the nexus of their group intelligence, to make ourselves known and beg their forgiveness. I should have known better and warned everyone, instead of always presuming (as ever) that my superiors know better than me. Metallic and technological though they appear, these 'cars' have always reminded me of the horseshoe crabs we have back in Japan. I thought it only a superficial observation, but perhaps I should have spoken up.

Breitlung: Nevada have sent us translation devices, but these differ from any used on previous missions: they will translate through time as well as through different vocabularies and phonetics. Dubceck tells us that to the Eridanians we appear almost static, so slowly do we move compared to their accelerated timescale. While we think they have ignored us, in fact they have probably viewed us, examined us, filmed us, had a national debate about us then agreed to ignore us, all in a blink of our eyelids. We must find their parliament and approach it, while broadcasting a signal of our peaceful intent.

Mashimoto: We thought we'd struck lucky at first, but the public building we have homed in on turned out to be a kind of sports arena where daily wars are held and televised for the entertainment of the citizens of Eridanopolis. Hundreds die, their purple blood stains the water, while the crowds cheer and applaud. All this we can only observe because the probes film it and play it back to us slowed down sufficiently for us to understand. We are broadcasting a new signal now into the waters around us, asking to be taken to their leader or governing council.

Breitlung: What a strange and savage world. Their leader is enormous, thirty feet long, the largest Eridanian by definition. He tells us that their world is one of supreme hierarchy, survival of the fattest. All Eridanians feed on blue suckerweed, which grows abundantly on the ocean floor. The food is nutritious but highly indigestible. The more they eat, the larger they become, but also the more methane they expel from their rear-ends, which also serves as a highly efficient means of propulsion. Thus are the people of this world propelled on their own flatulence. Their constant wars held in public arenas are to determine the fattest and largest among levels of apparently equally matched Eridanians. They are obsessed with these hierarchies and never stop trying to establish where they each sit within them. Apparently we are of no interest to them, because being of so different a species means they cannot place us within their hierarchical scale.

But don't you have religions? we asked. *Some species are tempted to regards alien visitors as gods or demons.*

No... their enormous leader bellowed and belched. *We worship only those who are above us, and fear only those who are below us, for the same reasons. Envy, admiration, revulsion, condescension: these are the gamut of emotions that our fellows awaken in us as we overtake them on the great scale of life, as if swallowing them and excreting them through our gut.** *We worship*

---

* A sinister metaphor which he told us had perhaps been literal for them in ancient and more primitive times.

only ourselves, and revile ourselves, in equal measure.

So are you never at peace then? – Never content within yourselves, never serene and at rest, contemplative rather than combative?

We waited for an answer, but by the time our technology had translated our question back, he had apparently lost patience and hurried on, leaving us abandoned, alone with our unanswered questions within the central room of his palace, whose every wall was a distorting mirror, some to make him look larger than himself, some to look smaller.

Mashimoto: We meant to leave this world as we had found it but something went wrong. The heat from our exit rocket, as we sought to return to the icy surface above the translucent sky, melted then broke the plates of ice we were approaching and fragments of white sky began falling down onto the city of the terrified Eridanians below.

The sun that they then glimpsed, for the first time in millennia, horrified their minds and scalded their pale and vulnerable skins. We thought they might ignore it as they had ignored us, but clearly its enormous power commanded their attention.

For several days (a couple of minutes of our time) they even ceased the endless wars inside their bloodthirsty arenas, and took to gazing upwards and guessing whether this great yellow stranger was to be worshipped or feared, tolerated or chastised.

In the end they sent their enormous leader out (or did he himself elect to go? we were not quite clear) and we watched him rising upward, leaping forwards out of the sea, thrashing his fins on the oxygen winds for the first time, propelling himself on great gusts of flatulent gas from his rear.

His wide eyes, dilated with madness and curiosity, unrequited love and envy, nearly reached us at the surface where we waited, before he was burned blind and exploded in the blaze of the ignited gases within himself, and fell back towards the grey seas below like a great ruptured dirigible, a punctured whale.

What did his people make of that? Will they merely go on feeding and competing as before until a new leader, as fat and flatulent emerges? Or will they revise their philosophy and each take on board the selfish little ships of their minds, the incredible notion that there exists something beyond themselves and their own appetites, then turn towards that thing to ask for an answer?

If and when they do, we will be waiting, to welcome them and help them.

*

Despite it making for spectacular television (through extensive use of slow motion), the 82 Eridani b mission brought Dubceck in for considerable criticism and nearly lost him his command before he'd had a chance to prove himself. The effective vandalism and violation of an alien world's environment, both physically and psychologically, was met with horror and consternation among the liberal educated classes across Earth.

But some small collateral good often comes out of apparent calamities. In the wake of the public outcry at the conclusion of the Eridani mission, a special committee was formed (to which Vesberg and Fording were seconded as 'invisible' partners) to draw up a new code of ethics, to moderate human interaction with alien worlds and prevent catastrophic 'world-changing' interference, accidental or otherwise.

~

20

REVELATION

Curiously, Jack Downey and Becky Lee Falconer's relationship ended as it had started: with a long drive together through the desert. The setting and the players were the same but, six years on, everything that one could not see with the eyes was different. A sinking gloom was filling the pit of both of their stomachs, long silences were taking hold between them, which once might have seemed peaceful or romantic, but which now seemed threatening. Falconer had been called before a congressional hearing, and in under twenty-four hours she would have to lie under oath or implicate Downey as her source for the leaked story of the Lecaux scandal. Gene Vesberg was about to go on trial and was in hiding, having been granted half a million dollars bail by the Supreme Court.

They talked openly about Downey's wife and children these days, the tacit pretence, in which they might have entertained some dream of mutual escape and starting again, was long since over. Today, Becky had promised at last to take Downey to meet Guy Lecaux's brother, one of her key sources who had fed her with research information across the years, driven by a messianic urge to bring justice to the memory of his forgotten blood relative.

Am I driving the right way? We're heading for your side

of town, is that right? This guy lives in Reno? I thought you said he was in LA or San Diego? Have you flown him over to stay in a hotel or something?

Becoming increasingly grim, Becky no longer answered these questions directly but said merely: *Right then left, then left again after the next intersection…*

Hey, wait a minute… Downey smelt a rat. *This is your neighbourhood, your house. Are we meeting him at your house? Is that wise, won't that be under surveillance by now?*

Uncomfortably, Downey parked the car and followed Becky up the driveway into her suburban bungalow. He had been there before, but was wary of the neighbours now, wary of the stories that he knew were about to break, some of which would involve him.

In the living room he expected to find some hunched middle-aged man with a hunted, not to say haunted look, in a grey shabby raincoat, perhaps unshaven, maybe a French accent, peculiar shoes. Instead he found nothing. The usual furniture. He expected Becky to call out to her guest, but instead she merely excused herself to go upstairs, maybe he was asleep in the spare room.

But when she came down, shaking, her eyes wet with tears, she held only two documents. She laid the first one down on the table in front of him and he read it, frowning, wondering if he should have asked her for a drink.

Why have you given me this? he asked.

You see what it is?

Sure, your birth certificate I suppose, that's your maiden name is it, before your first marriage, Rebeccah Lee Fournier… so what?

She placed the other certificate down in front of him and left the room saying *I'll get you a drink*. Mind reader. He needed it. Then he saw why.

Oh Christ. Guy Fournier. She came back in. *What does*

this mean? I thought you said he only had a brother, are you...?

I lied, Jack. He only had a sister...

And you're her?

She nodded her head. *He was born 15 years before me, when my parents were students, they couldn't have coped. Reluctantly, they gave him up for adoption. But years later when they were married and they'd had me, they got curious, they made enquiries.*

I see... Downey sighed, his head reeling.

Do you? By then he was already dead. How tragic can one man's life be? Abandoned by his parents, given up for adoption, then hideously tortured by an experiment gone wrong, then erased from history by powerful people to protect their own asses. He was my older brother, the brother I never knew I had, but always missed somehow, I always guessed in my heart that he existed, that he was the explanation for the sadness I saw in my parents as I was growing up.

I'm sorry, Becky, I'm sorry.

They're dead now too. My parents. My mom ten years ago, my dad five. He made me promise on his deathbed that I'd follow this story to its end, that I'd honour Guy's memory, call to account those who annihilated him.

Jack crossed the room and embraced her. *No, Becky... he wasn't annihilated...*

She drew back, eyes flaring. *Don't tell me that, I know what they did...*

No, that's not what I mean. I'm not a scientist but I've read the reports and seen some of the footage. It's not death, it's some other indeterminate state that nobody really understands yet, not even Vesberg.

You think that makes it better?! Her lips curled, disgusted. *That he can't even rest in peace?*

Well... Downey shrugged... starting to feel lost, out of

his depth. *Perhaps he's immortal... what is it that we all want really, life or immortality?*

Eternal torment more like... like a living hell. Jack... she was crying and shaking now, *I just want you to leave now.*

Maybe... he added as he picked up his coat, *...maybe they're the same thing. Think about it.*

I don't want to think about it! she howled after him as he reached the door, *I just want the people who did that to pay!*

Downey hovered at the door, thinking, realising he had something important to tell her, not to save their relationship, that was well lost, but to save her. He had made enough mistakes in his youth to know one piece of wisdom surer than any other:

Becky, the quest for revenge is a living hell for those who go after it, a thirst you'll never quench... but worse than that even, it's a poison. Forgiveness is the only peace you'll ever find.

Then he closed the door quietly.

Outside in the bright light, he looked at the white shiplap boarding of her house and something caught his eye. A curious black staining, an outline. It was very faint, insignificant to most people but he'd seen it before. He took a little of the dust off onto his fingers and tasted it. Ashes. It was the outline of a figure, pressing itself against her wall as if wanting to pass through it. If it rained that night, it would be gone by morning.

~

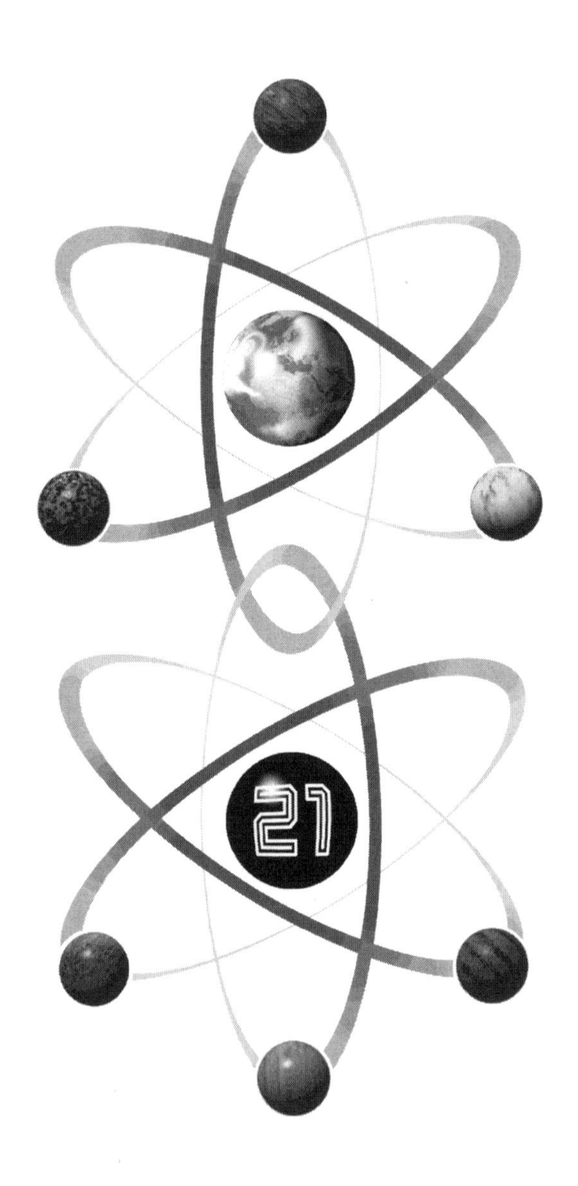
21

DIAMONDIS

It was well and good that Dubceck's first mission should have precipitated the Sanctity of Planets Protocol (SoPP) since his second might have gone even further wrong without it.

The dully-named planet of HD 217107 d was always likely to acquire a nickname, and that nickname became Diamondis, for reasons that will become obvious.

A carbon-rich world, but carbon has many incarnations of course, including graphite, buckminsterfullerene, coal, carbon nanotubes, not to mention its oxides and organic compounds. But Diamondis was something truly remarkable to human eyes: a world made of diamond, glistening, semi-transparent crystals, capturing and refracting light. The glassy surface of this world however, was a far from welcoming place. Criss-crossed by a trillion fissures, Diamondis was a world of towering cliffs and terrifying canyons, across which creatures leapt in death-defying bounds, some aided by wings, others only by glider-flaps between their arms and chest.

It was this second means of transport, aided occasionally by primitive ropes and bridges, that the Diamondans had evolved to deploy. A fairly intelligent and physically highly adept and agile species, their environment had apparently prevented them from building settlements of any great complexity and permanence, and so had inhibited their development of what humans would recognise as cities or civilisation.

The hunt for food necessitated their constant pursuit of winged mega-fauna from one cliff-edge to the next. The almost constant high winds meant that neither these, nor any other animals, could fly effectively for more than a few minutes at a time.

These circumstances meant that Diamondans valued bravery above all other attributes, and that diamonds, so valuable to humans on Earth, were as commonplace as dirt to them and of no economic value. That said, their cultural importance, the spectacular optical qualities of sunlight, particularly at sunrise and sunset, when seen through the narrowest edges of crystalline diamond cliffs, was deeply embedded within their religious folklore.

The Diamondan word for death meant both flight and light, as befits a world of perpetually frustrated would-be flyers. They believed that their spirits become motes of light upon death, able to ricochet endlessly between infinite rock faces, passing eternally around their world.

But with access to a planet of such abundance of diamonds, Dubceck faced a dilemma: how to resist the temptation to take some small quantity of diamonds back to Earth via Ansible in order to boost funding for future Telepedrome missions?

A short chat with the President hardened Dubceck's moral reserve (along with a pay rise), but in order to spare his astronauts the problem, a decision was taken to keep the mineral composition of Diamondis secret until the astronauts had actually 'touched down'.

Of course this was the dangerous advantage of the Entanglement technology over almost every other means of exploration and colonisation hitherto employed by mankind. The cost of transporting resources has always had to be weighed against the trading value on return to home, but with Ansible and a little patience, potentially no such constraint existed. Gold, silver, diamonds; however and whatever you choose to define as wealth, could now easily be brought to Earth from any or all of the numerous worlds that humans had now set foot on.

*

Dubceck's choice of 'landing party' were Valerie Romano and Claude Zwijic, two men for the first time in decades, causing the tabloid press to make various outmoded twentieth century-style jokes about NASA not being able to trust girls in the presence of so many of a girl's best friends.

This would prove ironic. How high are an astronaut's wages? How much can any man be trusted? Does each man have his price?

The probe landing site had been fairly arbitrary for the simple reason that there appeared to be no visible Diamondan cities for the astronauts to approach. Aerial reconnaissance had revealed only constant nomadic movement and large shifting settlements of animal-skin tents.

Romano and Zwijic emerged from the dupliportation chamber onto a high windswept plateau of sparse vegetation and fine grey soil (the powder form of the graphite state of carbon abundant in that world).

Within fifteen minutes they were able to intercept the head of an oncoming procession of running Diamondans, who simply attempted to run around them.

Zwijic knelt and tried to operate various hailing devices, while Romano jumped around, shouting and gesturing like a performance artist or a children's TV presenter.

The Diamondans were orangey-tan coloured creatures

with black markings somewhere between zebra and leopard. Their movement was semi-bipedal, but appeared most like rabbits or kangaroos on the move, both front and rear limbs occasionally touching ground in the process of a succession of rapid bounce-like movements.

Their speech was a fast chattering sound like excited chimpanzees, made as their jaws flapped together in a curious manner that exposed their oddly flat and outward-pointing teeth.

Their heads sported Mohican-like plumes of red and purple hair which blew eye-catchingly in the never-ending winds.

Romano and Zwijic were left staring after the procession like dazzled spectators, star-struck fans, jilted lovers. Hardly an interplanetary welcome.

During the next two days, the experience was repeated, and they increasingly took to concentrating on recording the chatter of the runners then transmitting it back to Earth as raw material from which translation software would hopefully evolve.

Returning despondently to the landing site each night, Zwijic couldn't help noticing the abundance of loose diamonds shearing off a nearby outcrop. Curious, he took a handful back into the base camp module to show to Romano.

Later that night under the porthole illumination from the quadruple moons of Diamondis, Zwijic turned the stones over in his hands, contemplating their potential monetary value, then on a sudden irrational impulse thrust some into his pocket before entering the dupliportation chamber for his statutory twelve hours 'shore leave'.

Whilst talking to his family through the glass back home that night, he surreptitiously transferred the diamonds into a haversack which he slipped beneath his bed platform. Of course the diamonds would now go on existing in both worlds, but Zwijic hoped to sell their terrestrial semblances on his official return to Earth at mission termination.

Despite Dubceck's express instructions against it, one of his assistants on night duty agreed to answer Zwijic's queries about diamond prices. *This rock here then, you can see it? The one I'm turning in my hands. About two inches across. How much do you think it would be worth on Earth, once cut and polished by suitably expert hands? Really? That much? Wow...*

And these little ones here? You see them? Size of kidney beans, what do you reckon? Yeah? Sure is a shame about that Sanctity of Planets Protocol of Dubceck's then, isn't it?

The turning facets threw fantastical light in fragmentary bursts of ethereal colours, momentary flashes into Zwijic's eyes, his pupils dilating in wonder.

*

The next day a new strategy was adopted in order to finally make contact with the Diamondans. Analysis of their language had revealed that they had been fully aware of the human presence, and even aware that they were probably visitors from another planet, but that they classed them as of secondary importance to their own religious rite of continuous running and cliff jumping.

On orders from Dubceck, Romano and Zwijic began jogging alongside the Diamondans as they hailed them in their own language from voiceboxes on their chests with the latest translator software downloaded. To their surprise and delight, the Diamondans immediately responded to this gesture of kinship, by slowing their pace in respect for the humans so that the conversation could progress without them getting too out of breath.

We come as brother creatures, from one of the stars in

your night sky, to greet you and learn about your world and your society and customs.

You are most welcome here if you are peaceful creatures. You must have travelled far and be weary, hence your reluctance to run. But those who do not run, do not catch beasts, do not eat, get sick and die. We will nurse you back to health until you can run at a proper speed.

Thanks, Romano coughed, *but we are quite happy at our lower velocity... it is what we are used to on our home star...*

You tàlk of stars and night, but only the sick and dying gaze upon those, my friends. By running we evade night, and stay always in daylight...

Of course, Zwijic slapped his head. *Why didn't I think of that sooner?! This planet's small scale and slow rotation... sunlight is continuously pursuable even on foot! That's what they're about here.*

To run is to breathe, my friend, but to leap is to be truly alive!

And at that the astronauts had to make excuses as the Diamondans sped up to make one of their spectacular leaps across a deep crevasse.

The sight was truly spectacular, and Romano and Zwijic wandered along the conquered edge in awe, filming the misty depths below where water roared and boiled. They watched the long leaps of the lithe Diamondans, bodies heroically outstretched, momentarily frozen paragons of youth and athleticism, as they flew between the sparkling diamond surfaces, faceted sunlight playing over them, refracted and magnified, prismatic, multi-coloured light.

*

Dubceck wanted a longer conversation with the Diamondans, and plotting their current choice of favourite running routes, suggested a meeting point some twenty miles further east, from where if a conversation were successfully started, at moderate jogging speed, one might expect to continue uninterrupted for the next hour and a half. Only one minor set of gullies would have to be leapt over by Romano and Zwijic, and their hosts would doubtless be greatly impressed by the prowess and kinship of their visitors thus revealed.

The astronauts waited for them at a particularly fissured rock outcrop, diamonds littering the ground.

What are you doing? Romano asked Zwijic suspiciously.

Zwijic straightened up and laughed nervously. *What do you mean? You don't think surely....? You know as well as I do how all our pockets are filled with vital instrumentation that we need. They're just pretty rocks anyway, what would I want with them?*

Romano stared at him for a moment, unimpressed, until he spotted an approaching running group over his shoulder and turned his attention to preparing himself to run.

Zwijic emptied the hand behind his back into a rip in his spacesuit, one he had carefully torn himself previously then repaired with *Autopatch*... a new pocket, deep and useful, a veritable kangaroo pouch.

The running match started. A different set of Diamondans from yesterday but a similar conversation. Greater insights into their culture were gained with more shared time available.

This time, various running mega-fauna were tracked down, killed and butchered by the Diamondans, even as they kept running with scarcely a stop, an astonishing feat of teamwork. Two bear-like creatures but blue with six legs, and something red the size of a rhino with two heads at either end of its body.

Even eating, it seemed, was performed on the trot, through the Diamondans' miraculously agile digestive systems, but the astronauts declined, pleading nausea and popping a few energy pills instead.

How are your children born? And what gods do you worship? Romano questioned them.

In the places of the night, where darkness dwells and our dead wait for the kiss of Saldaneytra, the goddess of cold blind rocks... there also is where the mothers wait for a moon season in order to bear child.

A gestation period of how long? That's equivalent to two Earth months. Astounding!

But lord of all gods is our sun god Varonelbta, who plays in the clear rocks of the truth cliffs.

Diamonds... Zwijic muttered.

You have these rocks on your star too? Their leader Parupanelyut asked, intrigued.

Yes, on our world they are of great monetary value, we mine them and trade them, make them into jewellery for rich kings and queens to wear.

What is money and what are mines and jewellery? Parupanelyut asked, puzzled now.

Romano then tried to explain them to the alien but after ten useless minutes decided he was wasting valuable time.

A gorge was approaching, halfway through their planned time with the running group, and the astronauts began to brace themselves for the leap, as Nevada started talking frantically into their ear:

It's a very short jump... Dubceck intoned urgently into the microphone at the Telepedrome. *Only three or four feet, and the probe-spores are on hand to boost your buoyancy if required. We've calculated your body mass and plotted it against your angular momentum and acceleration vectors, just keep running at about the speed you're both doing now.*

Parupanelyut was still talking as he (or she) ran effortlessly. *To steal a piece of sacred light-stone from the cliffs of truth would seem to us most perverse, blasphemy even. But to hang one around your neck sounds positively stupid...*

The gorge was upon them and the Diamondans were bouncing, leaping marvellously over the narrow gorge, their bodies dappled with golden light. Romano went first with the aliens, who were even holding hands with him, hands on his shoulders in camaraderie as the whole tableaux leapt, a profoundly moving sight, bringing tears to Zwijic's eyes.

Zwijic leaped next without hesitation, but found his body falling downwards with unexpected and terrifying force, his tears suddenly becoming those of terror and despair. A few Diamondans tried to help him up but their nimble limbs were built for speed, not for such heavy loads as he.

His fingers gripped the diamond cliffs, his face smashed into their facets, coming back bloodied. Diamond, the hardest material on his beloved home world, that no jeweller nor haughty countess could scar with her fingernails or teeth. Zwijic felt his nails break, his teeth slide on the impervious crystalline surfaces, as his strength failed and he fell towards the roaring water below. A hundred feet down and at a constant ninety degrees centigrade, he knew that he would be scalded and boiled alive before he would have the time to drown.

In vain, as he fell and writhed through space, calling out in terror, his voice ricocheting off the mute glittering rock around him, he reached a hand behind himself and ripped open his concealed pocket, then all his other ones, letting his stolen booty fall, returning it to its jealous creator. But the precious stones just fell with him, no more or less heavy, and moving ever further from the sunlight, no more beautiful than rocks.

~

22

AVIARISS

...But Thirty—thirty desperate draggled Things,
Half-dead, with scarce a Feather on their Wings,
Stunn'd, blinded, deafen'd with the Crash and Craze
Of Rock and Sea collapsing in a Blaze
That struck the Sun to Cinder—fell upon
The Threshold of the Everlasting One...
...And in the Centre of the Glory there
Beheld the Figure of—Themselves—as 'twere
Transfigured—looking to Themselves...

– Farīd ud-Dīn Attar, *The Conference Of The Birds*
(translated by Edward Fitzgerald)

The planet of Aviáriss was one whose life forms consisted almost entirely of what we would call birds. Sonya Clements had vivid memories of listening to the *Dawn Chorus* back on Earth as a child and being convinced in her drowsy state that the collective complexity of the sound had all the structure and majesty of a classical symphony. Here in this world of little land, but endless swamp forests swaying in acidic cloudy waters, it was easy to believe that those ideas had been a premonition, a foretaste of this world, where such wonders were not just possible it seemed, but an everyday reality.

Sonya had been a precocious musical prodigy, an award-winning cellist and pianist by the age of ten, but somehow subsequent years had side-tracked and diverted her into a no-less-stellar career as an astronaut. As usual, the deal had been that her quantum-entangled body would be created instantly on Aviáriss after the probe-spores carrying entangled ions had arrived here, and her mind would transfer at will between the two locations by sleep and wakefulness, monitored by NASA in Nevada. But something had gone wrong and she was now irrevocably marooned, or at least so for the next fifteen years until a manned flight from the neighbouring planet of Sentillos might be able to relieve her post.

Meanwhile back on Earth her shattered catatonic twin (she didn't want to think of it as her 'original' any longer) was strapped down in an endless twitching nightmare, eyes closed tight, moaning like an animal, partially brain-damaged due to the explosion that had killed her colleague Fred Diwani. His cruelly shredded remains had been buried on both worlds, in Earth in a grave, on Aviáriss in a silver body-bag, weighed down with imported stones to take him to the murky ocean floor. Sometimes she couldn't stop herself from thinking of Fred's body lying there, far beneath the pressurised aluminium tree-hut where she sat now, suspended halfway up a hundred-foot Palipandarus tree, between the sea and the forest canopy, with the wistful dawn sky turning pink then blue up above.

It was sunrise on Aviáriss again, each day taking an equivalent of 38 Earth hours. Dawn was a slower affair therefore, as was spring, giving the 'birds' more time to perfect their art… or was it communication? Along the treetops Sonya had seen what she was tempted to call *cities* of mud and stick construction of startling complexity, even written symbols on dried leaves, signs that the birds were teaching and recording knowledge, making tools and ornaments from wood carved by their beaks.

Nevada, still in touch daily by Ansible, thank goodness, had been analysing Sonya's recordings of the birdsong for fourteen months, trying to break it down into cogent phonemes of a useable language, but so far to no avail. Speculation was mounting on Earth, that if the same all-mighty software that had cracked the light-pulse language of Sigma Draconis d and the tap-touch tongue of Talluris f, was failing here, then there might well be no language to be found.

But Sonya was adamant. She had a lot of time to think about it, because she was of course incapable of sleep. To do so would have been to use the section of her quantum-entangled brain damaged on Earth. And according to the principle of neuron re-colonisation, this polarisation would only accentuate itself over time, in both bodies. Thus one would never sleep, the other never wake. While her colleagues back in Nevada were packing up and heading home for the night, she would be settling in for a long session of musical analysis, attempting to recreate sections of Aviáran birdsong, ready to broadcast back in the morning from the basecamp tannoys in an attempt to spark interplay and communication. She had even had Nevada dupliport out an antique violin just small enough to fit inside the foot-square Ansible chamber.

At dawn, she put on her oxygen mask and ventured through the air-lock to the balcony to play a phrase of Red Rufflebird song out into the forest around her. A few blue and white Scatterscrutches whistled by, non-plussed. Fragrant Salfrajas leaves swayed in a gentle breeze, brushing her cheek with their velvet tips. A family of yellow Goonbursts came and sat for a while on her handrail, as if listening, or perhaps they were only preening their feathers, removing and eating the parasitic

Ketchkupper flies that congregated around their pink gas orifices to feed on their iodine-rich excretions.

Suddenly they all flitted away in alarm as a three-foot long Gasspurger swooped down on his silver and purple wings, trying to ensnare a few of them in his wide-open beak. Sonya switched her playing to a Gasspurger call, three rapid trios, followed by a tritone, an arpeggio then a glissando end note, as she heard his distinct hooting starting up as he departed, but he either failed to hear her or was unimpressed with their likeness to his own. But they were more than calls. As the Gasspurger reached the treetop canopy he met another five of his clan and began a rapid series of interchanges with them, beautiful hoots and gurgle-swoopings that modulated and inflected too fast to seem like anything other than language.

Her playing was interrupted by the flash of the Ansible light inside, and she withdrew from the chill thin morning air, taking off her breathing apparatus. It was her husband. She checked her time-difference tracker and frowned: what was he doing up at this time of the night?

John seemed to miss her more than she missed him. Remarkable really, considering he had eight billion other humans around him while she had only alien birds and trees. He had been getting increasingly maudlin of late, wishing they'd had children before she signed up, even suggesting that eggs be taken from her Earth body for him to fertilise. A suggestion she found strangely distasteful, even threatening, considering it would be some other woman's body on Earth that would have to play surrogate to carry such an embryo. Only for Sonya to have to watch an entire family of unreachable loved ones every night, rather than the current painful, but containable, one.

Sonya... John began, *I've been thinking about your bird problem for you, like a crossword puzzle.*

Sweetheart... you should get some sleep, leave the music

and maths to me.

No, really, listen. I know I'm tired and my brain's addled but...

John, have you been drinking? You said...

No, no, not at all, I...

Are you sure?

Well maybe a tin or two, I'm finding it hard to sleep without something to...

Music. You need to stop listening to music, John. The phrases and rhythms, catchy tunes, they keep you awake.

Tell me about it. Listen, I was thinking, maybe it's a crazy idea but why don't you try playing something back to them, at high volume?

What do you think I've been up to, John? That's exactly what I have been doing.

No, no, not their stuff. Maybe that's where you've been going wrong. Why don't you play them Beethoven's Fifth or Schoenberg's Transfigured Night or who was that guy that copied birdsong again?

Messiaen.

Yeah. You think I'm crazy, right?

I never cared for Messiaen much. Great theory, but it sounded like guano.

Szymanowski then, or Roy Harris, whatever, one of your favourites. You've got time to try a lot of alternatives, right?

Sure, sweetheart, I've got a lot of time. No shortage of that whatsoever...

*

Sunset was also a good time for bird-listening on Aviáriss, as on Earth. Tonight Sonya ran through her usual cycle of learned local calls, with some Catchculker and Fivvydray calls thrown in, but to little recognisable response. Just to humour John inside her mind, she played the introductory phrases from Richard Strauss's Metamorphosen on her violin to no apparent effect, then enjoyed the music for its own effect on herself for a change, for the next five minutes, before pressing on with Schoenberg's Pelleas und Melisande, of which she could play a larger part from memory. By the time she stopped, a group of luminescent blue Shampuffs were glowing in the branches opposite and two squadrons of Red Kiterays were dive-bombing her and twittering promisingly. But she dismissed it as coincidence.

*

Nonetheless, by the next sunrise, she had scaled the treetops and set up further pairs of Ansibled speakers from Earth and downloaded several of her favourite classical recordings in preparation. Marc Dubceck, acting head of the NASA Telepedrome project had a few pointed questions to ask about this:

Clements? I know you're a big classical music fan and life is lonely out there, but you wouldn't by any crazy chance be thinking of broadcasting this music out to the Aviáran fauna, would you?

That would be an insane proposition of course, Marc. Highly unscientific. You know me better than that, surely?

You're not being sarcastic are you, Clements? I'm quite serious. You know we've consulted at length about this, and the consensus of biological and psychological opinion on Earth is that indiscriminate intrusion by an alien sound language into Aviáran could have highly unpredictable effects and risk doing untold damage.

But Earth's music, classical music, is not a language, sir, as I'm sure you'll admit. It cannot convey the time of day, the price of apples or the square root of 49. It is in short, practically useless as a language in any conventional sense.

To us perhaps, but to them, by accident, who knows? It could be like reading at random from a handful of books in Portuguese without having the slightest idea what you're saying. One might be a recipe for pizza, the other instructions on devil worship or nuclear fission, who knows?

Then they'll simply laugh at us.

They can't laugh.

Not as such, but who's to say what they feel and what all their sounds and gestures mean? Don't you see? We have to do something. I am dying of loneliness here, surrounded by vocally intelligent life, but unable to speak to it. If I can only break through then I will have contact, you will have contact, Earth and Aviáriss will recognise each other and talk.

Clements? I'm concerned by your state of mind and by your life-signs that I'm monitoring from here, your heart-rate and perspiration. I have reason to believe you are in danger of irrationality. Perhaps it's a light fever, a minor mineral imbalance in the brain. Please take some rest and desist from further experimentation for at least the next three days. That's an order.

*

The choice of music was critical, and Sonya agonised and dithered over it, but in the end came down on the side of pure emotion: what moved her most. This was her last stand, the way she was feeling. Her cry for help on behalf of all humanity across the vast blankness and silence of space.

She reverted to the simplest and saddest piece of music, and the first, that she had ever learned to play. The second movement, the *Affettuoso*, from Johann Sebastian Bach's Brandenburg Concerto No.5 in D Major. Its sadness was exquisite, old Bach had lost a wife and many children after all, and suffered as any intelligent man in a chaotic age, against which he built an aural bastion of optimism and order. The harmonious organisation of his work seemed almost a reflection of, a *paean* to, that of Nature itself, a glorification of God (as he himself would have stated it), but no less impressive now to discerning ears of a more secular era.

Sonya set the speakers to full volume and took to the balcony again, ready with her violin, to accompany and reinforce the melody with her own counterpoint and rondo, a few embellishments and improvised harmonies added in perhaps, as the mood might take her.

The impact of so terrestrial a sound shocked at first, as it made contact with the alien air, reverberated off foreign bark and leaves, rippled on exotic water. But then, as Sonya drew the bow and joined the melody, she felt something bigger take over. The spirit of Bach himself perhaps (crazy irrational thought), rejoicing at making contact with such marvels as these, the works of a God yet vaster than any one world, whose taste and wisdom could encompass this astonishing diversity of colour, shape, form and tone.

Silence seemed to answer the music at first. It was hard to tell of course, at the acoustic outskirts beyond the waves emanating from the resurrected voice of Bach, beating and throbbing like a proxy heart. But out there, she seemed to sense a fright, a recoil, a recovery then something else: a listening, attentiveness, curiosity and patience.

Something in the melody and arrangement, the interplay of flute and harpsichord, struck Sonya for the first time as somehow more than German, more than 18th century, more than Baroque, encompassing in its simplicity: elements of folk music from all across Europe, even the wider world.

As the glorious Affettuoso came to a close, Sonya was

struck a glancing blow on the side of her head. To her horror, she followed the dismal progress of the stunned bird, a green-crested Warbsedger, plummeting down far below her until vanishing into the water with a diminutive splash, a pitiful spurt of ripples from the lonely point of impact. To her dismay, more suddenly followed suit. Three Redrays, wings lifeless, dropped past, then two Starjewels, then four more, followed by a dense rain of black Stormspindlers, between twenty and thirty at once, some issuing plaintive little dying cries.

Sonya screamed and stood up, trying to get back into the tree cabin, but her fingers suddenly felt like butter, slipping and shaking uncontrollably, her heart fluttering like panicking wings, her mind blinded as if staring into the sun. Stunned, dead and dying birds ricocheted off her back and shoulders in ever-intensifying rain as she flinched and cowered.

Perhaps her pre-set music selection should simply have used the *Allegro*, the next movement of the same concerto, its joyously uplifting gigue just the trick to lift the wistful heart. But instead the computer now went on to the last movement of Shostakovich's eleventh symphony, dramatic, warlike and triumphant.

By coincidence or otherwise, the birds had now begun to peck and tear at Sonya, some even attempting to smash into the glass doors, potentially compromising the base's atmospheric integrity. At last Sonya unlocked the door, but was spun around by further impacts to see the strings of her violin being ripped from the bridge and pegs, a yellow Skewerpooly smashing headfirst straight through the sound box. A flock of tiny Gillypuffs were setting about the strands of her long blonde hair now with the same vehemence as that shown to the strings.

As the airlock closed behind her, she thrashed her hands across her head and body, and looked back to see a dozen twitching corpses on the floor, some having made it past the inner doors. Her immediate primal instinct was to stamp on them, in rage and revulsion, but remembering the danger of contamination (not to mention her erstwhile respect for life), she rushed to contain them each in sample jars, then vacuumed traces of their blood and feathers off the sanitized control room floor.

Then she threw herself onto her mattress and wept uncontrollably until she fell asleep exhausted.

*

Asleep? But wasn't that exactly what she couldn't or daren't do anymore? In the blackness into which she slipped, a hypnotic ocean lapped at the edge of her mind and grains of unseen sand slipped forever through her fingernails, which she found strangely extended now, turning into claws. She walked endlessly through a sluggish medium of murky water, or was it a walk along a twilit beach? Somewhere in the distance she sensed a figure she didn't want to draw close to, but however she changed direction she still found this spectre drawing near. She tried to push it out of her mind, to un-think it, but always it reappeared, closer than before. Sweating, crying out, she found at last it was in front of her: rotting, wrapped in black decaying cloth, the figure slowly turned as she screamed, unable to look away. Its face was her own, grotesquely damaged and distorted by age, a white beak-like section of skull emerging from below its putrid nose. The beak opened, and the screech blended with her own. It spread its black cloak out into two massive raven's wings and fluttered at her, and she woke up with her hands writhing over her face.

*

Men, indeed women, are not meant to live in isolation.

Robinson Crusoe after all, was based on a real castaway, who would have lost his mind on a South Pacific island had he not eventually been rescued. As with dogs, sheep and other pack animals, our surface appearance of individuality conceals some deeper and invisible requirement for connection, a profound need that if left untended will turn in upon its host and poison him in bitter retribution for its neglect.

When Sonya awoke it was to the sound of NASA's alarm signal and Dubceck's voice demanding an explanation of why her intercom had been switched off for the last three days. In the corner, a second Ansible webcam showed John, eyes bleary, voice pleading, in his neglected pit of an apartment in New York, open bottle of whisky at his side. But Sonya turned the sound down on all of them and walked towards the balcony doors.

Dubceck had thought they wouldn't understand, but they had understood too well. As she stepped outside, her heart leapt at what she heard now. Suddenly it dawned on her that despite its enormous strangeness and complexity, all the Aviáran music she had heard until now had been in essence: joyful, contented, celebratory, not unlike in that respect, birdsong back on Earth.

But now something was changed. The birds had listened and understood and digested, and after the shock, were now sending back their answer, what they made of the strange sound of life from Earth, the distilled wine of all its millennia of trials and suffering.

Incredibly, what they sang back was Bach, was Shostakovich, was Schoenberg, was Strauss, all of it mixed together, but sadder now, more so even than the saddest of what those great men had ever summoned up from their heavy hearts in their worst moments of despair.

Sonya fell to her knees amid the fragments of her shattered violin and wept, covering her ears. The volume of the sound seemed to begin intensifying, shaking the whole tree cabin, shattering the windows behind her one by one. But she knew she could not stop listening, because it was the most beautiful music she had ever heard, and so irresistibly sad now that it led her by the hand, helpless, towards her own imminent destruction. Her heart was breaking and this unbearable emotion, an exquisite blend of beauty and despair, would surely kill her any second now, long before the music ended.

So much for language. Everything means something, signals are everywhere. The name Sonya means *wisdom*. The new music was the sound of innocence shattered, of Paradise violated by the idea of another world, one of war and cruelty and a beauty possible only through tragedy, a bitter-sweetness never tasted before. The birds wept for those who could have brought such terrible knowledge, and for themselves, who would be forever changed now, with no way home.

~

23

TWO MILES DOWN

The strangest of all worlds was HD 160691 g, which quickly acquired the nickname of Enigma. Its apparently arid surface was covered by a myriad of black 'cacti', tall thin succulent spines that seemed to contain water. Moisture condensing each dawn and dusk also seemed to accumulate on the heavily pitted ground, leaching out from the water table hidden far below. With no other life forms present it was hard to decide whether Enigma was a barren or a fruitful world.

Dubceck felt he needed help, and when he accepted Nathan Fording's offer (without his mother's knowledge) it was with some irritation that he found Nathan had strayed from the meeting room he had been told to wait in, and was pacing the polygonal corridors of the Telepedrome 'beehive' instead.

He eventually found him outside the Zeta Reticuli cell, nose pressed to the glass, gazing longingly in to where the sleeping bodies of Nelder and Varinder still lay in darkness, only the dim 'pilot lights' of long-stay life support ticking in sleep mode.

Say, what fascinates you about that one, Nate?

Characteristically, Nathan didn't turn to acknowledge his presence, but eventually answered: *The unknown.*

Everyone else came back or got killed. It's like the penny you drop down a well to gauge its depth but you never hear anything.

Sandy bottom, Dubceck answered.

Nathan smiled, laughed to himself, and turned. The two men's deflective characters met somewhere on the far side of the obtuse. *No symbols where none intended.*

Samuel Beckett... Dubceck answered, and this caught Nathan's attention, who met his eyes at last.

Watt, by Samuel Beckett. A good book. My mother said you were too unimaginative to dig stuff like that.

I'm a scientist. I love what I can't understand. It takes all sorts. On a wild gamble he offered his hand and to his surprise Nathan shook it. The kid had grown up some apparently, or the weirdness had migrated to less obvious places.

He diverted him to the nearest meeting room he could find and laid out some photographs. *This stuff's not been made public yet, and there are films too, I'll show you. I'd appreciate your...*

Nathan lifted his strange grey eyes to look at Dubceck again in his usual unsettlingly judgemental way.

...Your unorthodox perspective on it. Dubceck continued. *You think differently. Our mass-produced world, mass-communications... originality and free-thinking seem to get rarer every year.*

Nathan smiled. *You're not like how my mom described you at all, you know that?*

Sure, Dubceck laughed. *I know that very well. I believe the men and women of the future will be ice-cold, analytical, not emotional maelstroms bubbling over with irrationality: dull but supremely effective.*

Nathan nodded as if he didn't even need to hear these words, had heard them coming years before. *This is interesting...* he said. *Show me the films, I'd like to see more.*

*

Pascall: It's the strangest thing. The ground ripples under us, weird mini-earthquakes. But only when we walk on it. We've been monitoring this for a week now, and there shouldn't be any seismic activity anywhere within a five hundred mile radius. It doesn't happen anywhere other than where we put our feet down. How can that be? Some kind of reflexive membrane beneath the topsoil, to repel meteor impacts perhaps? Far-fetched, but that would explain why we can find no crater evidence. A planet with a kind self-healing, foreign-object repelling, skin. Is such a thing possible?

Barolo: Nevada are going to re-programme the lander module and relocate it (and us) to a different region of the planet. We're getting nowhere with this here. They've mapped a region with an active volcano and two deep seas of methane-rich liquid nitrogen. Perhaps we will find more signs of life there and some more clues to how the eco-system of this place actually works.

Pascall: Incredible. When we landed on one of the lakes on our flotation device to take samples, it misted over within minutes, and the water clouded beneath us, preventing us from taking our readings and samples. Then a storm threatened to brew up. We only just got back to shore in time. We're back inside the lander now, analysing what we got, while the volcano throws lumps of ash on top of us. Hope we're not entombed by morning.

Barolo: Even stranger still. The probes have confirmed

it. The continuously wriggling soil beneath us has opened up, five hundred yards from here, to reveal a chasm two miles deep by a half mile across, a sort of grand canyon that wasn't there yesterday. What kind of planet, what kind of rock can accomplish that sort of change on so condensed a timescale without other widespread seismic effects? This planet makes no sense at all.

*

Nathan Fording sat in the control room at last, with Dubceck across the table from him. None of the other advisors recognised him, and they'd agreed to identify him as Nathan Dalzell, using his middle name as a makeshift surname. Dubceck mumbled his qualifications and banked on nobody bothering to google a name they didn't know how to spell.

Suggestions anyone? What kind of rock under what kind of pressure could behave this way? Our usual experts are puzzled.

Claire Reinhart from Geology shook her head in dismay. *If only we could get samples, but that damned wriggling soil always prevents the probes from digging.*

There is no rock. Nathan said quietly, and everyone looked astounded.

All planets are composed of rock ultimately, unless they're gas giants which this patently isn't. What are you suggesting, a molten upper mantle?

Nathan ignored the question and threw another curve ball: *Could we apply our linguistic analysis software to the weather?*

The weather? Dubceck himself was astounded now. Nathan looked him in the eye until Dubceck complied and wrote a couple of notes.

Analyse the weather as a language, Nathan reiterated,

and prepare aerial probes capable of seeding the clouds with silver iodide.

To cause rainfall?

To effect rainfall in the manner of a language.

Dubceck cut back in: *This new chasm that's appeared, Reinhart, do you think it's stable, should we risk sending an unmanned probe down to examine the valley floor? From what we can see the composition is completely different down there from the surface layer we've been struggling with so far.*

But Nathan answered this question too: *Send a manned probe down. You'll find it's quite safe. You need to dig there and look for fossils in particular.*

This was too much for Dubceck. He regretted his decision to involve Nathan and drew the meeting to a hurried close out of embarrassment. But, after a further week of stalling and wavering and doubt, quietly acted upon all his suggestions.

Barolo: Stable ground at last. Two miles down, surrounded by walls of that weird snakeskin surface-stuff, we found sand and pebbles, the rocky surface of an ordinary world. Nevada told us to dig and look for fossils. Better than that we found bones too, traces of real living creatures perhaps only dead for a matter of centuries. This curious planet gets curiouser still. These canyon walls creep me out though. I feel as if they could suddenly close over again without the slightest warning. That snakeskin stuff seems almost alive. Sometimes I think I see it wobbling a little, like jelly on a plate, like skin.

Pascall: Good to have Barolo back on the surface tonight after a day down there. She seems seriously spooked. The volcano has died down for now and we can concentrate on analysing this fossil record for Nevada. Meanwhile they've got the probes doing something really weird in the sky overhead, they're not even telling us about it. Why the secrecy? Something about cloud seeding. They had me filming cloud patterns all day for them up here for some reason. Have they all gone bonkers back on Earth?

*

Dubceck had been working too hard. In his dream that night he imagined himself as one of the aerial probes lifting higher and higher above the landing site on HD 160691 g, progressively seeing more and more of the alien landscape below him. There were the twin black lakes, the volcano between them, the deep chasm now opened up to the south. He screamed aloud in terror and woke up in a sweat, shaking, startling his partner Jeff beside him.

For a moment he had seen the planet's surface as the face of Gene Vesberg, old and contorted with wrinkles, crying out in pain.

*

Meanwhile, Nathan, a night owl by habit, sat in his student flat in Los Angeles and analysed the data stream Claire Reinhart was feeding him from Nevada. He knew it. The pattern was forming. Soon the fog and mist of HD 160691 g would clear away and reveal its astounding secrets at last. The planet had been alive once with flora and fauna, fish, insects, birds, rodents, apes or their equivalents. Food had run scarce over a fatal century and life dwindled, starved, fed on itself, resorted to cannibalism. What covered the planet now was not an upper mantle or a crust but a living epidermis with veins and perhaps muscles beneath. An enormous living being with a sentient mind that had consumed and destroyed everything that went before it, all its resources used up. Without hands or tongue, now it was talking, communicating with them in the only language it still knew: that of weather, squalls and storms.

Psychologists had told Nathan he lacked interpersonal skills. But he knew that what he must write next would have to be poetry to be written across the clouds, the sweetest words of wooing any human had yet devised. Humans had arrived on one of HD 160691 g's good days and seen the best of its sunshine and warm breezes. No one had yet seen its true anger, and he had a horrible feeling he could imagine what form that would take.

~

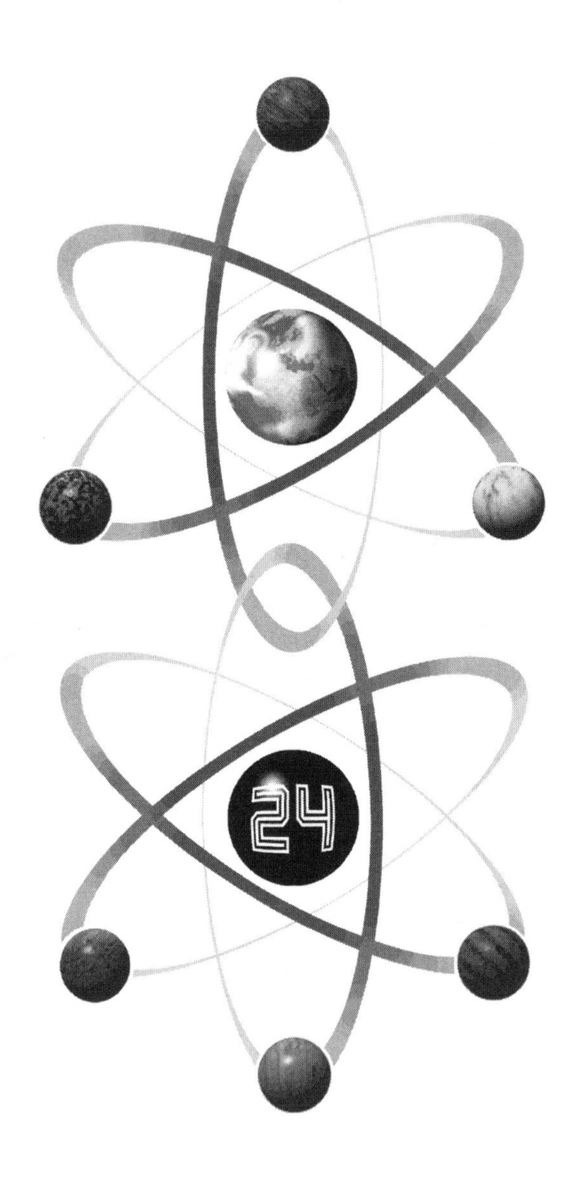
24

BOOKED

I would be glad to know which is worst, to be ravished a hundred times by negro pirates, to have one buttock cut off, to run the gauntlet among the Bulgarians, to be whipped and hanged at an auto-da-fé, to be dissected, to be chained to an oar in a galley; and, in short, to experience all the miseries through which every one of us hath passed, or to remain here doing nothing?

– Voltaire, *Candide*
(translated by Tobias Smollett)

Publicly disgraced and convicted of malpractice and obstruction of justice, what was the world to do with Gene Vesberg now? Already an old man (for the second time) who had proven that long-term solitary confinement presented no hurdles to him, it seemed pointless to consider prison. Fines and compensations had already been exacted to make him virtually penniless. It was a fine paradox.

Hillary Fording was now a pensioner herself, technically retired, but still attached as an occasional consultant to the Telepedrome, which was now ruled over by the successor to Dubceck, Carlo Serranto, her one time dirty secret, himself now fat, bald and middle-aged. So life goes, on

Earth at least.

42 years and 480 missions had been and gone. Spectacular achievements all of them, whose astounding finds in terms of biology, botany, psychology and archaeology were still keeping Earth's scholars busy with fresh interpretations of data, and would probably go on doing so for several generations to come.

What had humanity learned? It knew *what it thought it had learned*. It thought it had discovered that although life was relatively common, life quite like humanity was not. That particularly in our attitude to death, child-rearing and monogamy, humanity was really rather rare. And it dared to think that maybe there was something in these things, these peculiarities, that had made humanity uniquely dynamic and had got it to the stars before the stars got to it.

What tosh.

Now something unexpected happened to disprove all this, as is apt to occur when one starts making a lot of noise in one's galactic neighbourhood. Someone paid mankind a visit, a little house call, having received their calling-cards of probe-spores a century beforehand and not been greatly amused by them.

A fleet of complicated-looking space-going vessels arrived and began orbiting the moon. Each being a mile long, they were visible from Earth with telescopes, and visible to the naked eye on Luna (to the terror of those living there). But everyone's fears were unfounded. The vessels soon projected a message of peaceful greetings in 40 terrestrial languages and requested permission to land a delegation at any location of human choice, so that they could converse with the human species in general, the operators of the Nevada Telepedrome in particular.

The aliens were politely asked to move their fleet to Mars where it would stop scaring people, and to land only a small delegation without any weapons or potentially harmful technology on board, in the Nevada desert. They were asked to remain physically isolated at all times by means of bio-suits, so as not to risk contamination of the flora and fauna of Earth* (in which regard of course, a desert was also a good choice). Vesberg and Fording were both recalled, along with Marc Dubceck, to join a small welcoming committee led by Serranto.

The Creftlastrians were ten feet tall, ant-like upright creatures with 'flesh' of reddish-brown armour, green eyes and glowing red antennae. Extremely kind, gentle and immensely intelligent, they were somewhat upset to find how much their appearance and technology alarmed everyone. Their landing craft looked like a malevolent insect as it hovered down onto the Nevada desert, and the occupants visible within its transparent bridge made several grown men and women soil themselves upon sight, and retreat to the toilets, reducing in numbers the scientific team left quivering at the entrance to the Telepedrome with hands outstretched in nervous welcome.

We judged that your species would be more advanced than this, emotionally, they said, *less given to fear. Having seen the technological feats you have achieved and the other worlds you have succeeded in visiting. This level of sophistication does not usually occur in species still beset with superstition and primitivism. We are surprised for instance, that you still fight wars, and worship non-existent deities...*

Are there many species as advanced as you, as us? Carlo Serranto asked excitedly. *In our searches we have only found worlds of beings less sophisticated than us, with a small number of mysterious exceptions...*

---

* The reader will note here that such biological-isolation measures were not always adopted by the dupliported humans who visited the 480 worlds. Then the boot had been on the other foot.

But is that really what you've found, or have you looked too carelessly and selfishly I wonder? You say "sophisticated" but perhaps you mean "technologically advanced". Their lead delegate, Kelcanaldric replied. *Advanced species will mostly have acted as we have, that is to say: intercepted your initial probes, de-activated them, rendered them inert and stored them in museums or study facilities, or simply destroyed them as bad examples of uncouth interstellar garbage.*

Excuse me? Serranto stammered.

You're very welcome, Kelcanaldric replied, proud of his new mastery of human English language and etiquette. *You see there is a galactic-wide ban on the kind of invasive exploratory missions you have been staging. By visiting all these worlds you have been interfering in their development, however minutely, in ways that are not authorised, because they can be dangerous and destabilising to those worlds.*

Authorised? What authority are you speaking of?

The league of species who have developed technology sufficiently advanced to travel between stars.

We didn't know you existed. Nobody asked us to join.

No, of course not. I'm afraid you caught us all by surprise, that's why. Usually species master space travel before teleportation. You seem to have managed it the wrong way around. Vaguely impressive, but rather awkward and inconvenient I'm afraid. You're a real nuisance, make no mistake.

How many intelligent species like you are there?

Where? In this galaxy?

You've travelled to other galaxies!? Holy shit! How many in ours for a start?

In this, the Milky Way as you call it, we currently estimate there to be 410,458. The number of life forms of lesser technological advancement, as you have begun to notice, is a much vaster number.

Have you come here to chastise us? To ban us from further exploration? Fording cut in at this point, unable to restrain her incredulity.

***Laughter and ironical smiles**,* Kelcanaldric said, in an altered and robotic tone (his software clearly felt the need to put into words certain facial gestures and mannerisms so alien as to be incomprehensible, but the effect was disconcerting). *It is a highly amusing trait of your species that you assume that everyone else thinks like you. Childlike, if I might say so. You have been exploring because you seek answers, we presume. We have come to give you your answers, so that your desire to explore may cease to be so strong.*

In actual fact, we have found your violations of the code of the league of species quite interesting, having happened before we had the chance to dissuade you, and on the whole we see that they have done thankfully little harm. Your method of only landing tiny parties of explorers is admirable as has been your restraint in not seeking to plunder these worlds for large quantities of their resources. Your violation of space, although wrong, has demonstrated goodwill at the heart of your intentions, which we are now going to reward with trust.

Trust?

We propose to take two people, two only, a human male and female, and show them some of the rest of this area of space, give them some of the remaining answers that your species seeks.

But there are billions of us. Vesberg spoke up. *We are honoured by your offer of course, on behalf of all humanity, but how could we possibly make a choice amongst ourselves regarding such a privilege?*

Time is short, Kelcanaldric said (***sighing, not bitterly*** his translation software explained). *You are a male and* *female are you not?* he said looking at Vesberg and Fording, reading them as some sort of matching set, who then looked at each other in confusion.

Ugh yes, but...?

And greatly experienced in the appropriate sciences...

But we're old...

And therefore held in much respect and veneration by your people.

Well, not really... Vesberg started to protest, but Fording put her hand on his elbow to restrain him.

You are persuaded then. We leave in two of your Earth hours. Do you have space suits? Something a little less constricting than these that you have quite unnecessarily encumbered us with? Our bodies have an outer shell engineered for off-world by our ancestors, you see.

Marc Dubceck, perhaps a little jealous, subconsciously at least, intervened at this point in a state of agitation: *But surely there is a risk for us in this? These are two of our top scientists, not to say human beings with families, children and grandchildren who love them* (Fording frowned at this point, astounded by this uncharacteristic display of irrational emotion). *How do we know that you won't lead them on a wild goose chase, expose them to extraordinary risk, kill them even, inadvertently? They are not spring chickens any longer, not in prime health.*

Vesberg felt annoyed at Dubceck's stupid use of untranslatable idioms involving poultry, a sign of his state of excitement, as much as at his lack of daring. He was about to interject that he felt himself to be just an old man in everybody's way now, with nothing to lose anyway, when Kelcanaldric answered:

I can assure you, we have all the technology necessary to protect and even prolong the lives of both of these beings, and as collateral against any perceived risk, we offer you something else: an externalised abstract of their knowledge, their thoughts and memories. What you might perhaps call a computer file, but infinitely better. Although these two individuals must inevitably die in due course after their safe return to Earth, you will always have these mind-maps, copies of their intelligence, which we will make during their journey with us and present to them on their return.

Serranto, taking his lead from Dubceck, looked confused, and was speechless.

A kind of immortality then? Fording ventured hopefully.

Nothing so tiresome and painful, I can assure you. You will get to rest forever, as every being deserves to, but your genius, such as it is, (***smiles politely in mild irony***, the software intoned, sotto voce) *will be preserved for those who live after you.*

Fording slumped a little, then smiled again like a child on Christmas morning.

We have one somewhat eccentric request, the Creftlastrians now added, and Serranto raised his eyebrows. *Could you please give us what I believe is called a gun to take with us. Just one small one, the hand-held variety, and several bullets. You will understand later.*

*

The Creftlastrians set off in a direction that humans hadn't thought to look, at a speed that they hadn't thought possible. The first stop was a planet orbiting Betelgeuse, where they met another species: the Delmaryns. Pale, tall and sinuous as fish, they lived in beautiful cities like silver crystals, fabulously sophisticated, communicating by mind alone. They greeted Vesberg and Fording warmly apparently, but they were beyond warmth really, beyond all emotion so far had they vanished into the realms of pure knowledge. It was hard not to kneel before them as gods. They showed the human visitors and their Creftlastrian guides to a device at the heart of their capital city: and explained that it was their equivalent of a dupliportation chamber but developed and perfected further, more like a wormhole but safer than any black hole.

Vesberg wanted to know about the particle physics behind it but before he could understand the equations they flashed under his nose, he found himself standing inside the thing with Fording and Kelcanaldric, who gave a hand signal at which they watched the world outside dissolve in a blur of speed and distorted lights, accompanied by a noise like wailing ghosts.

They found themselves on Yamura, the fifth moon of Aurelia IV, in the heart of a city of whizzing metal objects like aeroplanes and cars, a bewildering 3-dimensional maze of constant movement and communication, except (Kelcanaldric explained) that these were not vehicles but all that was left of the Yamurans themselves, who had died out ten thousand years previously, leaving only their machines, which exceeded their creator's abilities in every aspect except emotions, and had forged the next link forward to the stars. After a short flight, cradled in the back of a speeding robo-Yamuran, the party entered a different design of portal and were transported again, yet further and faster to the edges of space.

In all, Vesberg, Fording, Kelcanaldric and his two assistants Symtoa and Tsolnad, travelled through five portals on five worlds, each of similar function but increasingly advanced design. They passed through the red desert world of Velamanacala, where people lived in curved geometric openings in the rock and had spent millennia gazing up at the stars through their clear desert night skies, evolving enormously advanced theories and philosophy. Then the Hanuncyan home world: part of a network of ten inhabited moons that wove complex and eccentric paths between two yellow stars and one red one. The history of the Hanuncyans had driven them to achieve space travel to connect all their moons and make sense of their complex astronomy.

The last portal lay on the deep blue oceanic world of Pelenassus, where people lived on countless floating cities, the survivors of a drowned world, who had used their science to escape but now returned with high technology capable of utilising their changed environment. Their portal was kept underwater to cool it, manned by Pelenassus's astounding natives: half human height with pink and grey heads with six horns, some of which were for sonar and echolocation, with dozens of tendril-like arms that could reach out to about thirty feet around them at a stretch. Again the button was pressed, the levers pulled, and Kelcanaldric turned to smile at his guests (or so his software assured them), as the now familiar whining and blurring made their stomachs lurch.

And now at last, for the world that will astound you most, my friends. One on which, incidentally, you may safely remove your breathing apparatus and suits.

How far have we travelled? Fording stammered, disorientated. *Where are we?*

Ahhh, but the question is flawed, as you are about to discover.

The portal doors opened and the party found themselves inside a large cave, near to its entrance. On uncertain legs, they staggered out and forward into the blazing sunlight of the world beyond.

The sky was blue, criss-crossed by white altostratus, the air balmy. The trees looked like giant palms, the grass looked like that on Earth.

Look up, Kelcanaldric prompted.

What? Vesberg puzzled.

Oh no, oh God... Fording gasped, as a very large scaly beast stumbled out of the undergrowth and roared at them.

That looks a bit like a protoceratops... Vesberg mumbled.

Not that, you fool. Look up, Fording nudged him.

It was a full daylight moon. But it wasn't just a moon. It was ***the*** moon. It was Luna. They were home. A herd of juvenile deinonychus emerged from the opposite flank of jungle and began to encircle the protoceratops.

How the devil can this be? Vesberg pleaded with the Creftlastrians. *Are we back in time somehow?*

Indeed we are, Kelcanaldric smiled (or so his software assured them). *You see, we have travelled very far, but by using what you would call dupliportation or teleportation as we have perfected it, you have in effect exceeded the speed of light. All those stars you gazed up at as children, that your parents explained were already dead and mere ghosts from thousands of years into the past, by going to those stars almost instantly you have gazed back on an Earth equally lost in the depth of its own past. Now by travelling faster than instantly back towards such an Earth, with some help from us, you have in effect entered your own past.*

So time travel is possible.

Yes, and your 'dupliportation' is the first step towards it. This is the logical conclusion of your discoveries and endeavours.

But if we can travel to our own past, who else has done so? What about retro-causality? Violations of timelines? Is this safe, our being here?

You have encountered the Zetans I believe, on one of your previous missions?

And found them remarkably unfriendly as it happens, do they have this technology?

Yes, they do. And it is of great significance that they

didn't welcome you, with open arms, as you say. Perhaps you thought it was because you are not important to them, but in fact the opposite is true. They are the human race in the future, your descendants in a sense.

Vesberg gasped: *Then surely there is real danger in their interaction with us? There have been rumours for centuries of them visiting us. Abductions and experiments.*

Our league of species has forbidden intervention on worlds as primitive as yours has been prior to now, but of course the Zetans bypass this restriction by virtue of their being the same species as yourselves. Although I can't say that we approve of it hugely, nonetheless.

What have they been trying to do here?

They have been seeking to perfect themselves by manipulating their own timeline and genetic heritage, by amending you, in other words, in a hundred tiny and covert ways. Also they are obsessive historians. They travel back to experience Earth's violent past, placing cameras behind people's eyes.

Time tourists... Fording frowned.

So the past can be altered, and when it is, the future instantly changes. Is that how it works?

My advice to you is to have as little as possible to do with the Zetans, for your own safety, but as to the question of causality and timeline violation... well, that is the reason we have brought you here.

Vesberg and Fording spun around as one of the deinonychus broke off from the hunting party (now harrying the protoceratops with a thousand tiny bites) and began to move towards them, looking dangerously interested, its nostrils flaring, catching their scent.

You will recall... Kelcanaldric said calmly, as Vesberg looked back at him with terrified eyes, *that I borrowed this device from your colleagues before leaving Earth?*

Y-yes! Vesberg stammered, while Fording screamed,

grabbing his arm and backing away.

An antique hand gun, a Walther P99 from the 20th century. Well, I think you might want to use it now.

Vesberg, hand shaking, incredulous, took the gun from Kelcanaldric. Fording took it from him, turned around and took aim, while Vesberg cowered behind her, while all the Creftlastrians' translator software cackled: ***laughter, general hilarity.***

Her first shot missed, but the second one hit the body, the next few lodged into the skull and heart. The beast fell almost at their feet, its charge interrupted, gurgling warm blood onto the Cretaceous soil between the wind-blown gymnosperms.

Well done! Kelcanaldric congratulated Fording heartily, whose body was now shaking violently. *We shall take this and lay it in a riverbed for you now.*

Riverbed? Vesberg was in tears, shivering uncontrollably.

To make a fossil. Then you'll have the answer to your conundrum. Such things can only be demonstrated by example, not by anecdote or theory. Come now, your adventure is nearly over. I see that our little bit of sport has quite tired you out...

Is there a Creftlastrian word for fucking bastards? Fording stuttered in a hoarse whisper.

They're actually quite small...up close, the deinonychus ... Vesberg marvelled, tentatively running his hand over the carcass, *and covered in feathers. Hey, could this thing fly?*

It was just about to... Kelcanaldric answered. *Most dinosaurs had feathers and could fly. But unfortunately most of your palaeontologists are idiots.*

But wait! Vesberg exclaimed, hurrying after the three aliens, who were now carrying the dead dinosaur between them using energy beams emitted from their foreheads, taking it down towards the sandy riverbank. *You say our adventure is nearly over, but what about the meaning of life?*

Kelcanaldric paused and his software muttered: ***looks puzzled, perplexed, confounded expression***.

What shape is the universe, how will it end? How big is it? How many other species are out there? Who or what created the universe and life?

*Oh, that stuff... (**shrugs shoulders, equivocal gesture**). Space is the shape of the inside surface of a sphere. The universe currently appears to be expanding only because we are approaching the equator of the sphere, having travelled from a pole that you call the Big Bang. In a few billion years we will reach this midway point and enter the other half of the sphere of space, where exactly the same motion will begin to bring all matter together rather than apart. Eventually all matter will drift together and begin attracting and contracting. You call this idea the Big Crunch, and from that singularity all matter will travel, conceptually, through the centre of the sphere to emerge at the Big Bang again, except that the two points are the same, time will have arrived at the start again. Everything will happen again, the same. Except that there is no 'again', since if things happen exactly the same then in a sense they happen only once, or an infinite number of times, but nothing in between. Thus 'once' and 'infinity' ultimately fuse due to the shape and nature of space-time. By the same token, the apparent vastness of space and the apparent tiny size of the individual portion of it that you occupy; these two ideas also fuse and collapse. Time collapses, once you realise that its only meaning is your location on the sphere of space. Importance and irrelevance also fuse and collapse. This conversation is no more or less important than the death of a star or the birth of an insect. All are critical and vital, all are supremely* *trivial, simultaneously.*

All events are merely geography on the sphere of space we travel across. So far we estimate that we have reached one ten-thousandth of the galaxies in existence, and one billionth of all intelligent life. These are vast figures but not insurmountable. We anticipate that by the time the Big Crunch approaches, all consciousness will have found and completed itself and reassembled, formed a vast compound brain. At that point we will know everything, be everything, and growing tired shall will our own destruction, meaning sleep. Who created the universe? You did. We did. You will. Whoever can ask the question, contains the answer, is a living fragment of it, what you would call a jigsaw piece, to be assembled in the future, to be hurled outwards from the past. Simple. Got it?

How many dimensions are there? Fording spluttered. *Is our String Theory correct?*

Only four... Kelcanaldric said, turning away again, *any child can see that. And we class String Theory as one of your religions. It is... I believe the polite term is... bollocks.*

*

President Ngobo insisted that Vesberg and Fording address the American people, even before greeting their own relatives. They had returned only three days after they left Earth, but utterly changed in ways that although primarily psychological, also seemed to shine out now through their physical bodies, elderly though they were. They had been brought straight to Washington.

With five minutes to spare before the official address from the White House balcony, Vesberg asked the President if he and Fording could have a few minutes alone in the Oval Room, to "pull themselves together".

What are we going to say to them all then? Fording

asked, straightening her hair in the mirror.

Who?

Them out there of course, the human race. Who else?

Oh them... Vesberg mumbled grumpily, looking over some notes in his diary. *Everything I suppose. The meaning of life, time and space, the universe.*

Do you think they'll be able to handle it?

Sure, why not? We can, can't we?

Can we? Tell the Christians there's no Jehovah, the Muslims there's no Allah. You don't see a problem there? Or that time travel is possible? And that we've already been fiddled around with in our history by aliens who are ultimately ourselves? A sort of cosmic child abuse? You don't think that's going to mess with some people's heads?

What do you suggest we do?

Keep quiet. Tell them some nice safe stories about cuddly aliens, benign ones as intelligent as us, who have shown us countless friendly worlds waiting to do business with us.

That's true as well though, isn't it?

Not quite. I'm not sure any of them want to see much of us ever again, never mind exchange goods and ideas, are you? We're not very interesting to them. We're only one of hundreds of thousands of promising civilisations, and we're ill-behaved and barbaric. They want us to just stay put and shut our mouths and stop making a din for the next five thousand years, until we're better evolved, and to leave everyone else alone.

It's kind of hurtful when you put it like that I suppose.

So why don't we lie to them, or be "economical with the truth" as some old British politician once said?

You know what I think? Vesberg sighed, standing up and parting the curtains a little, after which a wave and ripple of extra hysteria seemed to break from the crowd outside, as if he had been spotted. *I don't think they'll believe us anyway. A pair of crazy old gits. A disgraced bureaucrat, an ex-con like me, and a dirty old lady like you, with a name for putting it around with young Italian bucks in your better days, no offence.*

Fording laughed and choked simultaneously, beating her chest to get her breath back. *You cheeky devil. There's no way to say any of that without being insulting!*

I'm sorry. I'm just being honest. I think I owe you that. I think you know I... I... Vesberg considered his words while Fording knitted her brow in disturbance. *Fuck it, you know I love you, in the best sense, as a friend, as a woman, as a man with tits, as one of the best scientists I've ever worked with.*

Friend will do, thank you, Gene. I forgive you, of course. And, at my age even cast-up infidelities seem like some kind of backhanded compliment from fate. I'm not insulted.

Backhanded compliments from fate... nicely put. And who is Fate exactly? You see, can even we be sure we're not still residually religious ourselves? From one barbaric primitive to another?

Vesberg and Fording laughed together heartily, then embraced.

I love the human race... Fording said, drawing back, wiping a tear from her eye, *...even with all their flaws. In fact I love them more than ever now that I've seen some of the alternatives to them out there. They're more everything than anyone.*

Sorry? Vesberg frowned incredulously.

More violent, more loving, more stupid, more ingenious, more resilient, more full of ludicrous hope. More more.

That's just because you speak their emotional language of course, and can't understand that of other species so well. As a scientist, I am bound to point that out to you.

Yes, perhaps. But I think part of you agrees.

The emotional part. Hillary, if you don't think they'll

believe what we tell them, then how come they believed all those missions to all those outlandish planets with insane life forms?

Oh that's different. That was television. They believe two and two make three if they see it on television.

So it's agreed then, Vesberg clapped his hands and checked his watch. *We tell them everything, just how it is, and watch their jaws drop as they understand less and less, refute more and more, then finally reject and discard us and everything we tell them, even though it's the truth?*

Yes, agreed. That's a magnificently doomed plan, a blueprint for heroic failure. History will love us, but our peers revile us. Galileo and Christ move over. I'm up for that.

I can't think of better company.

Who? Galileo?

No, you, you silly cow. Will you take my arm, in a no-longer-socially-acceptable gesture of male superiority?

Sure, why not, now that we've proved your inferiority.

Touché. Here, I meant to say. It's really lucky don't you think, a big relief in fact, that our visiting Earth's prehistoric past with the Creftlastrians didn't change anything here in the future? You know, butterfly's wings and all that?

Yes... Fording mused, running the seven fingers of her right hand through her hair. *Either we were lucky or we've disproven all those pesky theorists and Sci Fi writers...*

Mmm... Vesberg frowned, swishing his tail absent-mindedly across the president's carpet. *As far as I can see... the world is just as we left it. Here,* Vesberg found something in his pocket and brought it out into the light. A black and silver cube of slots and buttons and lights.

Fording reached inside her pocket and brought hers out also. *Yes, our essences. Our uploaded souls and brains and experience. Interrogable computers of our consciousness for humanity to keep and consult from time to time, in all the centuries to come.*

These big red scary ants sure keep their promises, eh?

Vesberg laughed and nearly juggled the object in his hands. *Could just be a Rubik's cube for all we know...*

No, no, they said NASA would be able to read it, even now, with current technology.

Mmm... Vesberg turned it over, *I suppose a USB port would be too much to hope for...* then he sighed and looked up. *Mankind will ignore these, as much as they ignore us, you know, for a long time to come, until they discover a few clues for themselves and remember us and come back looking for these things, for the theories that explain it.*

The big guys never did give us a word for these objects, did they? They said we had to choose one for ourselves, an appropriate term. Solid-state souls. Our digital hearts. Our recorded nexus. Our mind matrix...

There was a knock at the door and President Ngobo and his men entered. He was straightening his shirt, clearing his throat, preparing to address the world with his two prize voyagers at his side, his Vasco da Gama and Marco Polo. They would be officially rehabilitated.

I've thought of a term. One word, four letters, Vesberg whispered as he stood up, narrowing his eyes, trying to look mysterious.

Hillary Fording smiled, thought for a moment, then took Gene Vesberg's arm and approached the balcony. *Yes, now I have too,* she said, *but you go first...*

~

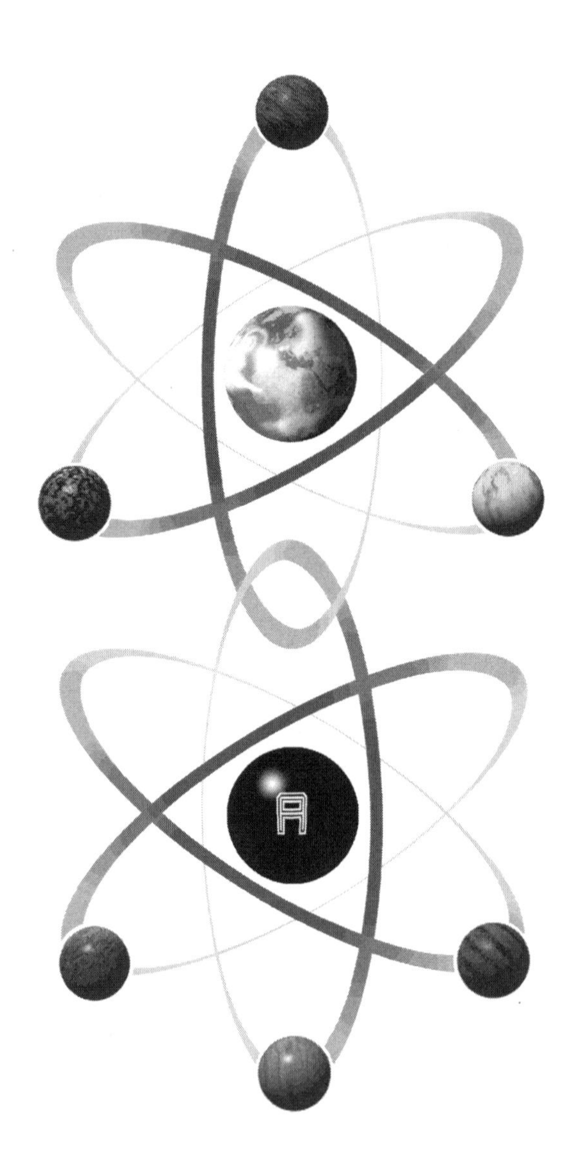

APPENDIX A

Missions to Gliese 581d and 581e revealed only semi-arid worlds with basic plant life and small rodents. A rocket was gradually constructed on 581e, by transporting materials in numerous small loads by Ansible. Six years later, in March 2218, a rocket was launched towards 581g (aka: *Somnos*) with Julia Pleznick on board, who hoped to lead a compassionate expedition to locate her husband's body on the dark side of the tidally-locked world, or at least erect a commemorative plaque. Safety dictated however that they land first on the day-lit and volcanologically inert side of the planet, from which to organise land transport.

Julia Pleznick and her two colleagues Greenberg and Nadurra were approached within hours of touchdown by a crowd of aliens (matching Walter Pleznick's verbal descriptions), one individual of whom rushed towards the party with such speed that his actions were interpreted as hostile. This resulted in him being 'accidentally' shot dead by Greenberg.

After a few days negotiating with the aliens, retrospective translation of their language and replay of film of the incident indicated that the alien had cried out: "I am Pleznick. I love you. Don't shoot."

Exploration of the dark side of Gliese 581g has so far been forbidden on religious grounds by the natives of the planet, although covert mapping by aerial reconnaissance of the area is scheduled for next year, subject to the hemisphere's unpredictable weather and cloud cover.

Julia Pleznick went missing from her diplomatic post on Gliese 581g last month. The life signs of her 'original' body on Earth so far remain normal. Although movement in her (restrained) legs suggest continuous walking motion of irrational intensity.

~

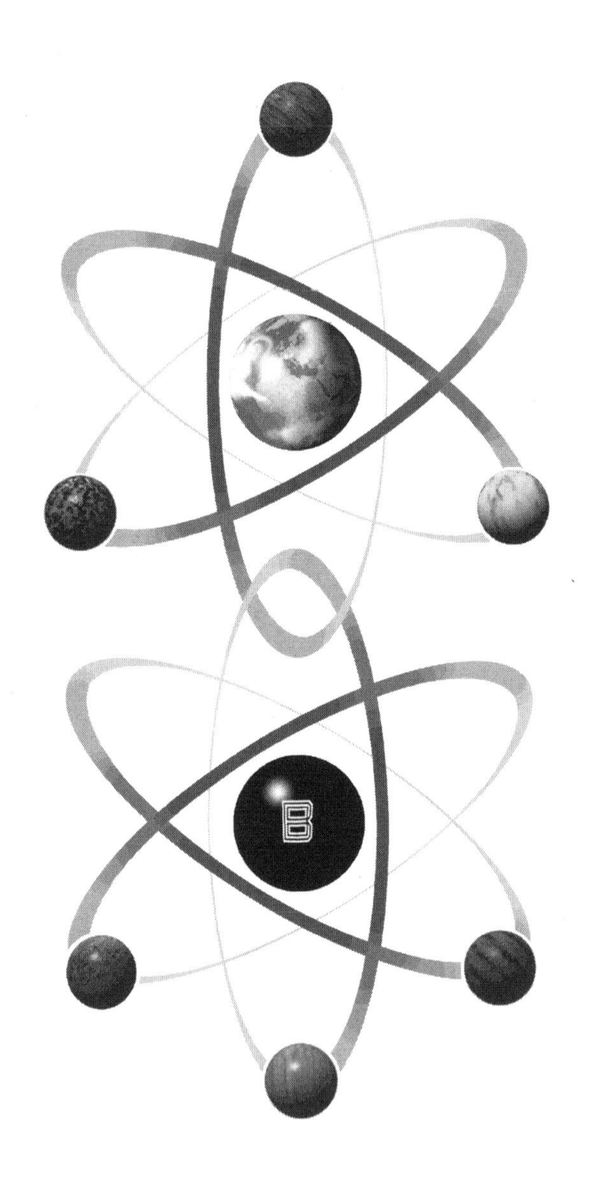

APPENDIX B

Once quantum-entangled, with Earth's current technology, there existed no safe method for disentangling astronauts. Thus after each mission, the Entanglement chambers on each distant planet had to be shut down and hermetically sealed to prevent attack and egress by a natural hazard or alien life form. This strategy was largely successful but with a few unfortunate exceptions. Whilst enjoying his retirement from NASA, aged 64, walking down a street in Baltimore, Jacques Filimore's left arm came off and hovered ten feet in front of him before he passed out and died. A Viragan scientific team had succeeded in gaining entry to his sealed Semblance Pod on Virago (despite it being concealed underground) after thirty years of trying different kinds of drill bit and were commencing their autopsy on what they believed was simply a dead body.

Similarly, Brenda Jeffries was split open from throat to abdomen in a crowded restaurant with her grandchildren in Seattle as a group of alien scientists on Sigma Draconis d began their examination, having dissolved her pod by use of an exotic acid known only on their world. Her internal organs began levitating around the room as the restaurant was evacuated.

Finally, during a volcanic eruption caused by a meteor

strike on Alpha Centauri A g, Fiona Yung caught fire and was compressed into a three-foot-long tube of ultra dense ash while walking her two poodles in Lafayette Park, San Francisco.

The Entanglement chambers which remain intact may theoretically be re-used after the death of the original astronauts. Thus all former astronauts must be cremated upon death by law. Their ashes which simultaneously appear within the sealed pods on their remote twinned locations, are automatically hosed down and blown out into the atmosphere of the surrounding alien environment. A fitting and symbolic end to the heroic lives of those who have served their country and the world, their essence commended not just to the soil and air of their home world, but to that of the partnered globe on which surely the most dramatic adventure of their lifetimes took place.

~

APPENDIX C

From Flickapedia, the free encyclopedia

The Grange Ridge Fossil Find was a disputed dig carried out by the British philanthropist and palaeontologist Raymond Gordons Ford in May 1927, in the Grange Ridge National Park area, some 14 miles northwest and downhill of the summit of Mount Tohado, in the state of Montana, USA.

The fossil bed uncovered by Ford included several deinonychus skeletons, one of which had two circular holes in the skull and one in the pelvis. The exact dimensions of these holes and the lack of surrounding fractures or scrape marks have since become controversial, leading some commentators in subsequent decades to speculate that these holes correlate exactly with the punctures left by .40 calibre bullets from a twentieth century handgun. Sceptics argue that the horns of a protoceratops or of some other smaller, as yet undiscovered dinosaur, could have left the marks as a result of some unusual encounter with a semi-conscious or incapacitated deinonychus unable to offer resistance.

Ford's daughter released hitherto unseen photographs of the dig site to the British Paleontological Museum upon her death in 2010, together with further handwritten documentation of the time and several fossil casts. Some of this data was leaked to International Geographic Magazine in Spring 2011, including a cast of an unidentified object, possibly made of heavily-weathered metal, found next to the skeletons. The object has been alleged by some to resemble a Walther P99 semi-automatic pistol and other small objects nearby .40 calibre bullets consistent with the circular skeletal punctures. If confirmed by scientific analysis, this model of pistol was not manufactured until 1996, in theory ruling out the possibility of contamination at the original site by Ford and his assistants. The Margaret Gordons Ford legacy was recently alleged to be a hoax by Stein Magazine, but the British Paleontological Museum's carbon dating and DNA tests are currently ongoing, and the Museum are said to remain confident of placing the artefacts on show sometime in Summer 2014.

See also:
Time Travel
Causal Paradox
Anomalous Archaeology
Fringe Palaeontology
Ooparts

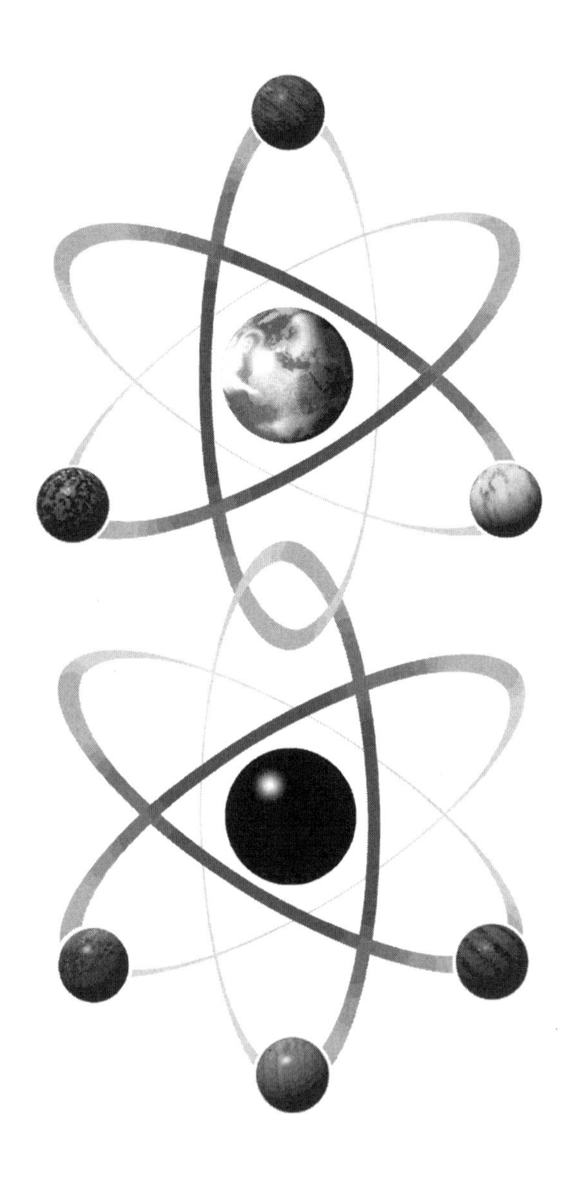

AFTERWORD

In August 2018, in the University Hospital of Geneva, Switzerland, the decision is taken to switch off the life support machine of a promising young scientist named Gene Vesberg.

For a month he has lain in a deep coma, attended by his parents and fiancée Hazel. The doctors tell them that Gene probably can't hear any of them talking and that there is little hope of his recovery. He has been severely burned and irradiated by collision with a beam of accelerated protons. Nobody can say where Gene Vesberg's thoughts and feelings are, if indeed he has any, in his persistent vegetative state.

But unknown to them, Vesberg has heard their voices from time to time and cried inside himself, cried for the numb passage of time and the future life he will never have, never complete as planned.

Instead, in desperation, he has voyaged to many worlds, dream worlds, imagining planets constructed from his fading life force, his drowning soul. Wonderful, enlightening worlds, full of strange meaning and the power to enlighten humanity as to what it is, and what it could yet be. Worlds that men and women could reach by the simple trick of sleep, strapped down in beds in antiseptic rooms, as he has been.

Will such worlds die, die with him now, as he hears his mother weep, the doctor's leaden footsteps move towards his life-support to disconnect the vital leads? Or are all dreams once dreamt, somehow alive? Who is to say that a man who walked on a distant world while he slept, was or was not dreaming? And who might each of us prove to be one day, and in what strange dream, should something wake us from these; our daily lives in which we move and love and hope and, stumbling, cry out, reach out, for something other?

~

ACKNOWLEDGEMENTS

Encouragers, heroes, and accomplices appreciatively
acknowledged alphabetically:

Nina Allan, Allen Ashley, Martin Bax, Peter Buck,
John Foxx, Victoria Hooper, Rachel Kendall,
Ursula Le Guin, Rona MacDonald,
Simon Conway Morris, Al Murray,
Ian Redman, David Rix, Ian Sales
& Stephen Theaker.

Elsewhen Press

a small independent publisher specialising in Speculative Fiction

BLUE FRIDAY

MIKE FRENCH

In the Britain of 2034 overtime for married couples is banned, there is enforced viewing of family television (much of it repeats of old shows from the sixties and seventies), monitored family meal-times and a coming of age where twenty-five year-olds are automatically assigned a spouse by the state computer if they have failed to marry. Only the Overtime Underground network resists.

Dystopian science fiction, *Blue Friday* tells of a future where many live in fear of the Family Protection Agency, a special police division enforcing the strict legislation that has been introduced to protect the family unit. Combining dark humour with a vision of the future that inverts the classic dystopian nightmare, this latest novel from Mike French follows in the tradition of great Speculative Fiction satirists such as Jonathan Swift. Thoughtful, while at the same time prompting a wry smile in the reader, it reverses the usual perception of a future regime driven by productivity and industrial output at the expense of family, demonstrating that the converse may be no better.

Mike French is the owner and senior editor of the prestigious literary magazine, *The View From Here.* Mike's debut novel, *The Ascent of Isaac Steward* was published in 2011 and nominated for The Galaxy National Book Awards. *Blue Friday* is his second novel. He currently lives in Luton with his wife, three children and a growing number of pets.

ISBN: 9781908168177 (epub, kindle)
ISBN: 9781908168078 (192pp paperback) November 2012

Elsewhen Press

a small independent publisher specialising in Speculative Fiction

The Lost Men

An Allegory

David Colón

In a world where the human population has been decimated, self-reliance is the order of the day. Of necessity, the few remaining people must adapt residual technology as far as possible, with knowledge gleaned from books that were rescued and have been treasured for generations. After a childhood of such training, each person is abandoned by their parents when they reach adulthood, to pursue an essentially solitary existence. For most, the only human contact is their counsel, a mentor who guides them to find 'the one', their life mate as decreed by Fate. Lack of society brings with it a lack of taboo, ensuring that the Fate envisioned by a counsel is enacted unquestioningly. The only threats to this stable, if sparse, existence are the 'lost men', mindless murderers who are also self-sufficient but with no regard for the well-being of others, living outside the confines of counsel and Fate.

Is Fate a real force, or is it totally imagined, an arbitrary convention, a product of mankind's self-destructive tendency? In this allegorical tale, David Colón uses an alternate near-future to explore the boundaries of the human condition and the extent to which we are prepared to surrender our capacity for decisions and self-determination in the face of a very personally directed and apparently benevolent, authoritarianism. Is it our responsibility to rebuke inherited 'wisdom' for the sake of envisioning and manifesting our own will?

David Colón is an Assistant Professor of English at TCU in Fort Worth, Texas, USA. Born and raised in Brooklyn, New York, he received his Ph.D. in English from Stanford University and was a Chancellor's Postdoctoral Fellow in English at the University of California, Berkeley. His writing has appeared in numerous journals, including *Cultural Critique*, *Studies in American Culture*, *DIAGRAM*, *How2*, and *MELUS*. *The Lost Men* is his first book.

ISBN: 9781908168146 (epub, kindle)
ISBN: 9781908168047 (192pp paperback)

For more information visit lost-men.com

Visit the Elsewhen Press website at elsewhen.co.uk for the latest information on all of our titles, authors and events; to read our blog; find out where to buy our books and ebooks; or to place an order.

Elsewhen Press

a small independent publisher specialising in Speculative Fiction

[RE]AWAKENINGS

AN ANTHOLOGY OF NEW SPECULATIVE FICTION

• ALISON BUCK • NEIL FAARID • GINGERLILY • ROBIN MORAN • PR POPE • ALEXANDER SKYE • PETER WOLFE •

[Re]Awakenings are the starting points for life-changing experiences; a new plane of existence, an alternate reality or cyber-reality. This genre-spanning anthology of new speculative fiction explores that theme with a spectrum of tales, from science fiction to fantasy to paranormal; in styles from clinically serious to joyfully silly. As you read through them all, and you must read all of them, you will discover along the way that stereo-typical distinctions between the genres within speculative fiction are often arbitrary and unhelpful. You will be taken on an emotional journey through a galaxy of sparkling fiction; you will laugh, you will cry; you will consider timeless truths and contemplate eternal questions.

All of life is within these pages, from birth to death (and in some cases beyond). In all of these stories, most of them specifically written for this anthology, the short story format has been used to great effect. If you haven't already heard of some of these authors, you soon will as they are undoubtedly destined to become future stars in the speculative fiction firmament. Remember, you read them here first!

[Re]Awakenings is a collection of short stories from exciting new voices in UK speculative fiction, compiled by guest editor PR Pope. It contains the following stories: Alison Buck: *Dreamers*; *Intervention*; *Mirror mirror*; *Podcast.* Neil Faarid: *The Adventures of Kit Brennan: Kidnapped!* Gingerlily: *The Dragon and the Rose.* Robin Moran: *The Merry Maiden Wails.* PR Pope: *Afterlife*; *Courtesy Bodies*; *On the Game.* Alexander Skye: *BlueWinter*; *Dreaming Mars*; *Exploring the Heavens*; *Worth it.* Peter Wolfe: *If you go into the woods today…*

ISBN: 9781908168108 (epub, kindle)
ISBN: 9781908168009 (288pp paperback)

For more information visit bit.ly/ReAwakenings

Visit the Elsewhen Press website at elsewhen.co.uk for the latest information on all of our titles, authors and events; to read our blog; find out where to buy our books and ebooks; or to place an order.

Elsewhen Press

a small independent publisher specialising in Speculative Fiction

THE ROYAL SORCERESS

CHRISTOPHER NUTTALL

The Royal Sorceress is set in 1830 in an alternate Britain where the 'scientific' principles of magic were discovered sixty years previously, allowing the British to win the American War of Independence. Although Britain is now supreme among the Great Powers, the gulf between rich and poor in the Empire has widened and unrest is growing every day. Master Thomas, the King's Royal Sorcerer, is ageing and must find a successor to lead the Royal Sorcerers Corps; most magicians can possess only one of the panoply of known magical powers, but Thomas needs to find a new Master of all the powers. There is only one candidate, one person who has displayed a talent for all the powers since an early age, but has been neither trained nor officially acknowledged. A perfect candidate to be Master Thomas' apprentice in all ways but one: The Royal College of Sorcerers has never admitted a girl before. But even before Lady Gwendolyn Chrichton can begin her training, London is plunged into chaos by a campaign of terrorist attacks co-ordinated by Jack, a powerful and rebellious magician.

The Royal Sorceress will certainly appeal to all fans of steampunk, alternate history and fantasy. As well as the fun of the 'what-ifs' delivered by rewriting our past, it delights with an Empire empowered by magic – all the better for being one we can recognise. The plotting and intrigue of Jack and his rebels, roof-top chases and battles of magic all add to the thrills; but it is by no means just a cosy romp, with many of the rebels drawn from the seedy and grimy underworld of London while their establishment targets prey on the weak and defenceless. Here, just as in our world, social imbalance and sexual inequality underpin society.

As an indie author, Christopher Nuttall has published five novels (so far) through Amazon Kindle Direct Publishing. *The Royal Sorceress* is his first novel to be professionally published. Chris is currently living in Borneo with his partner, muse, and critic Aisha.

ISBN: 9781908168184 (epub, kindle) October 2012
ISBN: 9781908168085 (208pp, paperback) February 2013

ABOUT THE AUTHOR

Douglas Thompson's short stories have appeared in a wide range of magazines and anthologies. He won the Grolsch/Herald Question of Style Award in 1989 and second prize in the Neil Gunn Writing Competition in 2007. His first book, *Ultrameta*, published in 2009, was nominated for the Edge Hill Prize, and shortlisted for the BFS Best Newcomer Award. *Entanglement* is his fifth novel.